Fated to be yours

Kendra

Fate has a plan...

Jodie Larson

JODIE LARSON

Prologue

THE CHILL OF THE NIGHT air sends a shiver down my spine. My arms instinctively wrap around my middle, warding off the impending cold as it blows over the balcony rails. My body senses him before he even touches me. His hard chest presses against my back as he wraps his strong arms around me, pulling me back toward our bed, our safe haven. Space which is only ours and no one can touch us. My eyes close as I deeply inhale a scent that is undeniably his, invading my every sense, straight down to my bones.

I crave him.

I want him.

I need him.

The pulsing throb between my legs grows exponentially as his lips press into the delicate skin of my neck, nipping and sucking before we fall into a tangle of arms and legs onto the bed.

"Tessa," he whispers against my skin. It pebbles under the warmth of his breath, laced with heat and desire. His hands roam curiously around my body with a familiarity only they know. A quiet moan escapes my lips as his hands continue their journey, finally landing on the soft curves of my chest.

My arms reach behind me, anxious to feel him beneath my palms. My fingers twitch with delight when I make contact with the massive erection in his pants. The sharp hiss in my ear allows me to know how much he wants my hands on him as well.

"I need you," he says, gently sucking on the lobe, causing spasms of pleasure to rocket throughout my body.

"I'm yours," I whisper.

Gently, he turns me onto my back. The bright sapphire eyes I adore beyond belief stare into my own, saying words that do not need to be spoken. My eyes search his face, wanting to see past the shadows cast by the candles surrounding us, dancing across his beautifully sculpted face, obstructing my view. Tentatively my hand cups his cheek, fingers lacing in the hair around his ear as I slowly pull his mouth down to meet mine.

"Shit!"

My body meets the hard, unforgiving floor as I fall out of bed once again. I'm stuck in this never-ending nightmare that is constantly teasing me with thoughts of someone out there who could love me. It plays through my mind every night, haunting my thoughts and causing me physical pain as my subconscious makes me so restless I need to throw myself from the bed for it to stop.

Fate has not been kind to me. She taught me long ago that bad things happen to the unloved. My mother rejected me, as did my father, abandoning me as a child, without reason. Every emotional relationship I've attempted to forge since then has fallen to the same fate, leaving me in isolation.

I dare not hope because it will ultimately lead to disappointment. And disappointment is something I already own in spades. Instead, I'll leave my future in the hands of fate and pray she's able to show me the way.

Chapter 1

"**D**AMN IT,"
I examine my latest bruise in the bathroom mirror, twisting my head from side to side while I dig out my supply of makeup to cover it up and make it less noticeable. It's part of my daily routine, one which I would be more than happy to get rid of.

That dream, that stupid, horrible nightmare has hurt me again in more ways than one. Besides the physical markers, the bruises on my face, and chronic headaches that follow, it also leaves emotional damage in the form of an aching heart. Why does it feel the need to torture me with thoughts of a handsome man who wants me? I'm single and alone, which I have been for years. Then suddenly, these past few months have been filled with intense blue eyes and a sexy voice always in the shadows. So intense that my body's natural response is to run away from them rather than to them.

And maybe nightmare isn't the correct term for this dream. To the normal person, it would be the greatest dream imaginable. One filled with happily ever afters and promises of a bright future. That is not true in my case. This dream, happy as it may seem, shows me a future that I don't see happening. A falsehood of hopes and dreams to never come true. Happily ever afters do not exist for those who were cast aside by people who were meant to protect and love you. Having never been shown that in the past makes me disbelieve of finding it in the future.

I know I shouldn't let my past dictate my present. I should just move on and get over it. Parts of it were good though, just not enough to outweigh the bad times. My parents divorced when I was around the age of nine, which is where I think my self-esteem issues stemmed from. Words were said, actions performed that cannot be undone, leaving me longing to have a normal home life, even though I never had it before. Home implies a place you can go to feel safe, where people will love you unconditionally and will treat you with respect. Instead, things happen and parents change. They leave or grow distant, pushing you away or forgetting that you exist.

They say that you spend your entire adult life getting over your childhood. I would have to agree. Overcoming your childhood is difficult, especially when you still struggle to overcome your failures and shortcomings, even with your best efforts to move past them.

But I can't dwell on the past right now. Now I need to focus on the present and get myself ready to begin my day while attempting to put my mystery man in the back of my mind.

I stare blankly into my coffee cup as I get lost in my thoughts again, until my phone rings and pulls me out of my head.

"Hello?"

"Are you on your way? Tell me you're on your way."

It's Kara, my boss, who also doubles as my best friend. And like the good friend that she is, she's always looking out for me, making sure that I don't fall behind or lose track of time. Which happens more times than not.

"Not yet. It's still early."

"Tess, it's almost quarter to eight. And you still need to fight the morning rush. You may want to start moving."

"No, it can't be that late." I glance up at the clock on the oven and almost spill my coffee over when I realize the time. "Holy shit, it is that late."

Kara laughs on the other end. "Like I said, are you on your way?"

I quickly dump my coffee into a travel mug and jump around while pulling my flats on. I press the phone to my ear as I gather my jacket and purse and fly out the door, locking it behind me.

"I am now. I can't believe I'm going to be late. I'm so sorry. I'll be there as soon as I can."

She laughs on the other end and I can hear her clicking away on her keyboard. "This is why I called because I've got some big news that I have to share with you and I need you here as soon as possible. So get moving, Chickie!"

I trip over a crack in the sidewalk as I fly out the front door of my apartment building and almost tumble into my car parked on the side of the road. "I'll be there as soon as I can. Thanks again for the call."

"It's what I do. Drive safe, but hurry. Remember, the speed limit is just a suggestion."

I start my car and pull into the driving lane. "I'm pretty sure it's the law, which would be illegal to break."

"It's only illegal if you get caught. I'll see you in a few. Bye."

"Bye, Kara."

I toss the phone into my open purse on the passenger seat and pull into the busy morning rush, hoping that it'll be a smooth sail to my building downtown.

Luckily it was only a twenty minute battle with the rest of the Friday morning workforce, as I enter the lobby and head toward the bank of elevators. There's a substantial crowd already gathered and waiting, which makes me cringe internally. I know what's going to happen before I even enter the car when it arrives. I'll get pushed into the back corner, too far away to press the button for my floor. And no one will be getting off on that floor either so I will end up riding the elevator until everyone leaves before riding it back down. It's a little pathetic, but I'm too shy to ask for help. It's something that Kara's been trying to work on with me. It's still a work in progress.

Ten minutes later I walk through the doors of Mattson and Associates and practically sprint to my cubicle toward the back. I avoid the stares of my coworkers, who know exactly how late I am and proceed to pass their silent judgment upon me. Again, nothing new. Just something else for me to compartmentalize and deal with at a later time.

I place my jacket on the hook and flop into my chair while noisily tossing my purse in the bottom drawer of my file cabinet. A few people walk by and eye me up with all the noise I'm making before walking past and continuing their duties. But I don't have time to give them a second thought. I quickly grab my notepad and pen and make my way across the hall to Kara's office.

Kara Thomas is one of Mattson's senior account executives. She's been making a name for herself by taking on the bigger accounts that we've been signing and was even featured in one of the local business magazines. She works hard and has the business savvy of someone who's been in the game for twenty years, but also has a heart of gold, as she often shows with me. Like my morning call, making sure that I'm getting to work on time because something important is happening. I don't know what it is yet, but I'm about to find out.

I enter her office and take a seat on one of the two chairs placed directly in front of her desk.

"I'm late. I know. I tried really hard to get here on time but, you know, things happened."

Kara looks up from her computer and smiles. Her green eyes are laughing behind her glasses.

"Which floor did you travel up to today?"

I readjust myself on my chair and look down at the notepad on my lap. "The twentieth."

She whistles softly. "That's a new record. There couldn't have been that many people left in the elevator at that point. Why did you wait so long?"

I shrug. "It was embarrassing enough to be caught riding it past my floor. I wasn't about to purposely highlight it by selecting a floor beneath where we already were."

Kara sits back and twirls her chair to face me. "Tess, what have I been saying to you?"

"That it's okay to ask for help. It's just, I don't know, embarrassing."

"They won't bite, you know." She pauses and then laughs. "Well, I can't actually say that because there could very well be people in this building who get their kicks by biting strangers. You need to watch out for those."

We both laugh and I feel better about my morning, which I knew I would because Kara always has a way to brighten my spirits.

"So you have something exciting to tell me?"

Kara practically bounces in her chair with excitement. "Yes! Have you ever heard of the Tree of Life Foundation?"

I shake my head. "No, I haven't."

She flips open a folder on her desk and hands me a pamphlet that I flip through quickly.

"It's a foundation which is based in London whose goal is to help underprivileged children by giving them a place to belong through private and government funded centers. They have several of them set up across Europe and are looking to expand to the United States. They heard about the work that we did for the Excelsior Foundation last year and knew right away that our company would be the perfect fit. And the Twin Cities is their first stop, which is quite an honor."

"I agree, especially considering they could have started in New York or Chicago."

"They said they prefer to start in smaller metro areas and Chicago and New York were too big. Either way it's good for us and good for the community."

"I agree. Any place that helps children is okay in my books."

I smile at the thought of someone helping kids who have very little and trying to give them a better life when no one else wants to or has the means to. Once again, my past comes into my thoughts but I quickly shake it off because now is not the time to dwell on it.

"Agreed. And guess who they requested by name to lead the project?"

With a smirk, I pretend to think of an answer. "Let me guess, Collins?"

A paperclip comes sailing by my head, making me bark out a laugh.

"Hilarious," she says, sticking her tongue out at me. You'd never guess she was ten years older than me by her actions. She acts more like a teenager instead of a serious, modern businesswoman. "I hope you have a passport because you're going to need one."

I blink several times. "A passport? Why?"

"Because you and I are going to London. They wanted to meet in person to sign the contracts, rather than conduct everything over the phone and emails. Which I completely agree with. It's easier to do business face to face. They also wanted to give us a first-hand look at the centers so we know what we're working for."

"They?"

"The Board of Directors. Well, not all of them. Just three of them. The president, vice president, and their head of operations. Here, I'll email you the itinerary so you can get everything prepared for next week." She quickly pulls up several things and after a few clicks on her keyboard turns back to face me.

"This is so short notice."

Kara nods. "I know, but this just fell into our laps and we

have to jump on this as soon as possible. So Chris authorized our business trip and has made all the essential arrangements. Now I just need to know if you have a passport."

I smile and nod. "I do. I picked one up a few years ago on the off-chance that I needed to go out of the country."

"Planning on doing a crime spree?"

"No, nothing like that," I say, shaking my head. "In case I ever wanted to go to Canada or Mexico I'd need to have a passport."

"So, crime spree."

I laugh. "No crime spree."

Kara sticks out her bottom lip and then rolls her eyes. "At least you have a passport so we're set there."

"When do we leave?"

"Sunday morning. I'll pick you up so we don't have to park our cars overnight. Can you be ready to go by eleven?"

I nod emphatically. "Of course! I just can't believe that you want to take me with you."

Kara tilts her head slightly. "What do you mean? When have I ever gone on an out of town business trip without you?"

"Well, never, but there's always a first time for everything."

"Nonsense. You are my best friend and the greatest assistant a woman could ever ask for. Of course you're coming with. I wouldn't hear anything else about it."

Tears threaten to well in my eyes, but I blink them away. "You're too good to me, you know that?"

She waves a hand in front of her face. "Think nothing of it. Besides, you could use a break. When was the last time you took a vacation that didn't involve you sitting at home because I forced you to take a day off?" I stay silent and she nods her head. "Exactly. You need this and I couldn't be happier to do it for you."

"Thank you, Kara."

Kara looks at her watch and smiles. "I'm also making the decision that we're having a short day today because we need to pack and shop for next week. So you are to leave this office at noon and not one minute over. Then you are to drive straight home and get packing."

I stand from my chair, noticing that I didn't even write one note down the entire time I was here. Kara rounds her desk and quickly hugs me. I squeeze her back and pull away.

"It won't take me long to get ready. I don't have many nice items so packing will be easy."

She walks with me out to my cube and stands at the edge of the wall. "That's not the only reason we're leaving early. I've also booked you a massage appointment with Jenny at Panache this afternoon. And before you object, I've already paid for it so you can't turn it down."

I bring my hands in front of my mouth and gasp. "You didn't."

"I did. Two o'clock so you better not be late. Do I need to call and remind you?"

I shake my head. "No call will be necessary. I'll be there. Thank you, Kara. You're too much."

"It was nothing. Now get to work because we're leaving in three hours." She smiles at me again and turns to leave.

I stare at my computer, still half in shock over her announcement. London. She wants me to go to London with her. I've always dreamed of going to London but never once thought I would be able to go. Since vacations were non-existent for me growing up, I just assumed they would be the same in my adult life. Not that this is a vacation. It's a business trip but knowing Kara she's still going to find a way for us to have fun and explore the city.

Opening my email, I glance over our itinerary and see we will be there through Friday. We meet with the board on Monday afternoon, then go on two different tours Tuesday and Wednesday before meeting with the board on Thursday for an all-day meeting. They probably wanted to block off the entire day because who knows how long the meeting will go. It's smart, that's for sure. Hopefully, it won't take all day so we can have some down time before we leave Friday morning.

Okay Tess, time to focus on your work I scold myself. Bringing my attention back to the task at hand, I start sending out my various emails for Kara, confirming appointments and sending contracts to all the necessary parties involved with her current clients.

Before I realize it, Kara is standing at the entrance to my cube, tapping the face of her watch while trying to suppress a laugh.

"What am I going to do with you? You're supposed to be gone by now."

I turn and shrug apologetically. "I got caught up in my work. It happens."

"You work too hard. This will be good for you because it's going to be a well-deserved break."

I stand and put on my jacket before grabbing my purse from the bottom drawer. "We're still working, just in a different country."

She shakes her head and walks with me to the elevators.

"No, this will definitely be different than your regular work. Did you read over the itinerary?"

"Yes. Meeting, site tour, site tour, meeting, then return home."

Kara nods as we ride the elevator to the lobby. "Yes, and somewhere in there we'll go out and see the city. We can't work the entire time we're there. That would be silly."

I laugh as we walk out into the crisp autumn air and cross the street to the parking garage. "That doesn't surprise me that you would want to find any loophole to have fun."

"Besides, we need to see the sights since you've never been there. And who knows. Maybe you'll run into the man of your dreams and fall desperately in love with him."

That makes me laugh. "You're crazy. I'm fairly positive it won't happen. We'll only be there for a week. That's not an ample amount of time to get to know someone and determine you're in love with them."

"You don't know that. The heart knows what it wants. Time is inconsequential when you meet the right person. Besides, wouldn't that be fun?"

"If you say so."

She walks to her car and opens the door. "Life is too short to not have fun. I suggest you try it sometime. Live a little. Put yourself out there by doing something crazy and impulsive. In the four years I've known you, you have yet to do something that will put yourself out there. And I know you're shy and don't like attention, but can you promise me one thing?"

"Do I dare?"

She leaves her car to give me a hug. "Promise me that you will do something impulsive and not think of any consequences that may arise from it."

I chew on my bottom lip and shrug. "I'm not sure I can promise something like that."

Kara holds me at arm's length and smiles. "Just take a chance. Please?"

I nod. "Okay, I'll do something impulsive while we're there. Will that make you happy?"

"Tremendously. Now hurry up and get ready. Don't forget your massage at two!" she says, climbing into her car with a wave.

I walk to my own car and start it up, eager to get home and start my preparations for the week ahead.

Chapter 2

I WALK INTO MY APARTMENT, feeling completely refreshed after my massage. I really need to thank Kara for the gift because it was exactly what I needed. I've never had one before, but I know that I will be putting money aside in my budget to get another one. Jenny had some magical hands and managed to ease all the tension from my body. Not an easy feat but she did it.

Looking around at the space I call my home, I decide that a good cleaning is in order before I leave for the week. Not that it'll take long. I'm not a messy person and I don't usually have people come over so nothing is ever out of place. But I love the reward of my house smelling of citrus afterward so I clean as often as I can.

A few hours pass by me with ease as I dance and sing along with the songs from my playlist. The Swiffer duster is acting as my microphone while I belt out each note from every song. I'm a bit of a nerd when I'm lost in my music, but it's a lifeline that I can't live without. Getting lost in the lyrics, imagining my life being told by my favorite songs and pretending that they're singing about me or to me is my reality escape.

Bon Jovi's "Living on a Prayer" is blasting through the speakers when all of a sudden the music dies and my phone rings. I walk over to the dock to grab my phone and look at the display, loudly groaning when I see that it's my stepmother calling. The phone rings once more before I reluctantly answer the call I already know I don't want to take.

"Hi, Sharon."

"Tessa, how are you? It's been a while since we've talked last. I figured I'd check to see how you were doing."

I close my eyes and let out a hushed sigh. She and my dad married a little over eight years ago, a few months prior to my high school graduation. My dad never really kept in contact with me after the divorce. There was the occasional phone call but after about a year it stopped altogether. It wasn't until after he married Sharon that I really spent any sort of time with him. And even then, our time together was quiet and strained. I tried to get along with his new wife, but Sharon had other ideas. Our contact has been as minimal as possible since Sharon has made it very clear from the beginning she thought I was a nuisance. She was his new life and there really wasn't much room left for me so I kept my distance and only came around when I was asked.

"I've been really busy lately with work so I haven't had the time to talk to anyone. How's my dad doing?" I say quietly into the phone.

"He's the only reason why I'm calling in the first place. He's working on another large case again as usual. He asked me to call you and see how you were doing. You know how his schedule is. He's always in court about something or traveling some-where because of it."

I sigh and can't help but wonder why he doesn't just call me himself? Why does he always have her do it? "I know. Well, you can let him know that I'm alive and well. I'll be out of town with my boss next week on a business trip so you can let him know that too." I purposely omit telling Sharon about London. Knowing her as well as I do, I'm not in the right frame of mind to listen to her gloat about her many trips around the world that she takes with my dad. She always loves to rub it in how they go anywhere and everywhere as they please and that I don't have the means to do so. It doesn't help that she looks down on my job, calling it menial work. Something no self-respecting indi-vidual would make for their career, according to her.

"They're taking you on a business trip? You're just an assis-tant. What could you possibly do?" she scoffs.

I hang my head and run my fingernails across the edge of the kitchen counter. "I help take notes and prepare everything for the meetings. I am very helpful during these business trips. Kara brings me all the time when she goes." My voice is small and I can't help feeling like an insolent child.

"Personally I think it's a waste of company money but I suppose it's their call." I can hear her flipping her magazine in the background, telling me that she's already bored with this conversation. "I will report back to your father that you are well. Goodbye, Tessa." Sharon ends the call before I get the chance to say goodbye back to her. I gently put my phone on the counter and hang my head in my hands. Whatever happi-ness and excitement I had before Sharon called has vanished into thin air. It's a specialty of hers. She's always looking for new ways to bring me down and remind me of where I stand in life. With my mood now dampened I decide to resume cleaning, only this time without the luxury of losing myself in the music.

Another hour passes by and my living room slowly illuminates from the street lights outside my window. Only then do I realize it's now nighttime and I haven't eaten anything all day, again. My stomach rumbles at my neglect as I walk over to the bread box to make a toasted English muffin with peanut butter.

As I walk in circles around my tiny kitchen area waiting for the muffin to toast, a song jumps out at me and I absent-mindedly hum along to it. Once again, music comes to my rescue, slowly relieving the tension that was brought on by my impromptu phone conversation. Don't ask me why "Jumper" by Third Eye Blind pops into my head at that moment but it definitely reflects my mood perfectly right now. I can understand the feeling of being out on a ledge, seeing there is no escape and wondering if anyone genuinely cares. I know all too well about having the past haunt you, torment you every single day, reminding you of who you are and where you came from. What I wouldn't give to escape that past and build a better future.

For now I'll settle for my other way to escape reality. I grab my meager dinner and trot over to the couch, flopping unceremoniously onto the cushions and tucking my feet underneath my body. I page through my Kindle to find my newest book acquisition and lose myself in the story of two star-crossed lovers, destined for each other, overcoming all obstacles while finding their elusive happily ever after.

Sunday greets me with bright sunlight peeking through the curtains in my bedroom window. The hard, unforgiving floor is cool underneath my heated skin as the images of my recurring dream play out in my mind. Why can't I stop dreaming about this guy? I don't even know who he is, but he is a constant presence in my subconscious. I pick myself up off the floor and jab at the alarm, silencing the annoyingly loud buzzing that is aiding my headache. I quickly shower and ready myself in record time because for once I'm actually excited to do something.

With my lazy day yesterday I was able to pack all my luggage and necessary items for the week, except what I was going to need for this morning. I decided that my laptop bag would double as my carry-on, only because I ran out of room in my suitcase and didn't want to check another bag. I gently place my laptop in a zippered pocket, along with my Kindle to keep me entertained during the long flight. We have a layover in New York for a couple of hours before we head to London so I'm definitely going to need something to do there. The files that I had to run and get from the office yesterday, which I had forgotten in my haste to leave on Friday, are secured in another zippered pocket, along with the flash drive containing the digital versions. Last, but not least, a bag of chocolate covered peanuts is tucked away into a side pocket, my guilty pleasure.

I sit patiently on the couch, glancing down at my watch every few minutes in the hopes time has sped up.

10:45 a.m.

I let out a sigh and bounce my leg up and down, staring out the window of my living room. The noise of the city buzzing by my window distracts me momentarily. My neighbors are yelling again and I can hear a dog barking down the street, probably at another squirrel running by as it gathers food for the winter. The leaves are starting to turn and my street is lined with vibrant colors of green, yellow and red. As much as I detest the drab and dreary winter months, I enjoy the prelude of fall, nature's one last hurrah before plunging us into freezing temperatures and a never-ending blanket of white.

Loneliness starts sinking in as I watch a couple cross in front of my first-floor window. They look so happy and in love. The guy pulls her close as a gust of wind kicks up, blowing the hat off her head. He laughs as he chases it down the street. She stands there, holding her stomach while grinning from ear to ear as he gently places it back on her head. She gets up on her tip toes and leaves a kiss upon his lips, causing him to smile when she pulls back. They lace their fingers together once more and continue their journey down the sidewalk.

"I want that," I murmur to no one but myself.

As the couple disappears from my sight, I shake my head to pull myself out of my newly depressed thoughts. *What time is it?* It feels like it's so late in the morning. Kara should be here by now. I mean, I must have wasted at least ten minutes just staring and daydreaming out my window.

10:48 a.m.

Ugh! I'm going to drive myself nuts if I keep this up. So I get up and do a final once-over on the apartment, making sure everything is unplugged and the heat is turned down. I've already arranged for my mail to be held at the post office while I'm gone. Not that I get much anyway, but I don't want it to look like I'm gone either.

My lamps are on a timer, which is programmed to turn on at six o'clock at night and then stay on until ten o'clock. It gives the appearance of someone being home; a trick my grandma taught me when I was little. It used to amaze me when her living room lights would magically turn on. She would tease me and say it was her special Grandma magic and it only happened when she had her good little girl visiting her. I would crawl up into her lap and she would tell me all kinds of stories about her childhood and my mom growing up.

After my dad had left, my mom changed and started to pull away from me. We would drive down to visit my grandma, but as soon as we would get there she would spend the entire time locked in her old bedroom. The only times I would see her was when she came out to get something to eat. Otherwise, it was like she was a ghost. You could feel her presence but never really see her. My grandma would keep me busy and ease my mind by letting me ride the metro with her to take me shopping or she would show me how to bake a cake from scratch. She even allowed me to stay up and watch The Benny Hill Show reruns that would come on around eleven at night. She would try to explain to me that my mom was just sad and how I needed to be a big girl and help her out.

After a while, our visits to my grandma became few and far in between. She would talk to me on the phone at least once a week until it got shut off because my mom didn't pay the bill. The last time I spoke to her she sounded so sad. She couldn't come up to visit me because she didn't have a car. I remember the desperation in her voice, wanting to do more for us. If I had known it was the last time I was going to talk to her, I would have said so much more than just making idle chatter. I would have begged her to let me stay down there. I would have promised the moon and the sky, been the best girl in the whole world if she would just take me away from the loneliness and isolation of my house. But instead we talked about what we always talked about: how school was going, what new adventures I'd managed to find around my house, or if I was helping my mom out. The ordinary and usual things we'd discuss.

And then a couple months later a policeman came to the door to let us know she had died in her sleep. I remember clinging to his uniform and crying into his shoulder. My mom came to greet him, looking completely disheveled and didn't show any emotion when he told her the news. She just nodded her head and retreated back into her room. The policeman asked if I was going to be okay and I couldn't do anything but nod my head. Once he closed the door and left, I sat with my back pressed against the closed door and cried. I was ten and my whole world was shattered again.

There's a knock on my door, breaking the silence and halting my dark thoughts. Placing my hand over my heart as it beats a mile a minute, I walk over to the door and open it. Kara bounces into my entryway, grinning from ear to ear.

"You ready there, Tess? Let's get this party started!"

I fumble with my purse and laptop bag, slinging them one by one over my shoulder while juggling my suitcase and keys as we step into the hall. A quick flick of the key in the lock and we are on our way.

"I'm really looking forward to this. Thanks again for bringing me with you. I'm sure you don't really need me, but I appreciate you doing it anyway," I say as I tuck my hair behind my ear.

"Of course I need you. And I wouldn't dream of going over there by myself. I need backup and you're it, Chickie."

She throws her arm around my shoulders and we walk out the front door of my building. My steps falter when I see the waiting limo parked in front of us.

"A limo? Really?" I stand with my mouth gaping open. Kara smiles and nods her head while shoving me to the massive car. "I've never been in a limo before."

"Well, now you have. No sense in paying for parking for the week at the airport. Besides, this is way cheaper and the company's paying for it. Now come on!" Kara grabs my hand and pulls me as the driver opens the door for us. He takes my bags and places them in the trunk and then shuts our door once we're inside.

Soon enough, we've pulled onto Hiawatha Avenue and are heading towards the Minneapolis-St Paul International Airport. It's not far from my apartment, which I'm grateful for, and traffic is pretty light for this late Sunday morning.

The loud jet engines alert us to our presence at the airport. Kara hasn't stopped talking since the door closed and I'm grateful for the distraction she brings. I'm nervous about this trip, but I don't want her to know. Having never flown on a plane across the ocean before, I really don't know what to expect. I did, however, bring a bunch of mint-flavored chewing gum. I read an article once that said if you chewed gum at takeoff and landing it's supposed to help with ear pressure. I just can't believe I've never heard of it until now. It could have saved me a few times when I've flown with Kara previously for meetings around the country. Plus I figured at the least the mint would help calm my stomach.

The driver gets our luggage for us and we head to the ticket counter to get our boarding passes. With our boarding passes in hand, we start weaving our way through the crowd to the security checkpoint. I look down at the paper in my hand for the first time and notice the two little words I never thought I would see in my life.

"First class? Oh my gosh, you're spoiling me, Kara."

"Not me, the company, silly. And since it's going to be a long flight they decided that first class would be better for us than coach."

"But what about business class?"

She gives me her devilish grin. "Yeah, well, sleeping with the boss has its perks every once in a while. I told Chris he was sending us first class and that was final. The blowjob sealed the deal."

"TMI." My face scrunches up as the unwanted mental images come crashing forefront into my mind. She laughs as we walk to the first class lounge with our carry-ons in tow. We go on and on about nothing in particular and she helps ease my mind about the long flight.

We watch the TV's that are set up in the lounge, one of them being tuned to Sportscenter. They start talking about the baseball playoffs and we both chime in our two cents regarding the Tigers making it again and our mutual distaste for the Yankees. I feel very fortunate that she's such a good friend to me and that we're able to share common interests while still keeping our professional relationship separate from our social one. We continue to gripe about how the Twins didn't do well again this year and discuss different players they should be going after now that we're in the off-season.

I was unprepared for what was waiting for me in first class. The chairs are larger than the ones I was used to in the coach section. Soft white leather covers each seat with a TV placed in the headrests in front. There are only two chairs in a row, compared to the three in the section behind the curtain. I always thought Hollywood had over glorified the first class section, making it into something it truly wasn't. Okay, so there wasn't a staircase like I've seen in some of the movies, but it definitely has a high society feel. If I were able to fly like this all the time, I wouldn't complain.

I pull out my Kindle before tucking my laptop bag under the seat in front of me and patiently wait for them to tell me I can turn it on. Kara's sitting next to me with a paperback pulled out and completely relaxed. Once we get the all clear, I dive in and start reading.

A couple hours later we land at JFK Airport and are waiting for our connecting flight to London. We're sitting in the first class lounge again and Kara is talking on her phone to someone. I'm not paying too much attention to her. The commotion and crowds around me have drawn my attention and I can't help but stare at the different array of people flying by us. I'm almost ashamed to admit this but people watching is one of my guilty pleasures. There's always something interesting to see or hear every time I do it. The stories I make up about the people I observe, I think, is where I find the most thrills or causes me to laugh out loud in public. That always attracts sideways glances and odd stares in my direction. Most of the time, people don't notice certain things that they do but as someone who is always alone I tend to pick up on these little tics quickly.

There's a woman who passes near us and every other step I can hear her sniff her nose as if there's something disgusting her. Or the little boy across the aisle from me who scratches his head as he rams his trucks into each other on the floor. A woman with a fur coat saunters our way and I laugh to myself as I imagine her sharing a space with the couple walking behind her, who are obviously from Texas. I can hear their slow drawl and the loud booming voice of the pot-bellied man from here, causing the corners of my lips to turn up in amusement.

As I fiddle with the clasp on my bag, I see out of the corner of my eye that someone takes the seat next to me on my left. Not wanting to invade the person's space, I pull my bag over towards the right to give them more room. But as I look to the side, my eyes are drawn to the nicely tailored pair of gray slacks and designer shoes. I'm not sure how I know the pants are tailored, but I do. There's just something about the material that says he didn't buy them from JC Penney. I can't help but admire his well put together attire and get confused when I feel my breathing start to speed up. My eyes roam over the slacks and the black sweater, causing heat to run through my system while noting that he obviously takes excellent care of himself. He has an athletic build, with his broad shoulders and lean muscular upper body. Even through his sweater I know that there is nothing but well defined sculpted muscles adorning his entire body.

My gaze slows as it passes over his chin, which is sporting some seriously sexy stubble, finally falling onto a pair of bright blue eyes looking intently at me. His face takes my breath away and it feels as if my heart has slowed its tempo. He has piercing blue eyes and dark hair that is styled like he just rolled out of bed. You know, that sexy way guys wear their hair that makes women turn into blabbering idiots. Chiseled cheekbones and a strong jaw complete the package. He screams yummy to my starving body. He appears to be in his late twenties or early thirties if I had to guess. I blink twice and then look back down at my bag, feeling shy and awkward all of a sudden.

"Is this seat taken?" he asks in his deep English-accented voice.

That voice. There is something about his voice that seems familiar to me. I know I've never met this man before in my life. I would most definitely remember meeting someone like him. I look up again into his kind eyes and he smiles at me, showing perfect white teeth. Oh my, the earth can swallow me up now.

"Um, no. No one's sitting there. Well, you are now, I suppose." Lame. Totally lame. Way to go, Tessa.

He gives a little chuckle, keeping the smile in place on his perfect face. I give him a slight returning smile and can feel my cheeks start to heat up. His eyes dance around my face and I swear I see something flash within them. Something familiar but I can't quite figure out why.

He looks as if he's about to say something, but the crackle of the speakers draw our attention to the airline desk attendant as she announces that our flight is ready to board. Kara is still talking on her phone but stands up with me as we make our way to the counter. I'm almost eager to get away from him, yet sad at the same time. The only comfort I can gather is he's going to be on the same flight as me. The mystery man follows suit and stands a couple of people behind me in line. As we board the plane, Kara ends her call and then turns around to ask me where I am sitting.

"Aren't we sitting together again?" I ask her.

"No. I wasn't able to get us a seat next to each other. I'm in row three, how about you?"

"Six."

"Oh well. Maybe you'll get lucky and the person you're sitting with is a mute. Or maybe they'll just be some hot eye candy that you can talk to and start an illicit affair with," Kara says, as she shrugs her shoulders.

"You're so funny. You know I'll have my nose stuck in my Kindle or I'll be sleeping." I laugh as I smirk at her. She gives me a grin back.

"If the person next to me doesn't show you can sit by me. Deal?"

"Deal."

I make my way through the aisle and find my seat. Row six, seat A. No problem. I sit down and pull out my Kindle, getting it ready for the long flight across the Atlantic. I'm juggling the device in my lap as I bend down to stow my laptop bag when I notice that someone is occupying the seat next to me. I inwardly sigh. Of course, I'm not lucky enough to sit by myself. I glance over to my right and see a newly familiar pair of shoes. I slowly straighten my body back into an upright position. With a small lump forming in my throat, I turn my head and there he is, my mystery man, sitting next to me and flashing me a smile that causes my heart to stop yet again.

"Hello, we meet again," he says in his sexy English accent.

"It appears so," I reply meekly.

He gives a slight laugh and sticks out his hand.

"Andrew," he says. I take hold of his hand and shake it.

"Tessa."

There's an electrical current that flows through our joined hands, causing my pupils to dilate and a breath to catch in my throat. I notice a similar reaction in him when I hear his faint intake of breath. I quickly pull my hand away, embarrassed that he's able to physically affect me like this.

"It's very lovely to meet you, Tessa. Is this your first time traveling to London?" His lips curve into a sexy smile and I can't help but focus on how his tongue caresses my name as he says it out loud. Is it possible to be turned on just by his voice alone?

"Yes, it is. I'm going on a business trip with my boss for the week. I'm really excited because I've always wanted to visit London. It has such a rich history that's always intrigued me." Why did I tell him how long I'd be there? I need to pull myself together.

"I do hope we can live up to your expectations then. It is a marvelous city. Tell me, what kind of business meetings are you going there for?" He clasps his hands neatly in his lap with each of his elbows placed gently on the arm rests. My gaze migrates to his hands and I can't help but notice his body again. He has a body made for sin. I can just tell. My mouth goes dry and my thoughts go dirty with that notion.

I clear my throat before I try to speak again. "I work for a consulting firm based out of Minneapolis. We're meeting with a foundation in London that wants to expand its business interests into the United States." I give him a slight smile as I'm drawn to the bright crystal blues of his eyes.

He looks at me and studies my face. "Really? Minneapolis you say. That is a very long way to travel. I must say I do adore your accent. It's very cute." He unclasps his hands and puts a finger to his lip. My eyes drop to his mouth and I can't help the involuntary shudder when his lips quirk up into an amused smile. Damn.

"Thank you. I like your accent too." Smooth Tessa. Nice comeback. Why am I so nervous around him? He's just a stranger. Granted I've never seen a more perfect stranger in my life, but still. His laugh pulls me out of my thoughts and I can't help but return the heart-stopping smile gracing his face.

"Why thank you, love. So tell me, what do you do for the firm you work for? Are you one of the executives?" He looks straight into my eyes and I can only keep contact with them for a few seconds before I turn away. There's something about the way he looks at me that has me extra fidgety around him and I'm confused by my body's reaction.

"Um, no. I'm just an assistant. My boss is one of the senior executives at our firm. I'm her right-hand man, er, woman I guess. I usually travel with her whenever she goes for long-distance meetings."

He's staring at me, not saying anything, but I can feel his thoughts as his eyes dance around my face, pausing briefly at my lips before swinging up to meet my own. I'm not sure what it is he's looking for, but he must find it because a smile brightens his face, making him even more arrestingly handsome than he already is.

"I hope you don't find this odd of me, but you have the most beautiful eyes I've ever seen. They are rather fascinating I must say. I've never seen a shade of hazel such as yours," he says softly. Our knees touch accidentally, but I don't pull away, shocking myself. Instead I leave the small contact where it is, not pushing or pressing, but enjoying the tiny buzz that's running through my system.

Gathering up the courage that I know is somewhere deep

inside me I glance up and smile into his kind eyes without blinking or shuttering away. "Um, thank you. I'm not sure how I got my hazel eyes because my father has brown and my mother has blue. I've always wanted my eyes to be green. Or at least I wanted them to be one color instead of both the brown and green," I say, as I chew on my bottom lip. I don't think that my eyes are that spectacular. Or any other part of me for that matter.

"Well, I think they're lovely. They fit your face just perfectly."

"Um, thank you." His words roll around my head and all I can do is look into his smiling eyes.

"I hope I'm not making you uncomfortable. That is not my intention at all." He runs a hand through this thick hair before placing it back in his lap while looking at me, his brows furrowed and a slight frown marring his perfect face.

"No, no of course not. It's unexpected that's all. I don't get many compliments so I'm not used to them." I play with the hem of my sleeve, embarrassed by what I just admitted to him. He stares at me and I notice his frown turning into a slight scowl upon his face.

"A beautiful woman like you should be paid compliments more often than not. Please believe me when I say that you really are quite enchanting." He dips his head lower to meet my gaze. I smile nervously and nod, turning my head in an attempt to stifle a yawn as I glance at my watch.

11:30 pm.

I guess this is what lack of sleep and a change of time zones will do to you.

"Judging by your yawn and the sleepy look you have on your face, you must be exhausted. I won't keep you up any longer. Would you like me to grab the stewardess to bring you a pillow and blanket?" he asks, concern etched across his face. His reaction confuses me slightly. I brush it off, not wanting to linger on it.

"No, thank you. I'll be okay, really. I'll just lie back a little and catch some shut-eye." I chew my lip again when our eyes make contact.

"Nonsense. You won't be comfortable that way. Please, let me have someone get you a pillow and blanket." He reaches up and pushes the button for the flight attendant. A beautiful redhead appears from around the corner where her prep station is at and approaches him with wide eyes. She hungrily looks over his body and gives him a full on dazzling smile.

"Yes sir, what can I help you with?" she says. She bats her eyelashes and leans down close to him. Andrew leans back into his seat, apparently wanting to get further away from her.

"Would you be so kind as to retrieve two blankets and pillows for us, please?" Andrew says as he looks at me and smiles. The attendant looks over at me and her smile fades away slightly.

"Of course, sir. I will be right back with those for you." She places her hand gently on his forearm and lets it linger there before she goes back to get the pillows and blankets. Within a few seconds she reappears with the requested items and hands them to him, her fingertips brushing against his as he takes them from her.

"Is there anything else I can do for you, sir?" She looks at him through her lashes and gives a slow sexy smile. He shifts in his seat before clearing his throat.

"No, thank you. We will be just fine now. I appreciate it,"

he says curtly.

"If you should need anything else my name is Laura and I will be more than happy to assist you," she says, as she leaves to go back to her little room. Andrew exhales quietly and then turns his attention back to me. I'm, of course, looking down at my fingers after watching the small scene she was making. He must find her beautiful and breathtaking. Why wouldn't he? She's tall with flawless skin and her face is perfectly made up. I must look downright homely compared to her.

"Here, love, one for each of us." Andrew reaches over and places the blanket across my body. He waits for me to raise my head so he can put the pillow behind it then smoothes my hair back into place as I lay my head against the pillow. Another strange spark happens inside me at his innocent touch, making me wonder if I'll be able to sleep at all tonight with him this close to me.

"Thank you so much. Really, I would have been okay without them," I say again, blushing as he looks at me.

"Since I need to get some sleep as well there's no sense in only getting those items for just myself and watch you shiver all night. It wouldn't be very gentlemanly of me." He places a pillow behind his head and drapes his own blanket over his body.

"Thank you again. You're really too kind."

"It's nothing really. Please, you're tired. Let us get some sleep. It's a long flight and you'll want to be well rested for your meeting tomorrow."

I recline my seat back a little and notice Andrew doing the same before I close my eyes. And for the first time in a long while I fall into a peaceful sleep due to the presence of the beautiful stranger next to me.

Chapter 3

SUNLIGHT INFILTRATES MY SUBCONSCIOUS, PULLING me from my dreams, as the clouds allow the day's first light to shine upon the left side of my body. My eyes flutter open as a yawn escapes my lips. There's a painful crick in my neck and I cannot figure out for the life of me why it hurts so much. Awareness causes my eyes to open wide when I realize that I'm not lying on my pillow anymore but on Andrew's shoulder instead. *Oh my God, kill me now.* My body jerks away from his, instantly missing the contact and the pull he has over me. Even in my sleep I'm somehow drawn to him. His face lights up with amusement at my knee jerk reaction as his rumbling chuckle fills my ears.

"Good morning, love." The gleam in his eye takes me off guard as he looks down upon my bewildered face. "I hope you don't mind, but I didn't have the heart to wake you. You looked so angelic and peaceful while you were sleeping," he says.

"I am so sorry Andrew. Honestly, I didn't mean to fall asleep on you like that." I attempt to pull myself together, praying that I didn't leave his shoulder covered in a puddle of drool.

"It's quite all right Tessa. You must have been dreaming something wild because you were tossing and turning during the night and only stopped when you landed on my shoulder. Once you finally calmed down, you had this smile cross your lips and at that point I knew you needed to stay where you were. I just couldn't move you away from me when you fit so perfectly against my body." That shy smile of his is back again and I can feel my face turning an unnatural shade of red as I realize what Andrew said.

"Was I really tossing and turning in my sleep? I hope I didn't keep you up all night," I shyly say as I avert my gaze to the knotted fingers in my lap, embarrassed that I must have had that dream again.

"Of course not. I was having difficulty sleeping myself and when I saw how distressed you were, I couldn't help but be concerned for you. Your dream seemed to really disturb you with how you kept tossing your head about." He looks at me with genuine concern in his bright blue eyes. How can he be so gorgeous this early in the morning? And after sleeping on a plane no less.

"Really, I'm all right. I don't even remember what I was dreaming about," I lie since it's always the same dream. "At least I didn't fall out of bed like I usually do. Thank heavens for seat-belts." I try to laugh off my night fit, but that just makes a frown appear on his handsome face.

"You fall off your bed during these dreams?"

I fidget with my sleeves again. Damn. Why did I say that? I really need to start using my filter when I'm speaking.

"Um, not all the time. Just sometimes. I don't hurt myself.

Really it's nothing," I say sheepishly looking down again.

The honest concern in his voice has me lifting my head and locking my eyes with his. "It seems like it's more than nothing. I don't like the thought of you hurting yourself due to some nocturnal struggle you are having."

Andrew's hand reaches out slightly as if to comfort me, but he returns it back to his lap just as quickly, folding it over the other. My brows furrow at the slight disappointment in not feeling his touch, assuming that's what he was going to do. This isn't the first time he's seemingly hesitated in an attempt to touch me. I noticed it a few times while talking last night he started to reach out to me. Maybe it was the lack of sleep making me see that or maybe it was wishful thinking. I can't help but feel as if I know him from somewhere, knowing full well that is impossible. I mean I would remember meeting someone like him. I just can't quite put my finger on it, but there's a familiarity there that I don't understand. *Maybe you just need coffee to wake up. Obviously your hormones are running your brain right now.*

"I'll be okay. I just hope I didn't talk in my sleep or drool on your shoulder. I would be mortified beyond belief." I try to lighten the situation again by giving a little laugh. His twinkling eyes stare right through me and I swear it's as if he can practically see into my soul. My breath catches as he grins at me.

"Now it would not be polite of me to divulge such things to a lady." Andrew sets a small tray in front of me when I fully sit up in my chair. "You slept through the breakfast they served, but I took the liberty of saving a blueberry muffin for you. I hope it is to your liking." He places a muffin and a glass of orange juice in front of me, making my heart leap at his completely thoughtful gesture. I give him an appreciative smile as my hand hovers over the muffin.

"Thank you so much for the thought. I really appreciate it since I skipped dinner last night." And right on cue my stomach growls loudly and I blush from the noise. My arms wrap around my middle as I silently will it to be quiet.

"Well, judging by the noise that just came from your stomach you must be famished. Promise me that you will eat a proper breakfast when we land."

Again the concern that Andrew is showing me is confusing but like before I choose not to dwell on it. Instead, I appease him by gifting a small smile and nod slightly. It's not as if I'm ever going to see him again so he will never know if I'm lying or not.

"I will try, but I don't make any promises. Is London home for you or do you live close by?" I ask as I peel the wrapper off the muffin and split it in two. Andrew gives me a quizzical look when he sees that I picked the top of it off and placed it on the wrapper.

"Yes, London is home to me. I travel quite often for business so I am gone most of the time." He continues to watch me pick at the bottom half of the muffin, bringing the tip of his index finger to the edge of his lips. "That is a very interesting way to eat a muffin I must say. Do you always eat the bottom of it first?"

I shove a piece into my mouth and chew slowly, watching him tap his finger against his full lower lip. A myriad of inappropriate thoughts floods my mind as I stare at them. His lips look so damn sexy. I can only imagine what they can do, what they would taste like.

Snapping out of my trance, I quickly glance away. I shouldn't be thinking dirty thoughts when I'm sitting this close to him. It's bad enough that his scent is invading every pore in my body, making me crave him more than I already am. I need to regroup and focus. But as I do, my eyes fall upon his, causing his lips to curl into a quirky smile. It's then I realize I haven't responded yet to his question as I'm lost once again in my fantasy.

"Of course. The top is the best part, you know with all the sugar and streusel on it. So I always eat the less desirable bottom part first to get it out of the way. Saving the best for last and all that jazz."

I pop another piece into my mouth and take a quick sip of my orange juice. Mmm, nice and cold still. Pulp free too. Just how I like it. I don't usually drink juice or eat muffins. They have too many calories for my liking, but I'm not going to let him know that. Plus he went out of his way to save this for me. It really was quite sweet of him, making me wonder if he's always this thoughtful and considerate to everyone he meets.

"I agree. The best should always be saved for last. I guess I've just never applied that theory to a breakfast pastry before." He chuckles and I take another sip of my orange juice. His eyes seem to be studying my face as we stare at each other over the rim of my glass, in a moment of comfortable silence. This is probably the most I've ever talked to a stranger, but he doesn't feel like a stranger to me. That feeling creeps back again, making it seem as if we know each other. I can't shake it, nor do I want to. Deep down I think there's a part of me that's relishing in Andrew's attention, grateful to be let out of the confined box

I've kept my emotions in for so long. But even as handsome as he is and how this little exchange is making me feel, we're still just two strangers on a plane, sharing a space for a period of time. Any delusion of something between us is just that, a delusion.

I gulp down the last of my juice before gently setting it on the tray. His clear crystal blues drop to my lips before slowly making their way back to my eyes. And that's when I feel something stir deep inside me; like a million butterflies have been released and are trying to escape all at once. Andrew doesn't look at me in a way I'm used to, one that feeds my fears and doubts. Instead, there's a heat in his eyes, along with a cool caution, as if he's not sure what's going on between us either.

I swallow loudly and return to eating my muffin, desperate for some sort of distraction. He watches me intently as I go about picking apart the muffin top.

"Would you like a piece of the best part?" I ask, turning my head and holding out a chunk of the muffin to him.

"No, thank you. With the way your stomach rumbled earlier you should eat the whole thing," he says. My tongue darts out of my mouth, wetting my lower lip in another nervous gesture, as I shake my head.

"Really, I'm getting quite full and I'd hate to see this magnificent muffin top go to waste," I plead to him with my eyes and he gives me a very shy grin.

"Well when you put it that way, how can I resist." We smile at each other simultaneously as I break apart a piece for Andrew. Our fingers connect, sending another jolt of heat coursing through my bloodstream. That one simple contact is enough to make me lose all my senses except for the ones that pertain to Andrew. The jet engines, the murmuring of the other passengers, even the annoying red-headed attendant all fall away as I solely focus on Andrew.

My eyes are drawn to his mouth as he chews, watching the muscles in his jaw flex with each small movement. He closes his eyes briefly and I take advantage of the moment to admire his features, especially his long lashes as they fan out against the rise of his cheekbones. The day old stubble on his chin has my fingers itching to run along his jawline as he finishes chewing the last of the muffin, his throat working to swallow the food.

Andrew slowly opens his eyes and I'm gifted with that heartbreaking smile once again, having been caught with my wide eyes staring at him. Crap. I quickly look away and pick off a piece of the muffin for myself and place it in my mouth. A satisfied humming sound echoes in the back of my throat as I savor the sweet and fruity taste. I'm amazed at how good the pastry is, especially for being airline food. He reaches over and lightly brushes away a stray crumb that was in the corner of my mouth with his thumb and I momentarily freeze. My eyes make contact with his, not knowing what to do or say at this moment. Andrew looks deep in thought but retracts his thumb as a flash of something crosses his face. I don't know what it was, but the lingering feeling of his skin touching mine remains.

"You had a little piece there on your lips. I hope you don't mind." His voice is low and seductive, like smooth dark chocolate, and my eyes follow the movement of his tongue as it gently sweeps over his bottom lip. Oh, why did he have to do that? The onslaught of images and scenarios begin running rampant through my overstimulated brain. Showing all the possibilities of what that tongue could do and what it would feel like as it traces the curves of my body. How it would worship every inch of me.

I suddenly feel overly warm as I squirm in my seat.

"No, I don't mind. Thank you." My voice is barely above a whisper as I take in a few short breaths, trying to re-inflate my lungs with precious air. *Get it together Tessa. You're going to scare the poor man away before we even land.*

I place the last piece of muffin in my mouth and quickly wipe away any stray crumbs from my face before he has the chance to do it. I don't think I can survive him touching my mouth again. I watch his hand start to rise from his lap, moving slowly toward my own but then drops back to rest on his thigh. The background murmuring that had disappeared begins to infiltrate my ears again, reminding us we're not alone on the plane.

Out of the corner of my eye, I see the red-headed flight attendant appear at his side. She's looking at me with a scowl on her face. I assume that it's because Andrew is intently looking at me and not paying attention to her.

"If you're all done with that *ma'am* I'll take the garbage from you," she says snidely. She accentuates the word ma'am to me, clearly indicating her displeasure of me getting Andrew's attention and not her. Her green eyes are drilling holes into my head, kind of like Superman and his heat vision. I swear I can almost see the red beams coming from her pupils. I slouch in my chair and put the empty wrapper into the glass before handing them both to her. Andrew just watches my hands while they move and he keeps a tapping finger against his lips.

"Thank you," I say timidly. Well, I guess she put me in my place. She obviously isn't pleased that Andrew is not giving her his full attention. The only reasoning behind this reaction I can think of is she saw me sleeping on his shoulder during the night. She must believe that we're a couple. Even though we're not, it appears that wouldn't even be enough to stop her blatant flirting with him.

"Is there anything I can get for you before we land?" She places her hand on his forearm again, flashing him an extremely saccharine smile in the process. I think I need to see the dentist after a smile like that. Could she be any more transparent? I mean I'm no ace with guys by any means, but she's making it way too obvious.

Andrew breaks his gaze from my eyes and frowns at the attendant. "No, thank you, ma'am. I'm perfect. I have everything I need right here."

She frowns when he calls her ma'am like she did to me. Apparently he must know younger women hate being called ma'am. And he must have seen the cringe on my face when she called me that before. I find it endearing he feels the need to stick up for me. I'm not anybody special, nothing more than a stranger he's known for less than twelve hours. Yet again, there's something about Andrew that makes me want to know him and want to be around him all the time. The draw to him is so high that I wonder if he feels it too. The way he's looking at me right now melts my insides and almost makes me believe there is something happening between us.

The attendant clears her throat next to us, drawing both our attention back to her.

"If you both could kindly put your trays up and lock them

43

we'll be landing in a little bit," she says through clenched teeth, even though a smile is still plastered on her face.

I put my tray up and can't help the giggle that escapes from me. "Well, I don't think she's a morning person. She definitely seems smitten with you though."

"So I've noticed," Andrew says while putting his tray away as well.

"I guess you must get that a lot. You know, women falling all over you and everything. Your girlfriend must get jealous all the time," I say, fishing to get more information out of him.

"No, no girlfriend Tessa," he replies blandly. Elation fills my insides and I can't withhold the smile that spreads across my face after his statement.

"Really? I would have thought a handsome and sexy man such as you would have a girlfriend waiting for him back home." Again, my brain to mouth filter is not working. I can feel the red creep up my neck and face. Once again, I've managed to embarrass myself in front of him. I quickly look down at our feet with the sudden urge to study our shoes.

He lets out a quiet laugh and I bring my head back up to meet his eyes. "Sexy you say?" The slow, seductive smile he gives me causes my insides to melt once again. How can he do that to me? How does he manage to pull such emotions and feelings out of me at the drop of a hat? I hardly know anything about him, other than he lives in London and travels around the world for his job. I don't even know his last name. And that's something important. I should at least know his entire name. Otherwise, we'll just continue to be two strangers who met in an airport, destined to be only that for the rest of our lives.

My teeth clamp down on my lower lip, resisting the urge to say anything else that could possibly embarrass me right now. His mouth opens slightly as if he's about to say something, but then he quickly closes it. We're lost in this moment and I pray that it goes on forever.

My stomach drops to my feet as I feel the plane start its descent, pulling me out of Andrew's trance. This is the part of flying I hate the most. My eyelids squeeze together tightly as I hold my breath.

"It's okay. Just take my hand. You'll be fine." Andrew reaches over and laces his fingers through mine, instantly calming me down, simply by his touch. I focus on his thumbs as he runs them rhythmically across the back of my hand. He gently tugs my hand into his lap and I risk a glance in his direction. He's looking forward acting as if holding my hand is something entirely natural. I glance back down at our joined hands and stare.

He's holding my hand. He is holding my hand.

Why is this beautiful sex god holding my hand? My self-doubt rears its ugly head as I continue to stare at our connected hands. I don't understand what he could possibly see in me. I'm just a plain Jane from the middle of nowhere.

A lowly assistant who lives by herself.

A nobody.

What could I possibly bring into a relationship with someone like him? I have nothing to offer other than a black cloud that seems to follow me wherever I go. I'm just an unloved being floating invisibly through life, never once getting a second glance from anyone, undeserving of attention by the people who are supposed to give it to me unconditionally. And yet, this beautiful man sitting next to me is holding my hand, calming me down, making me feel as if I matter in this world.

The plane jerks and bounces slightly as the wheels make contact with the ground and taxis toward the main terminal of Heathrow. I look out the window and watch with childlike excitement as realization sends my brain to its happy place. London! I'm finally in London!

I bring my attention back to Andrew, who has yet to release my hand even though we've landed safely on the ground. My fingers flex around his strong hand still in my grip and I stare at his beautiful profile, etching it into my memory. My thoughts are sober as I realize our journey has ended and soon we'll be leaving each other. This magical connection we shared on the flight seems so perfect and natural as if we were two pieces of a puzzle that are supposed to fit together. I don't want to lose this. I don't want to leave him.

As if sensing my inner turmoil, he turns his head towards me and gives me a smile. I return his smile with one of my own and a slight blush that's slowly heating up my face.

"I do love your blush. It's so sweet and innocent the way it softens your features, giving you just that extra splash of color across your cheeks." He releases my hand with a final squeeze. My hand feels cold and I'm saddened by the missing contact. But I put on my best mask in an attempt to hide by feelings and guard my heart.

He checks his watch and slowly stands up to retrieve his carry-on from the above compartment. I lean forward to get my laptop bag from where I stowed it and slowly begin to rise. The attendants start dismissing the passengers from the plane and Andrew steps to the side to allow me to exit first. We walk past a jealous Laura, who is still shooting daggers at me while undressing Andrew with her lusty green eyes. Without even looking, I know that he never acknowledged her. Call it a woman's intuition but I could feel his eyes never leaving my body.

As we round the corner onto the ramp, he swiftly moves to my side and places his hand at the small of my back. Tingles shoot up and down my spine at the intimate contact. I give myself a secret smile knowing I must be affecting him. I wonder if he's as nervous about leaving me as I am about him.

"So Tessa, you say you'll be in London for the week?"

My neck cranes back slightly as I get my first full glance of him standing next to me. He seems so much taller than when I first saw him back in New York. My best estimate puts him at about six foot three. I nod my head in response to his question.

"Yes, I will be leaving on Friday to return back to the States." I chew my bottom lip and wonder where he's going with this. We reach the end of the ramp and I step to the side to wait for Kara.

"I'd really like to see you again while you're here. There's something about you that's calling to me. I don't know how to explain it. All I know is that I have this urge to see you again and I'm hoping you do too." There's a flare of hope shining through his bright blue irises as he silently makes his plea.

"I don't think that's a good idea, Andrew. Unfortunately, I'm here for business and not pleasure. Besides, there's an ocean between us, literally. I appreciate your company on the plane and for everything that you did, but I believe it is best if we just part ways."

"I don't believe you," he says with a slight scowl. But then his face perks up with a determined look and I arch an eyebrow in response. "I guess I will have to prove you wrong." I sigh and try my hardest to fight the feelings that are running through my body for him.

"Again, thank you, Andrew, for your company on the plane. I really enjoyed it." I stick out my hand, but he just stares at it. He must see through the charade that I'm giving him. His lips curl slyly into a smirk and I hear the low rumbling in the back of his throat. He refuses to shake my hand though. Instead, he brings my hand to his lips and places a soft, gentle kiss on the back of it. His lips linger on my skin, making my stomach flutter and my breathing to hitch.

"Are you sure you don't want to see me again Tessa?" Andrew smiles and kisses my hand again. He's toying with me. He saw my reaction to his kiss and now he's going to play it so I can't deny it.

I pull my hand from his grasp and give him a smile while tucking my hair behind my ear. I contemplate my answer for a moment before deciding that honesty is the best route to go, especially since he seems to be able to know when I'm lying.

"I would be lying if I said no but that still doesn't mean it's a good idea. I'm only here for a short amount of time and my schedule will more than likely keep me extremely busy. Besides I'm sure you must be busy too since you're just getting home from a business trip yourself. Anything extracurricular just isn't in the cards for us." Andrew's hand brushes slowly down my arm and I'm about to cave into his request.

He gives me a smirk and a devilish smile creeps across his face. He leans in close, allowing his scent to wash over me again, sending my body into a frenzy of hormones and lust. "We will see about that, love," he whispers into my ear before he turns to walk away.

And just like that he disappears into the crowd. I can do nothing but stand there and stare at the spot that I last saw his retreating form, silently wishing I could have just one more minute with him. And then the paranoia sets in. What if I never get to see him again? What if this is all just some horrible waking nightmare and none of this is real? He sounded so confident that we'll see each other again that I have to believe it'll happen.

A pair of arms suddenly shakes me out of my reverie as I stare into Kara's bewildered face.

"Who was the hot piece of ass that you were just talking to? Tell me you got his number!" Kara squeals. Looping my arm into hers, we slowly make our way down the crowded halls to find the customs desk.

"All I know is his name is Andrew. We met at the airport in New York and then coincidently his seat was right next to mine on the plane. I don't know why but I have this crazy feeling like I know him from somewhere." Kara raises an eyebrow to that, but I just shrug in response. "Besides, we're only here for a week and I'd be setting myself up for heartbreak if I even entertained the thought of something more between us."

Kara looks at me like I've grown a second head. "Are you crazy? You could have a week fling and then part ways. In the four years I've known you I have never seen you with a boyfriend, let alone have a conversation with a guy. You need to put yourself out there girl or you're going to end up being the crazy lady with seventy cats in the house. Besides, there's no better sex than vacation sex."

"Thanks Kara for putting that into my head now. As if I

needed sex on the brain even more than it already is. And, believe me, I know how unused my lady parts are."

"Well then fix it. Hunt that beautiful god of a man down and rock his world."

I fish my passport out of my bag as we approach the customs desk. "Highly unlikely. So chalk it up to never going to happen and focus on why we're really here."

"Man you're a Debbie Downer. Fine. Business it is then. I'm just saying, the way he was looking at you was screaming hot steamy sex. He wants you. What did he whisper to you before he left?"

"He said that he'll see about that when I insinuated that we wouldn't see each other while I'm here."

The blues of her eyes narrow on me as she slaps her passport on the desk, causing the poor old lady behind the counter to jump slightly. Kara gives her an apologetic smile.

"Smart man. I have a feeling about him though. I wouldn't count him out just yet."

She gets her passport stamped and moves to the side, allowing me to place mine on the counter.

"Whose side are you on?" I ask. The lady hands me back my stamped passport and I thank her before we head to the baggage claim area to retrieve our luggage.

"Yours, but I'm just saying to keep an open mind. If the man is determined to find you, I wouldn't doubt that he will. And if he does find you, please just go with it. You need some fun in your life."

I puff out some air in frustration and sigh, knowing I'm not going to win this conversation.

"Fine. If he finds me, I will try my best not to fight it or him."

Kara claps her hands together as she quickly finds her luggage on the rotating belt. "That's all I ask. Now get your crap and let's get going. There's a hotel bed calling my name after having to sleep in that airplane chair all night."

Chapter 4

A S PER THE STYLE AND sophistication that I'm not used to whatsoever, it shouldn't surprise me that there's a waiting town car for us as we exit the airport. Kara just smiles that knowing grin of hers and allows me to have my moment. Once we've pulled into the bustling traffic of mid-morning London, I can't help but plaster myself against the window, taking in everything that's around me.

It still seems almost surreal that I'm actually here, in London, and not in Minnesota. Of course, I've dreamed of going overseas when I was younger but never did I actually expect to have it fulfilled. I want to think I'm dreaming. That this is not real or I'm a princess in one of the fairytale books my mom used to read to me before she pulled away from me. Good things like this usually don't happen to people like me, a child from a broken family with the broken life to follow it.

The busy city hustling by my window amazes me. The lush green parks we pass have my feet itching to ditch my shoes and walk barefoot through the blades of grass to find a nice shady tree to read under. Or the older brick buildings filled with rich history that I would love to wander through and lose myself as I study the times long passed. There are all the touristy things I would like to do as well: Big Ben, Buckingham Palace, and the Tower of London. So much has happened in just this one place. I'm not even sure the amount of time we'll actually be here would be enough for me. I could spend weeks here and still probably not see everything.

Silently I wonder what it would be like to live here, to be a part of the world's history every day. But I don't think that would ever happen. I don't know anyone here and there's no reason for me to be here. Except Andrew. And I don't really even know him that well. But yet again, he pops into my thoughts. I close my eyes briefly as I picture his features, the smile that graces his face whenever he looks at me or his low rumbling chuckle that I woke up to this morning. My hand instinctively goes to the spot above my heart and I let out a small sigh. In less than twenty-four hours, I've managed to strike up feelings for a stranger. This is so uncharacteristic of me. But still, there's that familiarity about him, drawing me to him, almost on a cosmic level. It's as if fate is tying us together. But I know that's impossible. Fate doesn't work like that. And I'm probably not going to see him again so it doesn't matter.

Kara is still engrossed in her emails as the city passes by us with me acting like an excited eight-year-old watching everything in rapt awe and wonder. The River Thames is next to us and the sun shines perfectly on the calm water, causing me to squint from the glare.

"Kara! Look at this!"

I can't help but bounce in my seat as we pass a few more

landmarks I recognize. She barely looks up from her phone and shrugs her shoulders. With a heavy eye roll, I turn back to the window and try to take it all in. Heaven knows I'll never get to do this again.

"So where are we staying?" I ask, sitting back in my seat.

She finally looks up from her phone. "The Four Seasons Hotel London at Canary Wharf."

"Yikes, that's a mouthful," I say.

She laughs as her phone beeps again. "I know. But since this is your first time here I figured you wouldn't know what I meant if I said Canary Wharf."

"You could have just said the Four Seasons Hotel though," I respond.

"Yeah, but where's the fun in that? Trust me. You'll understand when you see it."

We round the corner and our hotel comes into view. Wow. She wasn't kidding. It's absolutely incredible. Right along the river, it's a picture of modern architecture with the most fantastic view. The skyline of downtown London is displayed right behind the river. Looking to the left and right I can see the Tower of London and the famous London Eye. Kara really did her homework when she booked this hotel. But then again, it screams high class and Kara accepts nothing less than the best. Her idea of camping is staying at a three-star hotel.

The driver pulls to a stop and opens the door for us. I do a quick spin in place, looking over everything, still awestruck by the splendor and beauty that surrounds me.

"Pretty amazing, huh?" Kara says.

I turn to face her as tears threaten to appear from being completely overwhelmed. She slides her phone into her purse and links her arm through mine as we head to the grand entrance of my new home for the week.

"Amazing doesn't even cover it."

"Well our meetings will be held just across the river in the business district so we don't have far to travel and this hotel has the absolute best views of London hands down," Kara says.

Nothing could prepare me for what I was about to experience when I walked through the doors. Luxury at its grandest is the first thing that comes to mind. My heeled shoes echo and click against the intricately polished white marble floors. My jaw slacks open but I quickly pull myself together so I don't stick out like some hillbilly that's never been in high society before. Everything just screams opulence, from the elaborately carved pillars to the burgundy seating areas, all leading up to the grand staircase. I know some people look at stairs and wouldn't get that excited over something so simple and ordinary. Those people have obviously never seen these. A silver and glass banister, intricately designed with etching made to look like tall grass or tree branches, flank each side of the marble staircase. Beautiful yellow flowers paired with delicate branches sit atop two wooden stands on either side.

I stand near a small round table decorated with beautiful fresh cut flowers while Kara checks us in at the front desk. The lobby is relatively quiet with just a few people sitting about, reading newspapers or talking quietly off to the side with each other. Kara pulls me back to the here and now by handing me my room key.

"I asked that we had separate rooms when everything was booked last week. I hope that's okay. Not that I wouldn't mind shacking up with you, but I figured you might want your own space," she says as we walk to the elevators.

"That really wasn't necessary. I mean it just costs the company more money."

Kara flicks her wrist at me, waving off my concern. "Don't worry about it. There's plenty of room in the budget for this. You'll thank me later."

"Are we at least close to each other?" I ask.

She hits the button for the eighth floor as we walk into the waiting elevator. "Yes, we're right next to each other. Don't worry, if you need me to check for monsters under the bed, I'll do it for you. Or better yet, I'll find that hottie you were sitting next to on the plane and he can keep the night terrors at bay."

My face instantly heats up at the thought of Andrew. I can see Kara smirking out of the corner of my eye, knowing that she's hit the nail on the head. "Well it's a good thing he was just a stranger and I don't know where to find him. And I can scare away my own monsters, thank you very much. I've been doing it by myself for quite a while now."

Her face softens at my statement and we exit the elevator, heading down the brightly lit hallway. "I know. I'm just saying that it would be nice to have someone around to keep you company, even if it is just for a short period of time."

We stop in front of our rooms and Kara pulls me into a quick hug. My arms wrap around her shoulders to return the gesture. "No more depressing talk of my pathetic life now, please. I want to enjoy this time over here and not think about how lonely and sad I am."

She releases me and nods her head in agreement. "So we've got a few hours before we need to meet with the board. That should give you enough time to get settled and relax. I'll stop over and get you in a bit."

I nod my head and smile as she disappears into the room next to mine. I open my door and am surprised when I see my suitcase already sitting at the edge of my bed. Boy, they sure do have wonderful service here.

It looks like a standard hotel room, except it's completely extravagant. I poke my head into the bathroom that's directly on my left. It's immaculate. Pale green tiles, dark wooden furniture, fluffy towels and a marvelous glass shower make up the space, creating a calming and homey feel. It looks like one of those bathrooms you see on HGTV or in magazines. It's definitely something I would never see in my own apartment.

I walk into the main room and take note of everything around me. It has everything you'd expect a hotel room to have. A giant king sized bed covered in a soft cream colored duvet is located in the middle of the room with nightstands on each side. A large wooden dresser at the foot of the bed with a flat screen TV hanging on the wall above it and, of course, the standard desk area for the traveling business person. But that's not what draws my attention. No, it's the large sitting area in the corner and the massive bay window behind it that brings me further into the room. Magnificent views of the river and London are the backdrop to this quiet little area. I could see it as a space to sit and read a book or take an afternoon nap in my downtime while I'm here. I run my hand over the large cushioned bench showcasing the serene area. All the furniture in the room is light in color, giving it a very relaxing feel. The designers definitely outdid themselves when they thought up this room.

Needing to focus and keep myself from getting lost in the

excitement of being here, I decide to unpack my things and get situated into my temporary home. Once everything has found their proper place, I snatch my Kindle from the top of the desk and settle on the bench with the intent to start my new book. But my gaze falls upon the gardens below and I see lots of happy couples down there, holding hands as they stroll about the grounds. One couple, in particular, holds my attention. A taller man with dark hair is walking along the path with a young woman when suddenly he gets down on one knee holding out what I assume is a small black velvet box. I watch her reaction as she brings her hands to cup her mouth. He reaches forward to brush away a few stray tears from her face as her head nods up and down. With a shaking hand, he places the ring upon her finger and picks her up off her feet, smothering her face with his lips.

A sad smile forms as a new ache takes place near my heart. Such a sweet and romantic gesture.

"Congratulations," I whisper, wiping my own stray tear from my face.

Being the sucker for romance I am I decide to neglect my Kindle and watch the happy couples below me, wishing for just a few moments I could be one of them. Not wanting to sit in complete silence I pull out my phone and start up my playlist. I draw my knees close to my chest and watch the people down below as music fills the quiet space. My eyes slowly close as I allow myself the brief moment to pretend that I could be one of the lucky ones, finding that perfect someone and be completely happy and in love.

Before I know it, Kara's knocking on my door. After I sat and people watched during most of my downtime, I climbed into the massive shower and readied myself for our meeting. Unsure of how I should dress, I erred on the side of caution, choosing my gray slacks paired with my dark pink lace cami and marled three-quarter length cardigan. Light makeup and my favorite green jewelry set complete my look. I give myself a quick once over before opening the door to greet Kara.

She's dressed to kill in her navy blue suit that accentuates her slim physique perfectly. Her blonde hair is done up in an elegant chignon, causing my hand to try and smooth down the flyaway strands of hair that I know I have. It's no wonder she got to where she is in the company. She looks ready to rule the world. And she does. I have yet to see a client or coworker, say no to her. There's just something about her that commands excellence. I'm sure it's just her confidence in everything she does. It's definitely a must in the business world and something I just don't possess.

"Ready to go? We don't want to keep them waiting." Kara gives me a quick look over and smiles. "I love that outfit on you. It's one of my favorites."

"Thanks. You look great too."

"Do you have all the files?" she asks as she walks over to my desk.

"Yes. They're all set and ready to go. We can just bring my laptop bag if you want since I have everything right here."

"Good idea. Less is more. I knew there was a reason I brought you along." She winks at me before shoving me toward the closet to put my shoes on. "The car is waiting for us downstairs so let's get a move on it," she says with a bounce in her step.

"You are way too perky. How much coffee did you drink when you woke up from your nap?"

"Just enough."

I grab my stuff and we head down to the elevator. Kara's cell rings as we make our descent to the lobby. It shouldn't surprise me that it's Christopher Mattson, our CEO. Of course, he's concerned about our meeting this afternoon with the board. But probably not too much since it is Kara who's heading up this project. I half listen to their conversation while humming along to the music that's being pumped out of the speakers in the elevator.

I look up at the massive building that the town car has stopped in front of. It's definitely old world architecture, with the brick front and bronze rooftop. People are walking quickly up and down the sidewalk as we enter and make our way up to the fifteenth floor. Now that we're in the confines of the elevator, my nerves kick in and I begin to fidget with my clothes and bag.

"Nervous?" Kara asks me. I chew on my bottom lip, more than likely taking off all the lipstick I had applied before we left and nod my head.

"A little. So what exactly are we going to be doing in there?" I tuck a piece of hair behind my ear, mindful I should really stop the nervous gesture.

"Basically this is just an introductory meeting. They'll let us know what they want us to do and what we expect from them. A meet and greet of sorts I guess is a better way to put it. It's not much different than the other meetings we've been to before."

I give her an incredulous look and she laughs. "We've never had a meeting span over a week before Kara. This is way bigger than just flying out to Dallas to seal the deal."

"Fine. It's a little larger than you're used to, but it's a good thing. Besides, I believe afterward we're going out to dinner with them to relax a little and get to know each other more casually. Chris says this foundation is really laid back and admires hard work and dedication. So that's what we'll show them." Kara takes a brief moment to straighten out her skirt from any wrinkles that may have formed in the car. As if wrinkles would even dare form upon her clothes. I'm fairly sure she'd put the fear of God in them as well if they ever decided to show.

When the elevator doors open, I half expected to see a blank hallway with maybe a few paintings lining the walls, leading to multiple office suites. Instead, we're gifted with a beautiful entryway leading into their office, the only one on the floor. The glass doors are frosted with large modern silver handles. Their logo and the words Tree of Life Foundation are etched directly in the middle of each door. Pale blue walls greet us as we walk into the sitting area of the office. Small potted trees of all types are placed in every corner and comfy oversized chairs make up the rest of the room. Soft classical music is being played overhead, creating a peaceful environment. There's a large marble desk located in the middle of the room. A petite young woman is stationed there and looks up as we approach the counter. Her bright, friendly smile, as she stands to greet us, helps calm my nerves a little.

"Good afternoon. You must be Ms. Thomas?" Her voice is soft and light with an almost ethereal tone. There is absolutely no way that she's more than twenty years old with her flawless complexion and light brown hair.

"Yes, I am Kara Thomas. This is Ms. Tessa Martin," she says as she waves her hand next to me. I give a nod and a quick smile. Her petite little frame comes to life as she giggles while scrunching her shoulders together. The way her nose wrinkles in the process makes me want to adopt the girl. She reaches over the desk to shake each of our hands. I'm almost afraid to do so for fear of breaking her dainty little wrists.

"Of course. It's a pleasure to make both of your acquaintances. Right this way, please. I'll show you to the boardroom where they are waiting for you." She walks us down a short hallway and holds open the last door on the right while she ushers us inside.

"My name is Annabelle. If you should need anything, please just let me know."

"Thank you so much, Annabelle."

With a nod and a smile, Annabelle turns and gracefully moves back to her desk.

The boardroom is a smaller room with a solid oak table in the middle with around ten leather bound chairs that are placed around it. There's a wall of windows directly behind the table with a gorgeous view of the river. For a large foundation such as theirs I would have expected something a little more elaborate than this. But according to Chris this foundation is very laid back and I can most definitely see that. I know very little about the Foundation other than it's multifaceted in its works and projects.

There are only two people seated at the table, a man who appears to be in his fifties and a woman who looks to be in her mid-forties.

"Ah, Ms. Thomas I presume?" the gentleman says as he rises from his seat.

"Mr. Wallace. Mrs. Hughes. It's a pleasure to meet you both." Kara walks forward and shakes both their hands.

"Please, call me Charles," Mr. Wallace says, reaching over to shake my hand next.

"Allow me to introduce my assistant, Ms. Tessa Martin." Kara smiles in my direction. "She's my lifesaver."

"And we all need one of those. Pleased to meet you, Ms. Martin. I'm Priscilla," she says. She reaches her hand out to mine, encasing it with a firm grip. She and Kara will get along just swimmingly based solely on that handshake.

"Please, call me Tessa, thank you. It's nice to meet you both." My nerves strike up again as I sweep a section of hair behind my ear. Both of them smile at us and seem like genuinely happy people.

"Are we waiting for the other party to join us?" Kara asks, taking a seat at the table.

"Unfortunately no. You'll have to excuse Mr. Parker's absence. He's unable to attend this meeting but said that he will join us for dinner afterward," Charles says, reclaiming his seat.

"I'm sorry that he's unable to make this initial meeting and look forward to meeting him later this evening." She looks between Charles and Priscilla, who gracefully lowers herself back into her seat. Rather than be the awkward one still standing, I sit next to Kara, setting my laptop bag on the floor next to me. "It's my understanding that Mr. Parker is the one who will be foreseeing the project taking place in the States, correct?"

"That is correct. Mr. Parker is our head of operations and he likes to take a hands-on approach when we open new centers around the world, which is part of the reason he is unable to join us right now. He's just returned from several meetings with other similar foundations over in the United States and he had a few loose ends to tie up prior to this meeting," Priscilla says with a smile at Kara.

"I assure you that you've made the best choice in seeking out Mattson and Associates. As you know, our record speaks for itself. I know you're familiar with the Excelsior Foundation's success and what an integral part we played in their campaign," Kara says warmly. A smile comes across my face because I love seeing Kara in her element. She may come off as sweet and dainty but when it comes down to the brass tacks, she means business. This is her baby, her calling. I only wish I had half the determination and control that she possesses.

"Yes, we are quite familiar with the successes of your company and are extremely eager to begin this venture with you. Now let us get down to the nuts and bolts, so to speak," Charles says with a slight chuckle.

As I sit and listen to everyone discuss contracts and building requirements, I determine that I'm going to like working with this foundation. Charles is so cute in a grandfather type way. He's a balding man, a little round in the belly, but still seems so worldly. And Priscilla is very proper with her blonde hair cut in a very elegant bob. She reminds me of Mary Poppins a little with her mannerisms and gestures. I silently giggle to myself as I picture her standing on a roof, singing with Dick Van Dyke covered in soot and two small children running around jumping from chimney to chimney. She's almost what I anticipated a typical British woman would be.

"Well I think that was an extremely productive meeting, don't you?" Charles says.

When I look down at my watch, I'm amazed that an hour and a half has flown by. All I did was sit and listen while taking a few notes for Kara regarding the foundations needs and what they expect from us. Kara did everything to ease their minds and assure that we have a plan in place to make everything happen.

"I agree. I believe with all the information from today's meeting we'll be able to type up our formal proposal," Kara exhales with a smile.

"Shall we continue on to dinner? I'm eager to get out of this office for the night," Charles says as he stands from the table.

"Those exact same words echo through my brain every day," Kara says. The entire table laughs as the rest of us stand to exit.

"There's a restaurant not far from here that we've made reservations at. A local place that I think you'll both enjoy," Priscilla says.

"Sounds great." I inwardly roll my eyes at the minimal contribution to the meeting. Kara bumps my shoulder, flashing me a smile. I'm sure she can hear my thoughts and knows that I need a little encouragement.

We meet up with Charles and Priscilla at the entrance of an alleyway after being dropped off by our driver. Kara and I look at each other, shrug our shoulders and follow them down the narrow corridor, unsure of what to expect. Generally I would expect a dive bar or tavern if I'm heading down an alley but since it's London I'm trying to keep an open mind.

Charles stops at a set of wooden doors, holding them open for us as we all walk inside. Thank heavens I didn't pass judgment too soon because I would have been sorely mistaken. The restaurant is beautiful. It's tastefully designed with a flare of elegance in a partially finished industrial space. The vast open space has more tables than I would have guessed judging by the outside appearance of the building. Each one is draped with a neatly pressed white linen tablecloth and surrounded by polished black wooden chairs. The contrast between the black and white makes it aesthetically pleasing to the eye. Beautiful drop lights hang from the ceiling and fresh calla lilies in crystal vases adorn each of the side tables around the room.

Charles gives his name to the hostess, who informs us that our other party is already seated and waiting our arrival. She escorts us to the back of the busy room where we see a large table that is occupied by a single male facing away from us. My steps falter as we come closer to the table. There's a change in the air that has my skin erupting in goose bumps and my heart beating slightly faster. I don't know what's happening or why I'm reacting like this until I see Charles walk up to the man and firmly clasp his shoulder.

"Ah, Parker. I see you made it."

The mysterious Mr. Parker stands from his chair and turns to greet the rest of us. But when his beautiful face comes into my view my heart stops beating as I stare into the crystal blue eyes of someone whom I didn't think I'd ever see again.

Holy shit. It's him.

Chapter 5

He's really here, standing in front of me in all of his beautiful glory. Andrew, the mystery man who grabbed my attention and stirred up something dormant inside of me, bringing up feelings that I had pushed away and didn't even realize that I was still capable of having. But yet he easily drew them out of me with little to no resistance. Strange.

He's impeccably dressed, of course, sporting a perfectly pressed gray suit with a light green button up underneath it, sans tie. The top two buttons are undone, allowing his golden skin to peek through, giving me a slight glimpse of smooth muscle underneath. Niagara Falls has taken a permanent home in my mouth as he straightens to his full height while threading the button of his suit coat through the hole. My eyes follow the movement and my tongue involuntarily darts out to wet my bottom lip.

I feel Kara's elbow jab sharply on my side as my head tilts slightly toward her.

"Isn't that the guy from the airport?" she whispers.

Words have escaped me as my eyes finally meet his. The sapphire blues pull me back into the comfort zone that he had established the last time we saw each other. I've never felt so safe, so comfortable with a stranger in my entire life. And yet, I knew as long as I was with him I was going to be okay.

I nod my head and swallow thickly. "Yes, that's Andrew."

She grabs my elbow, holding us back slightly from the rest of the group. "Did you know he worked for the Foundation?"

Cautiously I shake my head, trying not to draw attention as everything seems to pass by in slow motion. "No, I had no idea. I never asked what he did or what his last name was. I assumed that we'd never see each other again."

"Well, lucky for you, it looks like you're going to be spending the week with him."

The knot forms in my throat again as I watch Charles and Andrew exchange pleasantries. Kara and I move forward to join everyone else.

"Andrew, allow me to introduce Kara Thomas. She's the senior executive in charge of the project for Mattson and Associates."

Andrew stretches out his long arm from his side. Kara's small hand is engulfed by his much larger one as they greet each other, formally this time.

"Ms. Thomas, it's a pleasure."

"Likewise Mr. Parker. And please let's ditch the formalities. I always feel like I'm too young to be referred to my last name all the time."

"Agreed. A first name basis is preferred anyway."

His tall body turns toward me, sending a round of tingles

up and down my spine as his soft smile floats across his face. He reaches down to gently grasp my hand, pulling it to his lips as he places a kiss on the top.

"Tessa. I'm so happy to see you again."

Heat rises up my face as I focus on his lips that linger just a beat longer with a second kiss to the top of my hand.

"Mmhmm," is all I can muster. My voice has left me, as well as most of my function to move. I'm grounded to the spot as he moves a step closer to me. Releasing my hand, I take the opportunity to brush a few tendrils of hair behind my ear, allowing my eyes to be free of their protective veil.

Charles and Priscilla look at each other in confusion. I'm sure they had zero idea that Andrew and I had previously met.

"Andrew, do you know Ms. Martin?" Charles asks.

My gaze is drawn to his lips as they curl up into a heart-breaking smile. I know he recalls our chance meeting at the same time that I am.

"Yes, I had the privilege of sitting next to the lovely Ms. Martin on the trip over here. Out of sheer luck, my plane to New York was delayed, causing me to miss my original flight so I had to catch the next one."

"Sheer luck indeed that you two were able to meet beforehand."

The men pull out chairs around the table for us women, just like every description of a perfect gentleman I've ever read about. I didn't know men still did that. Andrew, of course, pulls mine out so I'm seated next to him. His fingertips brush my shoulders lightly as he reclaims his place. The scent of his cologne permeates my senses and forms a cocoon around me, surrounding me with his clean, masculine smell and something that I can only describe as simply Andrew. My heart flutters and pounds wildly inside my chest. Not from nerves though but from the sheer excitement of seeing him again.

Small talk ensues around the table as we informally get to know each other. Everyone candidly discusses their families and hobbies, regaling the group with story after story. I, of course, stay silent and only respond to questions directed to me. My fingers are tightly laced in my lap as I take in my surroundings. The murmurings of the patrons in the restaurant pose as an excellent distraction from the thrum of desire coursing through my body due to the man seated to my right.

Out of the corner of my eye, I notice Andrew sitting in rapt attention, his finger gently placed in front of his full and sensuous lips. I reach forward to take a sip of my water, feeling the need to keep my hands and mouth busy.

The waiter appears at our table and Charles orders two bottles of a Cotes du Rhone for us. I've never heard of it but am assured that it's a superb red wine that can be paired with just about anything they serve here. I glance back down at my menu to study it, finding myself faced with two problems. My first dilemma is that everything on the menu looks so mouth-wateringly appetizing that I have no idea what I should get. And secondly, I have no idea what anything costs because I never took the time to learn the exchange between British Pounds and American Dollars.

Andrew leans toward me as my eyes continue to move quickly through my choices.

"May I recommend the filet? It's quite delicious and would go well with the wine selection."

I turn my head slightly to meet his gaze. "Um, thank you."

Priscilla notices our small exchange and I can see the smile on her face.

"Tessa, have you been to London before?" she asks.

I shake my head. "No. I've never traveled overseas before, but I've always wanted to come here. I'm hoping I can see some of the sights around town if my schedule allows it."

"I'm sure we can work something out so that can happen. It can't be business all the time," Charles joins in.

Kara nods her head in agreement. "Absolutely. We're all still young and spry. We can party all night and still make the eight o'clock meetings."

Charles lets out a deep laugh. "Speak for yourself. I don't think I have that kind of energy anymore at my age."

Kara smirks at him. "One night out with me and I can change that for you."

"I don't think my wife would be too keen on that idea."

"Bring her along! The more, the merrier. I love corrupting people and if I'm able to have fun in the process, I consider that a win-win situation."

The entire table erupts in laughter as the waiter arrives with our two bottles of wine. He takes our orders and quickly scurries away. Charles picks up his wine glass, holding it in the air for a toast.

"To our new business venture together. I have a feeling that great things will be happening for both our enterprises."

We chant our agreement before I take a sip of the deep burgundy liquid. The rich, fruity flavor dances across my tongue and I hum my pleasure. I listen as Priscilla regales the group of her family trip to Paris over the past summer and her children's addiction to Harry Potter books. Ah, books. Now there's a subject that I can get into.

The mood of the table is calm and relaxing. It truly is a wonderful way for five complete strangers to get to know one another. I don't know what it is about being over here that has my guard slightly down and the bricks of the carefully constructed wall that I keep up starting to chip away. But whatever it is, I think I'm enjoying it.

Kara is as animated as ever as she talks about an embarrassing story, thankfully about her, and I close my eyes when Andrew laughs next to me. A warm, fulfilling sensation travels through my bloodstream as the deep baritone of his voice fills my senses. He's just so perfect in everything that he does. It makes me wonder if he has any flaws whatsoever.

Our food appears and all conversation halts as we dive into the delicious food before us. My stomach rumbles as the aroma invades my nostrils. I just pray that I was the only one who heard that dreadful noise. But I'm wrong because Andrew turns his head marginally toward me. His eyes narrow a little, which in turn causes his forehead to wrinkle. I sheepishly duck my head low and stab a forkful of green beans, quickly shoving them into my mouth to avoid any conversation about my lack of eating habits that apparently he's been noticing.

Oh. My. God.

The food is incredible. The beans are so crisp as they snap inside my mouth, exploding with a flavor that I never knew they could even possess. My stomach rumbles again, but it's more of a satisfied noise than an angry one. The baby red potatoes are lightly roasted and I can see the sprinkling of rosemary on top of them. The steak, if I can even call it that, is smothered with a creamy béarnaise sauce and topped with crunchy fried onions. My fork nearly falls onto my plate as the first bite lands on my tongue. The delicious flavor sends my taste buds on a wild ride. It is hands down the most succulent piece of steak I have ever had in my life. I don't think I'll ever be able to have another steak again as long as I live because nothing will compare to this.

Once all the plates have been cleared and we groan our discomfort of overeating, Andrew turns his body to me, his hand cupping his chin.

"So how was the filet?"

My hand rests lightly on top of my stomach. The waistband of my pants feels tight, even though I didn't completely empty my plate.

"It was unbelievable. I'm pretty sure you've ruined me for all other steaks now."

He laughs, letting his hand fall to the table. Our fingers brush against each other, playing with the tips in a seemingly innocent way. The electricity that travels between our fingers has me taking a sharp intake of breath. I risk looking into his mesmerizing eyes and notice the same reaction. Another chip falls from the wall and I sigh.

I pull my gaze away from Andrew because I know that if I don't I'll be looking at him for the rest of the night. It's then that I notice Kara staring intently at the two of us. There's a gleam in her eye, which can only mean trouble. If there's one thing I can count on from her, it's a push in a direction that I'm not comfortable taking myself. And right about now I know that's coming.

I shake my head so only she can notice, silently willing her to stay out of it. Her red lips draw upward and the gleam turns into a full-on sparkle. *Oh shit.*

"How long have you been with the Foundation, Andrew? You don't look to be much older than your mid-twenties and yet here you are in the position that you're in," she says, her hands neatly folded underneath her chin.

Andrew's quiet laugh resonates through me once again as he shifts slightly in his chair. "Well I'm not that young, but definitely not much older. I've had the joy of working for the Foundation for the past six years now. It's the most rewarding job I've ever had and am thankful that Charles and Priscilla decided to take a chance on me."

"Well believe us, we were the lucky ones who snatched you up before someone else got to you," Priscilla adds.

"And I appreciate it every day." His smiling eyes make contact with everyone around the table, lingering just a tad longer on mine. "The projects we fund and the places I'm able to travel to, ensuring the children of the world have a place to go and be safe is rewarding all on its own. Getting paid to do it is just the icing on the cake."

My heart aches slightly as flashbacks enter my mind of my own sad childhood after my dad left. The loneliness of playing by myself because the other kids would tease me crawl forefront in my mind. Then I had to learn how to take care of my mom at a young age, which didn't help matters much. I loved my mom, even though she was neglectful and pushed me away often, leaving me scared and confused while trying to figure things out on my own. The nights were always the worst though. I'd listen to her cry down the hall, cursing my name and the situation she was now in. I'd stare out my window, looking at the stars in the night sky as they twinkled above me.

There was nothing more that I wished for other than to join them as they watched down on the people below, protecting them from the darkness of the night. Most nights I would cry myself to sleep, clutching my pillow tight, praying for a miracle to come take me away.

I should have been more specific about my miracle.

Kara's voice pulls me from my moment of darkness. "I agree. The work that your Foundation does is truly amazing. But with all your hard work and traveling you must be away from home quite often. Your girlfriend must get upset that you're not there all the time. I know that I would be."

If my eyes could burn a hole into her, I swear they would at that moment. Kara's eyes quickly dart to mine and she flutters her eyelashes in an innocent manner. *Innocent my foot.* I know exactly what her game is and I can't believe she's playing it in front of Charles and Priscilla.

"Since I do not currently have a girlfriend it's a non-issue." Andrew's eyes meet mine and the air charges between us. I'm graced with a shy smile from him as he clears his throat. "But you are correct about my travels. They do take me away from home more often than not, which sometimes does present a problem in meeting that special someone."

"Well someone as good looking as you shouldn't be alone. I'm sure the right girl is out there. Closer than you think even."

I nervously begin to fidget with my hair, tucking and re-tucking it behind my ears. My teeth work tirelessly on my lower lip as I try not to imagine Andrew meeting someone else. An unfamiliar emotion crawls into my chest as I pause to think about that situation. Jealousy perhaps? Even though I have no reason to be jealous. He's a stranger still to me. Well, not completely but we definitely do not know much about each other. We've never even been on a date.

I think I'm getting a little ahead of myself here.

"I have that same feeling too."

Satisfied with his answer, Kara leans back and resumes her previous conversation. Damn her. My foot lightly taps up and down under the table. Andrew reaches out and gently places his hand on my thigh, just above my knee, halting the movement. I feel his eyes on me as I reach for my wine glass that was just refilled in hopes to avoid him.

No such luck.

His fingers move in small circles on my knee, coaxing me to look his way.

"You look beautiful tonight, in case I failed to mention it earlier," Andrew whispers in a low voice so only I can hear.

"Thank you. You look very handsome yourself. Not that you didn't look handsome before. But now that we're not on a plane you look better. I mean, oh boy, I need to just stop talking."

His chest shakes slightly as he lets out a small laugh. "There's no need to be nervous, love. We're going to be working closely together all this week. There's plenty of time to get to know each other better."

"I guess so."

He gives my knee one last squeeze before removing his hand, causing that area to grow cold from the lack of contact. My body sags slightly in my chair, fighting with itself at the need to touch him and the need to keep a modicum of professionalism between us. If we're going to be working together, I shouldn't get into some sort of romantic relationship with him.

That just screams bad idea.

I reach for my glass of water to take a quick sip. Then Kara decides to open her mouth again, looking straight at Andrew.

"So Tessa's single, by the way."

I choke on the water in my mouth, causing me to spray it on the tablecloth in front of me. My face turns red as Andrew pats my back. Kara flashes her trouble-maker smile before returning to her conversation. Charles and Priscilla are looking at me, concern etched on their faces.

"Are you all right, dear?" Priscilla asks, passing me an unused cloth napkin.

I hastily take the napkin, covering my mouth while coughing into it. My eyes start to water and burn from embarrassment and mortification, not to mention the fact I almost drowned from my drink. My eyes fly up to Kara, who just shrugs her shoulders. I kick her shin under the table and she reaches down to rub the abused spot.

"I'm fine, thank you," I choke out.

Andrew is still rubbing my back as I clear my throat one last time.

"I apologize. I guess it went down the wrong pipe."

Smiles flank each side of me as I look at each person around the table. Charles takes this opportunity to check his watch now that I've completely destroyed the mood of the table.

"Well ladies and gentleman, I hate to leave but if I don't get home soon, the wife will start to worry."

The chairs scrape across the floor as we all stand in unison.

"Yes, it is getting a tad late. Tessa and I should get back as well."

The five of us walk to the entrance, falling back into small talk about the tentative plans for the week. Andrew walks beside me, his arm brushing against mine as he holds the door open for me.

"It was a pleasure to meet you both. How about a tour of one of the facilities tomorrow?" Priscilla says.

"A tour would be great. I'd love to be able to see what your Foundation does first hand. It will give us a better idea of what we're working towards," Kara says, shaking both their hands.

"Wonderful. I'll be in touch with the address. Shall we say around eleven o'clock tomorrow morning?" Charles asks.

"Eleven sounds perfect."

A car pulls up to the curb and a man stands to open the door for Charles and Priscilla.

"Until then. Goodnight, Kara. Tessa."

We watch as the two of them disappear into the back seat, leaving just the three of us standing on the sidewalk. My fingers pull at the lace of my camisole as Kara and Andrew flank each side of me.

Our town car pulls up and the driver opens the door for us.

"Andrew, it was a pleasure to formally make your acquaintance. I know Tessa is looking forward to spending more time with you." She laughs at her own joke before quickly adding, "And I am too, of course."

"Yes, I'm excited to be able to spend more time with the both of you as well."

With a nod of her head, she slips into the back seat, leaving me alone with Andrew. His hands are shoved into his pants pocket as I focus on a pebble next to my shoe.

"Tessa."

The way my name rolls off his tongue has the muscles in my stomach clenching with delight. I close my eyes and take a slow steadying breath. A slight breeze sends his cologne wafting through the air, invading my senses and drawing me closer to him. My eyes travel slowly up his body, relishing each inch they pass over until our eyes lock onto each other. The smile that appears on his face has my heart beating faster again and I know at that moment that I'm a goner.

I think I like him.

There, I've admitted it. I think I like him. I find him fascinating. His handsome features have danced through my brain the past twenty-four hours and I can't help but want to get to know him better. I've never wanted to get to know another guy before. Not after the last time. But Andrew is different. He makes me want to be different, to break out of my shell and be normal. I don't know why though and it confuses me. How can someone that I've known less than a day make me want to be stronger?

"I look forward to spending the day with you tomorrow." He reaches down to gently clasp my hand in his. The thrumming in my veins causes my fingers to tingle with the contact of our skin. He steps closer to me, never once breaking eye contact. "I think the fates are conspiring to bring us together."

I swallow past the lump in my throat because at this point I have to agree with him. I mean, he shows up in New York, we're seated next to each other on the plane over here and now I get to spend the week with him. Things like this don't happen to me.

Fate you better not screw me over on this one. I think I de-

serve a break for once.

"Me too."

He smiles, giving me a genuine megawatt grin. "Until to-morrow. Goodnight, sweet Tessa."

He leans forward and places a kiss on my cheek. Blood rushes to that spot, heating it instantly and fueling my desire for him. A slight moan escapes my lips as he pulls back. I can still feel him there even though we're not touching. I feel off-balance and place my hand on his chest, feeling it rise and fall as I steady myself.

Then I decide to do something completely out of character for myself. I swallow hard, gearing up for what I'm about to do. My eyes fall on his full lips. Lips I want to taste for myself and to have them touch my skin again, in any way, shape or form.

Now's my chance.

I lean forward, closing the distance between us and press my lips to his. It's impulsive. It's not something I would do, but there is no denying I want to do it, I need to do it.

I'm kissing a stranger. And I like it.

His lips are soft and sweet, the residual wine still faintly present on them. Slowly my lips move against his, careful not to push it further than I'm prepared for at the moment. Instinct takes over and I move closer to him, seeking his warmth and comfort, knowing it's him my body craves. The blood rush-es through my ears as the world drifts off into nothingness around us. It's hands down the most perfect goodbye kiss I've ever experienced in my life.

Reluctantly I pull back, missing the contact instantly. He reaches up and cups my cheek, pressing his forehead against mine. Our noses touch. His breath is warm against my lips. I feel something pass between us, something pulling me further into him, telling me that I need to be with him. I know he feels it too because his free hand rests on my lower back, pulling me closer to him. I grab the lapels of his coat as I close my eyes and regain my composure.

"You feel it, don't you," he says, breaking the silence. It isn't a question, so much, as it is a statement of fact.

The world restarts around us, the noise coming back into my senses, reminding me we're standing on the street in a very public display of affection. Embarrassment sets in as I risk the glance into his eyes, knowing full well that I'm helpless to resist him.

I nod my head and pull away slowly, needing to put some space between us so I can regain my thoughts.

"Goodnight, Andrew."

His fingers drag slowly across my lower back as I turn toward my car. Risking a glance over my shoulder, I can't help the smile that appears when I see him place his hands in his pockets. A satisfied smile beams back at me as I disappear into the back of the car, sliding next to Kara. The door shuts and we pull away into the late evening traffic, leaving the beautiful man who has captivated me standing there alone.

Not more than two seconds pass before Kara grabs my shoulders and shakes me. "Oh my God, Tessa! He is so fucking hot. Tell me his lips are as kissable as they appear."

She's bouncing up and down on the seat next to me. My eyes roll at her childish behavior.

"I'm not telling you that. That's a personal matter."

She pouts, sticking her bottom lip out in an over exaggerated gesture.

"Oh come on. Throw me a bone here. I am so jealous of you right now."

Again, my eyes roll up to the ceiling. "Whatever. You have a guy. There are zero reasons for you to be jealous."

"Yeah but he's back in the States and Andrew is here with you. And you, you lucky bitch, get to spend the entire week with him. Score!"

"Please don't make a big deal out of this. And I'm still pissed at you for that stunt you pulled at the table."

She feigns ignorance, but she knows she can't fool me. "Let's face it. You needed a push. And it got his hands on you so you can thank me anytime you're ready."

"Don't hold your breath. That was mortifying to say the least. And completely out of nowhere, mind you."

"Oh well. What's done is done. Now you just need to focus on having fun with the hot COO."

Truth be told, I haven't been able to *not* focus on him since I first saw him. But I'm not about to add fuel to the fire. She has enough ammunition that I don't need to give her more.

"How about we focus on the reason we're actually here in this beautiful city and not on my sad and pathetic love life, or lack of."

We pull up to the entrance of our hotel and the driver lets us out. Kara links her arm through mine as we make our way to the elevator.

"Well, that could very well change. He's completely smitten with you. I can see it in his eyes when he's looking at you."

"He doesn't look at me like that."

She turns to face me in the confines of the elevator, thankful that we're alone. "He does. You didn't see it, but he was looking at you every chance he could all throughout dinner. I swear I saw something in his eyes as I watched you two."

I shake her off as we exit into the hallway. "You're delusional. He couldn't possibly want me like that. I mean I'm an assistant and he's one of the heads of a company. What could I possibly bring into a relationship with him?"

We stop in front of our doors and she lets out an exasperated sigh. "You are more than what you give yourself credit for Tess. Believe me. You're not some unwanted waif drifting through life. You have a lot to offer and anyone who sees it should consider himself lucky to have you."

I shrug my shoulders, unsure of how to respond to her kind words. But she doesn't see me like I do. Even though she's my boss, Kara's still my best friend and the one who's always looking out for me. She knows more about my past than most people, but she wasn't there to live it.

She wraps her arms around my shoulders, pulling me in close for a hug. "I love you, Chickie. You know that right?" She pulls back again and slides her key card into the slot. "Get some sleep. We've got a busy day ahead of us tomorrow."

"Okay. Night, Kara."

"Oh, and Tess?"

I glance over at her, my key card suspended in the air above the slot. I raise an eyebrow to her, waiting for her to speak.

"I liked seeing you like that tonight when you let go and followed your heart. Promise me you'll keep doing that while we're here."

My teeth clamp down on my lower lip as my eyes divert to the floor. "I'll try," I whisper.

"That's all I ask. Goodnight, Tess."

"Goodnight, Kara."

I walk into the darkened space of my temporary home, realizing I'm alone once again. My phone beeps in my purse and I pull it out to see who it could be. I laugh as Kara's name flashes across the screen.

Breakfast is at nine. Be ready.

Securing the lock on my door, I type my one-word reply and flop unceremoniously onto my bed. I stare blankly at the ceiling, recounting the events of tonight. And all my scattered mind can focus on is that goodbye kiss. I can't believe I kissed him. My hand reaches up and touches the spot where his lips last were. I smile against my fingertips as his eyes and smile come into focus behind my closed lids.

My phone beeps again next to me. With a heavy sigh, I look at the screen and am surprised to find an unknown number there instead of Kara's name. My brows furrow as I open the message from the mystery caller.

Every time I close my eyes I see your face. I can't stop thinking about you or that kiss you left me with. ~A~

Holy shit. How did he get my number? My brain rushes into overdrive as I think of ways that he could have found it before realizing, duh, he's the COO of the Foundation. He has all of my contact information at his disposal.

My fingers hover over the screen of my phone, unsure if I want to type a response or if I should just let it go. Deciding to stay on my impulsive streak I type my reply.

Me too. I know that I will be having pleasant dreams tonight because of it. Goodnight, Andrew. ~T~

Surprise hits me as I smile at the screen. He's reaching out to me. He says he's thinking about me.

Holy shit he's thinking about me.

This is too much for me to process. How did I go from being alone to having someone admit that they're thinking about me? This is something that I'm not used to. Affection. Want. Lust.

Okay, so the last part is completely on my end but still. It's foreign but most definitely welcome at this point. I stifle a yawn while getting ready to call it a night. It's been a busy, tiresome day for sure.

I click off the light next to me and pull back the covers before crawling into the insanely soft bed. The dim light of my phone on the nightstand draws my attention, casting a soft glow on the side of my face along with a little glimmer of hope and anticipation. The incoming beep has my hands itching to see if it's Andrew.

As will I. Until I can see your beautiful face tomorrow, the dreams will have to do. Goodnight, sweet Tessa. ~A~

My heart skips a beat as I read and reread the words on the screen. Maybe Kara's right. Maybe he does like me. I quickly save his contact information and set the alarm before placing it back down on the nightstand. With my brain trying to process the events of the last day, the need for distraction is there and I seek out my Kindle to get lost in my fantasy world of perfect men and relationships. But my heart isn't in it. All I can think about is a bright pair of sapphire eyes, soft, kissable lips, and the gorgeous man that's attached to them.

Chapter 6

THE CHILL OF THE NIGHT air sends a shiver down my spine. My arms instinctively wrap around my middle, warding off the impending cold as it blows over the balcony rails. My body senses him before he even touches me. His hard chest presses against my back as he wraps his strong arms around me, pulling me back to our bed, our safe haven. Space which is only ours and no one else can touch us. My eyes close as I deeply inhale the scent that is undeniably his, invading me down to my bones.

I crave him.

I want him.

I need him.

The pulsing throb between my legs grows exponentially as his lips press into the delicate skin of my neck, nipping and sucking before we fall into a tangle of arms and legs on the bed.

"Tessa," he whispers against my skin. It pebbles under the warmth of his breath, laced with heat and desire. His hands roam curiously around my body with a familiarity only they know. A quiet moan escapes my lips as his hands continue their journey, finally landing on the soft curves of my chest.

My arms reach behind me, anxious to feel him underneath my palms. My fingers twitch with delight when I make contact with the massive erection in his pants. The sharp hiss in my ear allows me to know how much he wants my hand on him as well.

"I need you," he says, gently sucking on my earlobe of my ear, causing spasms of pleasure to rocket through my body.

"I'm yours," I whisper.

My body is gently turned onto its back. The bright sapphire eyes I adore beyond belief stare into my own, saying words that do not need to be spoken. My eyes fall on his perfect lips while the shadows cast by the candles surrounding us dance across his beautifully sculpted face. Tentatively my hand cups his cheek, fingers lacing in the hair around his ear as I slowly pull his mouth down to meet mine.

"Shit."

The pain slicing across my face is excruciating. Slowly my eyes open to register what I already know. My legs are tangled within the mess of sheets, which are still firmly lying on top of the mattress. The plush fibers of the carpet tickle my nose, causing it to scrunch up as I rub my face against it. Another bout of pain goes through my head and my hand cautiously reaches up to touch it. The same dream, only somehow slightly different. Regardless, the end result is the same. Once again, I'm on the floor.

Somehow my legs manage to disentangle themselves from the sheets as I slowly rise from the floor. Why does this keep happening to me? Why can I not escape the torture of thinking there's some guy out there who actually wants me?

Andrew instantly comes to mind and a slow smile creeps across my face. Andrew wants me. And he's real, not some mythical figment of my imagination. I stumble over to the nightstand to turn off the alarm on my phone and notice a missed text message.

Good morning, Tessa. I hope you slept well. Would it be too presumptuous of me to invite myself to breakfast with you this morning? ~A~

He wants to have breakfast with me. He wants to see me. I glance down at the time and see that I've got a little over an hour to get ready. My fingers are typing the response before my brain even registers the need to.

Not presumptuous at all. I would love for you to join me and Kara for breakfast. Can you meet us at our hotel around 9:00? We're staying at the Four Seasons Canary Wharf. ~T~

Love? My head rolls back as I squeeze my eyes shut, reminding me again of how I woke up this morning. I flinch as my fingertips lightly graze my cheek. One can only imagine what this bruise is going to look like. Within seconds, his response appears on my screen.

I will meet you in the lobby promptly at 9:00. I am looking forward to spending the day with you. ~A~

If it were possible to pass out while still being completely awake, I could do that right now from the sheer joy of knowing I am spending the day with my gorgeous mystery man. My shaky legs carry me to the shower as my mind races at a mile a minute.

I shouldn't feel this giddy about seeing him. We barely

even know each other. But then again, that's how it always is when you first meet someone. You don't know them. You have to spend time with them to learn their little nuances and the special things about them that make them the person they are, the person that attracted your attention in the first place. And yet somehow this beautiful man has me craving more of him. This draw I have to him elates me, an emotion that's confusing yet exciting me at the mere thought of him.

The soft knock on my door announces Kara's arrival as I crack the door slightly, using it as a shield against my mostly naked body. Somehow she manages to squeeze her body inside and shakes her head at me.

"What the hell? You're not even dressed yet?"

"Andrew is coming to breakfast with us and I have zero idea what to wear."

The Cheshire cat grin that appears on her face should have me worried, but I brush it off since I have more pressing issues currently flooding my brain.

"Andrew's coming?"

"Yes, Andrew's coming. Help. Me. Please!"

She turns to my closet, rifling through the few things that are hanging up before handing me my tan sweater dress.

"Here, wear this one. It'll be perfect for today since it's a little chilly out. Plus you'll look smoking hot in it."

She hands me the hanger with the dress on it and I hastily grab it from her. She finds a wide black belt to pair with it, along with my knee-high boots, tossing them both to me as I slide the dress over my semi-naked body.

Kara looks at me in the mirror at the same time as I do.

"Okay, I admit it. This looks good," I say, twisting my body around to get a look at all angles.

"Good? Please. You are hot! He's going to melt right on the spot when he sees you."

She picks up the curling iron and starts playing with my hair while I focus on putting my makeup on.

"Don't be nervous. Remember, you have all day to spend with him. Take a deep breath and relax."

My eyes close as I do what she asks. Somehow that makes me feel better. Kara digs through the small travel jewelry case and pulls out some bangle bracelets, along with my silver hoop earrings. She leans against the wall as I put on the finishing touches, spraying a fine mist of my favorite perfume across my body.

"Perfect."

I roll my eyes. "Not quite but it'll do."

"Whatever." She glances at her watch. "And with minutes to spare. Come on let's not keep the handsome man waiting."

My hands nervously fidget with my dress the entire way to the lobby. Kara looks over at me and shakes her head.

"Will you knock that shit off? You look hot. You couldn't look any hotter if you tried." She pulls at my hands and holds them steady as we exit the elevator. I can feel my breathing start to pick up and the onset of a panic attack slowly rises through my body.

"Look, there he is. Go get him, Tiger."

Kara pushes me playfully into the open space and I stumble forward. Then I just stop. Andrew is sitting in one of the wingback chairs, reading the newspaper. My hand hovers over my heart as I watch him nervously chew on his thumb, my eyes drawn to his mouth. He's dressed in a pair of khaki pants paired with a green sweater that clings to his chest, giving me an excellent idea of what lies beneath.

The rapid beating of my heart pounds a tattoo against my palm. He's just so elegant and refined, sitting there so calm and collected. The nasty thought of why he's interested in a nobody like me enters my head and my hands begin to twist into each other.

But then he looks up, sapphire eyes locking onto mine. Time stands still as he smiles in my direction. Andrew's entire face lights up as his eyes hover over me and I can almost feel his attraction from here. The air becomes thick making it almost hard to breathe. Or it could just be me as my breath is stolen from my body when he stands to his full height, gently placing the folded newspaper onto the table in front of him.

Kara nudges me from behind even though I'm rooted to the spot. My eyes never once leave his as he approaches us, moving with the same refined elegance I was admiring while he was just sitting there. He's completely out of my league.

"Good morning, ladies," Andrew says. The sound of his deep masculine voice washes over me, causing heart palpitations once again. My eyes roam over his features now that he's standing within arm's reach of me. Clean shaven, hair impeccably styled, unwrinkled clothes. Just sheer perfection in my book.

My eyelids flutter slightly as the first smell of his cologne hits my nose. The knots in my stomach pull tighter and I swallow past the newly formed lump in my throat.

"Well, good morning to you, Andrew. You look very handsome today. Doesn't he Tessa?" Kara says, elbowing me in the back.

It's then I realize that I have been mute and statuesque the entire time. But my body doesn't seem to want to cooperate. All I can do is stand there, silent, and look at him. He leans in close, giving my body another reason to tremble.

"Tessa, you look even more beautiful than yesterday," he says, grasping my hand. My eyes follow his lips as they gently land upon my skin, leaving a trail of warmth and fire in their wake when he pulls up. Heat rises in my cheeks, making me glad I skipped applying blush today, probably knowing I wouldn't need it as long as he was around me.

"Thank you, Andrew," I say quietly on an exhale. He smiles and once again my body reacts to the sheer beauty of him near me. He keeps my hand in his as Kara clears her throat behind me.

"So glad you could make it this morning. Unfortunately, I have a conference call I was made aware of at the last minute so you two are on your own."

My head twists to the side, trying to see if she's doing this on purpose or not. Although knowing her, she's lying so Andrew and I can be alone together.

"I wasn't aware of a conference call." She smiles her mischievous smile and shrugs her shoulders.

"Like I said, it was last minute. So I'll leave you two to it. Ta-ta!" she chirps, waving her hand over her shoulder as she quickly retreats to the bank of elevators. Mischievous little tart. I don't know whether to thank her or throttle her. The jury is still out on that.

My eyes fall onto our joined hands again until Andrew's voice draws my attention upward.

"It appears that it's just you and me then. Shall we?" he

asks, releasing my hand and offering his elbow instead. My arm slips easily into the crook of his as my head nods in agreement.

We glide across the marble floor toward the in-house restaurant, where we're ushered immediately to a quiet table in the corner, giving us some privacy from the rest of the crowd. It doesn't escape my attention that every female's eyes follow Andrew as we walk through the restaurant, allowing myself to receive a few glares at the same time. Not that I blame them. I'd be staring at him too if I weren't the one currently attached to his arm.

Being the perfect gentleman that he is, he holds out my chair for me. I give him my silent appreciation, still unable to find my voice as I watch him lower himself into the chair next to me. Odd that he doesn't want to sit across from me, but I quickly understand the reason why as his leg brushes up against mine. My stomach flutters again at the contact.

"So Tessa, tell me a little more about yourself," he says as he picks up his menu.

I watch as his eyes scan over the choices and I feel myself relax a little.

"Well, there's not much to tell really. I'm twenty-six, I live alone in a small one bedroom apartment close to downtown Minneapolis, and I go to work then come home and read. I'm really quite boring, believe me."

His quiet chuckle pulls a smile from me as I scan the menu in an attempt to avoid eye contact.

"I find that hard to believe. Have you lived in Minneapolis your entire life?" The genuine curiosity in his voice pulls my head toward him. My bottom lip disappears between my teeth.

"No. I grew up in northern Minnesota until I graduated

from community college with my AA degree and my certification as an Administrative Office Assistant. It's not much, but it was all I could afford at the time. Some people would look down upon my job title, but I truly enjoy it. There are so many people out there that have their jobs simply because of the money and are miserable doing them. It may not be the highest paying job ever, but it covers my bills and I'm doing something that I love, which makes getting up every day worth it."

Typically I go on the defensive about my job because most people do look down upon it. They feel that being a lowly secretary is just some position for people who have no talent or purpose in life. But as Andrew looks at me, I don't see the pity or disappointment in my life choices I see with some others. There's a sparkle in his eye as he just sits and listens to me describe my somewhat pathetic life.

"It's not often you find a person who enjoys what they do in life. You are most definitely a rare one Tessa, in more ways than one." He places his hand over mine and the familiar tingling travels through my veins.

The waiter arrives at our table, jotting down our order quickly as if sensing we wanted to be alone. It isn't lost on me Andrew has yet to remove his hand from the top of mine, making my soul sigh as it chips away another brick in the wall I've constructed around me.

The awkwardness I usually feel leaves me as we sit in a moment of comfortable silence. He obviously must be comfortable as well because he doesn't make a move to fill it. My eyes fall upon our joined hands and I notice he does the same. He lightly squeezes it, causing another spark to travel through my body.

"I hope you don't mind this Tessa, me holding your hand. It's just that I haven't been able to stop thinking about you since we first met. There's this overwhelming need to touch you as if to make sure that you're real," he says quietly.

That low timbre in his voice stirs emotions inside me again and I feel the heat rise in my cheeks as he verbalizes what I'm thinking in my own head.

"Well, to be completely honest, I have the same feeling as you. Every time I'm near you there's this attraction I just can't place. It's very new for me and it scares me a little."

"While we're honest with each other, I admit that it scares me a bit as well."

I watch as he lifts his free hand and lightly traces my cheek with his index finger. My heart beats a pounding rhythm in my chest as I watch his brows furrow in concern.

"What happened here? You have a slight bruise on your face." The tip of his finger crosses the discolored skin again, causing me to flinch slightly as he hits a sensitive spot.

"Oh, that? It's nothing." My attempt to play it off as nothing fails as a frown crosses his beautiful face.

"It most certainly is something. How did you hurt yourself? Please tell me that something or someone didn't hurt you after we parted ways last night."

"No, it's nothing like that Andrew. Do you remember on the plane when I said that I fall out of bed at night?" He nods his head. "Well, that's what happened. Apparently I really did a number on myself this morning."

His fingertip brushes the abused spot once more before his hand slowly retreats back. "I hate to think of you falling and hurting yourself this way."

"It's nothing really. It barely hurts. And besides, I'm used to it."

"What are your dreams about, if I may ask?"

How do I answer this question without sounding like a complete nut-job? How do I explain to this gorgeous man, who is obviously way out of my league to begin with, that there's a dark-haired man who visits my subconscious every night? Putting my mind into such a fit I willingly throw my body from the bed to crash back down to Earth.

"It's nothing really, just a silly dream I often have. But enough about me. I'm more interested in learning about you," I say, changing the subject to take the focus off me.

"Where shall I begin? I was born on the fourteenth of June on the second floor of St. Charles' Hospital in Kensington."

He says it with the utmost seriousness in his face and I can't help myself when I break out in laughter.

"Not that far back. How about something a little more recent," I say, wiping at an invisible tear. He graces me with that panty-dropping smile, lighting up his face once again.

"Something more recent you say. Well, I went to university at Oxford where I received my MBA. I started working for the Foundation while doing my studies and actually used it for my thesis paper. They had me do small things as I was learning about what exactly the Foundation is involved in, like volunteering to work in some of the centers around the city. When I graduated, the Board was quite happy with all I had accomplished so they decided to make me the head of operations. So now I'm in charge of traveling to each site, making sure they have everything they need and then coordinating funding and overseeing all the details for new centers to be built around the world."

The passion for his job is evident as I look into his eyes, mesmerizing me completely. He gives me a smile followed by a playful wink as he leans in closer.

"And just so you know, I'm thirty, I also live alone in my flat and am quite boring as well."

"I hardly doubt that you are boring. Your life is way more interesting than mine by far."

Unable to hold back any longer I let the laugh escape my throat, causing him to laugh in return as the waiter arrives with our food. Andrew reluctantly releases my hand as the delicious aromas cause my stomach to grumble once again. He gives me a look out of the corner of his eye and I quickly shove a forkful of food into my mouth to quiet the noise.

"So what do you do for fun?" I ask.

Andrew takes a sip of his coffee and wipes at the corner of his mouth with his napkin. "Let's see. Several of my mates and I started an intramural rugby league a few years back. It started out with just two teams and now we're all the way up to eight."

My eyes widen slightly. "Wow, that's amazing. When do you do this?"

"Normally we play during the summer months on the weekends. We schedule games on Saturday and Sunday, making sure everyone is able to play. We treat it like the professionals do, finding referees and having playoffs and the sorts. It's a lot of fun and everyone always has a good time."

I nod. "So you played rugby in college then?"

Andrew smiles and nods. "I did. My mum was less than thrilled about that because she felt I was distracting myself from my studies. So I did the logical thing and got A's in all my classes."

I laugh and take a drink of water. "Overachiever."

He shrugs his shoulders and chuckles. "Possibly. I like to think of it as determined."

"Do you always get what you want?"

He leans toward me slightly and smiles. "Yes. If I see something that I want, there isn't much to stop me from pursuing it."

I flush at his words and tuck a piece of hair behind my ear. "Oh." He laughs and I look back up into his eyes. "Did you play any other sports?"

He shakes his head. "No, just the one. It was enough to get me by though. Kept me active in between my studies. It was more of an outlet for me than anything else. There's nothing better to relieve your frustration then by running around and trying not to get killed."

My fork pauses in front of my face with my mouth wide open. "Please tell me you're kidding."

He laughs and chews the bite he just took. "Not literally killed. It only feels that way when people are chasing after you."

"I see."

"What about you?" he asks. "What do you do for fun?"

I quietly laugh to myself as I think of something good to say. "Not much. I go to work and then come home. Every once in a while Kara will drag me out somewhere or we'll have a movie night at my place. Otherwise, I just sit at home and read."

"Ah, a book lover."

"Yes, very much so."

"Tell me, what's your favorite book?"

My eyes draw up to the ceiling before finally shaking my head. "That's a difficult question. I have so many books that I enjoy that it is hard to pick just one."

"I bet I could guess it."

I quirk an eyebrow to him and smirk. "Oh, really? Okay then, what would it be?"

He leans back in his chair and taps his chin with his index finger. "I would imagine that you are a lover of romance and of the classics. You enjoy the stories where the male lead woos the female until they can no longer deny their attraction and succumb to it. With that said, I think I'd classify you as a Janeite. So my guess would be Pride and Prejudice."

I place my fork down on the plate and cross my arms in front of my chest. "That's too obvious of a pick. Everyone loves Mr. Darcy. But, no, not Pride and Prejudice."

"But was I right about being a Janeite?"

I laugh and nod. "Yes, on that you were correct. Actually, Sense and Sensibility is my favorite Austen book."

He laughs and takes another sip of his coffee. "I knew you were the romantic type."

I blush and take another bite of my food, not admitting that he's right about that.

"What about you?" I ask. "Do you have a favorite book?"

"I do actually."

I mimic his thinking pose from before, tapping my index finger against my chin. "I don't see you as a Janeite, or any other female author of that era. You probably like action and suspense with little mushy stuff. Although I think you're a romantic at heart too. But if I had to guess, I'd say Tolkien or Wells."

Andrew's lips quirk up into a smile and he shakes his head. "While I do enjoy reading Beowulf and The Hobbit, they're not my favorite. Actually you may be surprised to hear what my favorite book is."

"Don't keep me waiting. I'm on the edge of my seat."

He ducks his head to the side, looking at my chair and I laugh. With another chuckle, he smiles and clears his throat. "Actually I love the works of Charles Dickens. Bleak House, David Copperfield, Great Expectations. Pick one and I would happily read it for eternity."

I blink several times and smile. "You're right. I am surprised. But I have to agree, Dickens is a good author. I would read A Christmas Carol every year during the holidays."

"Another excellent work. Glad to see I'm not the only person who loves the written word."

I shake my head and smile. "No, you're not alone in that area."

We continue to eat while still falling into discovery mode for our conversations. In the back recesses of my mind, I notice how natural this feels. How compatible we seem to be. I feel like I've known him my entire life, which is ridiculous considering we've just met. But the familiarity is there once again, pulling at my heart, pulling me towards him and I'm unable to stop it. Not that I would want to anyway.

We sip our coffees once our plates have been removed. A comfortable silence has filled the space again. He reaches over, pulling my hand into his, lacing our fingers together. I watch as he examines our joined hands, marveling myself at the heat I feel coursing through my veins at this simple touch.

"Will you do me the honor of joining me for dinner tonight?" he asks.

Our eyes make contact. The butterflies in my stomach flutter uncontrollably as he silently speaks to me. Taking the risk,

I lean my body closer to his so our faces are only mere inches apart. Dragging my bottom lip through my teeth, I swallow hard and nod my head with a smile.

"I would love to join you for dinner tonight Andrew."

My fingers squeeze his and his face lights up with excitement. But it's short lived because before I realize it, he's closing the distance between us and his lips softly find mine. They're warm with the faint hint of coffee between us, but still it's a taste that's all Andrew. It's brief and I instantly miss the contact when he pulls back, tucking a strand of hair behind my ear, allowing my eyes to be unobstructed from his.

He glances down at his watch with a frown. With a wave of his hand, he flags the waiter, handing him a credit card to pay for the bill without looking at it.

"We should go get Kara and be on our way. It's almost time to meet up with Charles and Priscilla."

He signs his name on the receipt with the same fluidity and elegance that he emanates in everything that he does. I move to stand from my chair, but he's instantly behind me, pulling it out as I rise to my full height. He runs his hand down the length of my arm before clasping my hand in his, leading me out of the restaurant so we can retrieve my troublemaker boss.

Chapter 7

NDREW PULLS UP IN FRONT of an enormous building about a half hour away from our hotel. There's a fenced in yard with kids of all ages running all over, playing on the equipment and with each other. Their joyful laughter fills the air as we exit Andrew's car. Of course Andrew is the perfect gentleman, opening the door for both Kara and I before we have the chance to do it ourselves. Who says chivalry is dead?

Andrew holds his arm out to me once again and without thought, my arm links with his. His head turns marginally towards mine, giving me a wink as his arm flexes slightly. He offers Kara his other arm and I can't help but laugh.

"What's so funny?" he asks me. I shake my head from side to side, trying to allow my laughter to subside.

"You are, walking into this building with two women on your arms. It must be quite the ego boost for you," I tease.

Kara and Andrew join in my moment of laughter as we walk across the parking lot toward the school-like building. He slyly smirks and my insides melt just a little bit more.

"With women as beautiful as you two any man would be a fool not to have you hanging on his arms."

"You are quite the character, Andrew," Kara says, placing her hand on his strong bicep. "But don't get any ideas mister. You're hot and all but totally not my type. Plus I'm already taken."

She gives me a wink across his body and I can't help the eye roll that follows. It's my turn to flex my arm around Andrew's, reveling at the firmness of it as he flexes against me. My other hand instinctively comes up, gently lying on top in a familiar gesture. Warmth spreads through my body, thinking to myself how natural and effortless it is to act like this around him. Emotions that I'm afraid to acknowledge come creeping to the forefront of my mind and I quickly shake them off, not ready to accept what could potentially be happening here.

Kara laughs again and releases herself from Andrew's arm, giving us her customary wave over her shoulder as she climbs the front steps. I shake my head at my friend's apparent attempt to force us together. I will give her this; she's nothing less than tenacious when she has her mind set on something. And apparently that something is forcing me to be alone with Andrew whenever possible.

His warm breath at my ear pulls me out of my head once again as we climb up the steps behind her. "I think the fates have also enlisted Kara in pushing us toward each other."

My skin pebbles as his lips inadvertently graze my overly sensitive flesh. The scent of his cologne wrapping around me once again causes my eyelids to flutter with delight. It should be a crime for someone to smell this good all the time. He opens the door for me, again another thing for me to get used to if I'm going to be around him this week.

We enter the building and I suddenly flash back to my school years. It's a large hallway, filled with many doors all leading to what I assume are classrooms. But it doesn't have that edge like a regular school would. Music and laughter fill the halls, something I never experienced when I attended in my younger years, or at least that I never stopped to pay attention to. My mind was always focused more on surviving the torment I endured day after day at the hands of my peers.

I move away from Andrew, my fingertips dragging along his forearm as I walk over to one of the doors to my left. Looking through the window I see a group of little children circled around a young woman who is reading a book to them. They sit quietly with their chins propped up against their tiny fists as she animatedly tells the story from the pages, each of them sporting bright smiles and laughing eyes.

Andrew moves behind me, his hand gently resting upon my hip. He leans into me, his mouth once again near my ear.

"This is what we've dubbed the story room. All of these books have been donated by multiple families and libraries from around London. Most of the children you see here are around four or five years old. Their parents either are struggling to find a job or have multiple jobs but cannot afford standard daycare. That's what we do here. We are a place for children to go who don't have much of a home life and we give them a place to feel welcome."

His whispered words cause my breath to catch in my throat as I continue looking into the room. Hundreds of books line the shelves that circle the room. Multicolored bean bag chairs occupy the corners and small tables with chairs are set up in the middle of the floor. The children are sitting on top of a large plush area rug off to the side, a few of them curled up with blankets and pillows looking ready to take a nap.

My heart aches as I watch them enjoy their story, wishing that circumstances could have been different for me when I was growing up. I would have loved coming to a place like this, even if it were just to escape my life for a little while.

The heartfelt smile crossing my face and the regret over my lost youth has a small tear threatening to fall from my eyes. I quickly blink it away, not wanting to cause a scene or give Andrew any reason to look into my thoughts.

He's still pressed against my back, his fingers flexing gently upon my hip as I turn to face him. Reaching down, I tentatively lace my fingers with his, removing it from my hip. His eyes sparkle in the lights as I look up at him.

"This is amazing what your Foundation does for these kids. I know all any child wants most in life is to feel welcome and safe." I pause, suddenly fascinated with my boots so he doesn't see the pain behind my statement.

His free hand reaches up and softly drags the knuckles of his hand down my cheek. It's a loving gesture that also shows the compassion I'm not quite ready to accept from him yet. My chin lifts slightly, allowing me to see his brows furrow as he contemplates the meaning behind my off the cuff comment. He shakes his head then leads us down the rest of the hallway toward an office at the end.

As we walk down the hall, he explains some of the programs that they offer here. There's a tutoring program in place for all subjects and grade levels, working in conjunction with the public schools. There's an arts program with varying classes between music and painting to sketching and choir, allowing the kids to explore their creative sides. They also house a large gymnasium where the kids can come and burn off some energy while trying out different indoor sports. It allows them to hone their skills for organized teams at their regular school or just a safe place to hang out with other children like them.

We enter the office area, only to be greeted by the smiling faces of Charles, Priscilla, and Kara. Andrew tightens his grip on my hand as I try to pull it away from his, not wanting the others to see. Charles looks us over, his eyes landing on our joined hands as a smile crosses his face.

"Ah, there you both are. So glad you could make it Tessa," he says with a wink to me. My cheeks flush as I notice Priscilla's eyes also locked on our joined hands.

"Yes, so glad to see you again Tessa. Kara was just telling us about her morning."

Kara's hand moves to lightly cover her mouth in an attempt to stifle a forced cough. I can hear that she's on the verge of laughter as she clears her throat once more.

"Yes, I was in desperate need of a massage after flying over here. Thank goodness the hotel has an excellent selection of spa services available."

I narrow my eyes at my best friend. My lips are at war over whether to scowl or smile at her blatant lie to me this morning.

"I thought you said you had an urgent conference call?"

"Did I say that? No, I meant an urgent massage. Whoopsie," she says with a shrug of her shoulders.

The room erupts in laughter at the ridiculousness of Kara's statement and brush off. If she's trying to make it obvious that she wanted Andrew and me to be alone this morning she's definitely succeeding. Even still, I can't help but laugh with everyone else, especially when Andrew's thumb gently strokes the back of my hand. How upset can I truly get at her matchmaking ways? I really should be thanking her for allowing me to spend as much time with Andrew as I can while I'm here without the eyes of everyone else around us.

"Shall we begin with a tour of the grounds? I think you both will be quite pleased with what we do here at this Center," Priscilla states.

We spend the next few hours moving from hallway to hallway, classroom to classroom. We're introduced to several children in passing and even are invited to partake in one of the projects in the art room. Of course, we respectfully decline, using the premise of a lack of time.

Andrew's hand never once leaves mine throughout the tour. My heart beats wildly, wondering what Charles and Priscilla must think of their COO holding hands with a potential business associate. A wave of fear spreads through me as I dwell on that a little longer than I should. What would happen to us when the contracts are signed? Is there a no fraternization policy that would prohibit us from being together?

My fear is short-lived as we enter the gymnasium. There is a handful of teenage boys playing basketball toward one side. A small group of little girls are playing with hula hoops in the middle and over on the far right is a mix of boys and girls playing volleyball. My mood lightens considerably as I watch and listen to the laughter that echoes through the gym.

A basketball rolls toward me and I reach down to pick it up. A taller than average teenage boy jogs up to me, sweat dripping from his brow and slightly out of breath.

"Pardon me Miss but could I please get the ball back? We only need one more point and then we win," he smiles at me.

Inspiration strikes me as I hold the ball out to him. After our conversation this morning, I feel the need to step out of my comfort zone and try doing things that I may not normally do, per Kara's instructions before we left the States.

"Here you go. But I call the winner."

He stands there almost in a daze before he blinks back to life. "You play basketball?"

"I've played a little, but it's been a few years."

He looks down at my feet and starts laughing. He doesn't look to be more than fifteen or sixteen.

"But you don't have any trainers."

I look down at my knee-high boots and laugh. "I'll improvise, don't worry about that. But if you're not up for the challenge . . ." I say, leaving the sentence hanging in the air between us. He stands a little taller and takes the ball from my outstretched hands.

"Play a game with you? I'll make sure we win."

He runs back to his friends and tells them the offer. All at once they turn their heads toward me, each beaming brightly. Andrew laughs while looking down at me.

"Are you sure you want to do that? You'll kill yourself with those boots on."

"Oh don't worry. I'll manage," I say.

I bend down and start unzipping my boots, gently bracing myself on Andrew's arm as I slide them off my feet. He stares at me with heat in his eyes, giving me an appreciative grin while he follows the movements of my hands. I look up and notice that the group of boys have stopped playing too, carefully watching me as I strip out of my oppressive boots. I stand upright, placing my hands on my hips as I look in their direction.

"No one is going to win if no one plays, boys," I mock scold them. They unfreeze themselves and resume their game. I can hear the other three laughing behind us as I turn slightly toward them. They appear to be lost in conversation, occasionally glancing at Andrew and me.

I bend down again to remove my stockings, thinking that it would probably be in my best interest to play barefoot, especially since I know how coordinated I am. I risk a glance up at Andrew through my lashes, throwing him what I hope is a seductive smile. Once again, I see the heat in his eyes as they lock onto my hands, sliding underneath the nylon being drawn down my legs. My breathing accelerates and my stomach clenches as I hear a faint groan coming from him. My lower lip disappears between my teeth as I notice his breath catching when we lock eyes.

He gives me another appreciative grin, his lips curling into the smile that I have come to adore since I first met him. He opens his mouth, looking as if he wants to say something, but nothing comes out. Instead, all I hear is a loud thud due to the basketball hitting him in the side of his head. He stumbles a little and then looks over at the offenders after regaining his composure. They sheepishly murmur an apology to Andrew as he bends down and tosses the ball back to them with a laugh.

"I think you're going to have an unfair advantage over them, Tessa." He looks over his shoulder as the boys take several shots at the basket. It doesn't go unnoticed that they also look over at our direction often while they're playing. "It also appears that you may have a few admirers."

I boldly place my hand on his firm chest as I straighten upright. "Jealous?" I ask.

My eyes fall upon his throat as I watch him swallow hard at my comment. The joyful commotion coming from the boys behind us fades to a dull roar as the sexual tension flowing between me and Andrew occupies my senses. I blink hard, hoping it's enough to pull me away from him. He runs the pad of his thumb down my cheek as his eyes search mine. I need to put some distance between us, not wanting to draw any attention our way.

I step back and begin walking toward the boys, the winning team cheering loudly for their victory.

"Who's ready?" I ask.

Three of them walk toward Andrew, leaving me surrounded by five sweaty and panting boys. Apparently everyone else in the gym has caught on as a small circle forms around the six of us. Andrew winks at me and I take it as a silent gesture of encouragement. Whether it was or not, I have no idea but at this rate I could use all the help I can get. I wasn't prepared to do this in front of an audience.

"So who am I partners with?" Each of them raises their hands and I laugh.

"Well, you all cannot be my partners. How about you two are partners with me to make it an even three on three," I say, pointing to two of them. They eagerly spring to my side as the other three retreats to huddle around each other, more than likely devising their game plan.

I shake each of their hands as I introduce myself.

"Peter," says the one that I made the wager with.

"James," the other boy says.

"Nice to meet you both. Are you ready to play?"

"Yes!" they both exclaim at the same time. We join the other three in the center of the court, getting into our positions as I push up the sleeves of my sweater dress, ready to start the game.

After about twenty minutes, it's tied with a score of eight each. My hair is clinging to my head with a thin sheen of sweat. The boys are not holding back whatsoever, giving me a good run for my money. My feet ache slightly, but the smiles plastered on their faces keep me going. So does the one that Andrew keeps throwing my way, even though he's actively engaged in conversations with the other kids near him. I try to regain my focus as we resume action, quickly stealing the ball away from one of the boys. If I didn't know any better, I'd say he did it on purpose so I'd have to brush up against him. I run back to the line and pass the ball to James, who effortlessly sinks it into the basket. Peter runs up to us as we give each other high fives.

"One more then that's game," I somehow manage to say in a panting breath as I'm completely exhausted by the physical activity. Nothing makes you feel old more than playing basketball with a bunch of teenagers, especially when all the exercise that you do consists of walking from your couch to your bed during the week. If what Kara says is true about the hotel having spa services available I may need to look into that.

The other team takes a shot, but the ball sails over the rim, landing in Peter's waiting arms. He dribbles back to the line and quickly passes it to me. I drive the net, planting my feet before taking the shot. The ball bounces off the rim one, twice and then slowly sinks in. Peter and James come running up to me, wrapping their arms around me tightly in a celebratory hug.

"We won Tessa! That was so brill," Peter says.

I laugh because I have no idea what he just said. "I hope that means good."

Peter nods his head and smiles. I try to pull back from them, but they just wrap their arms tighter around me. I give an awkward pat on their arms with the limited mobility that I have.

"You both did an excellent job. Do you play for the team at school?" I ask as they finally release me.

"No, we don't have the money for the sports fees to play at school. But that's okay. We enjoy playing here with everyone else," James says.

My heart breaks a little as they talk about the lack of funding for them to pursue their favorite pastime sport. But they don't seem down about it. In fact, it's quite the opposite. The beaming smiles they have on their faces tell me they're not going to let it stop them from doing what they love.

I don't hesitate when I lean over and kiss both of them on the cheek. It's hard to tell if they're blushing due to my kiss or from the exertion of the game, but their faces are definitely red. Andrew comes up behind me, his hand gently placed on my hip, pulling me into his side. Without thinking I wrap my arm around his back as if it's the most natural thing to do. James and Peter take a step back as Andrew bends down, grazing his lips across my temple.

"Well done Tessa. I would never have guessed you were a basketball player," he says, amusement lacing his voice.

I pull back slightly from him with a raised eyebrow. "Are you saying that I'm not a sporty type of girl?"

"No, I never said that. It's just that you don't see many women play basketball in their bare feet while wearing a dress," he laughs.

I join him in his little joke at my expense. "You're lucky you're so cute. I will take that as a compliment then."

He reaches down and brings my free hand to his mouth, gently kissing each of my knuckles.

"And you should."

He helps me put my stockings and boots back on, holding me up as I hop from foot to foot before zipping them up. We turn to the five teens that haven't stopped staring at us. I shake each of their hands, giving a wink to James and Peter.

"Thank you for the game. I had a lot of fun."

"You can come back anytime, Tessa. We'll always be ready for you," James says.

I give them a final wave goodbye as Andrew and I start to head to the door where the other three are waiting for us.

He leans down and whispers in my ear. "I definitely think you have a few admirers now my sweet Tessa."

My head tilts back as I trace his features with my eyes. He truly is quite handsome.

"They're just little boys. It's only a crush. I'm sure they'll get over it."

His eyes dilate as his chest expands and his nostrils flare slightly. His voice drops low, deep and seductive. "I think it's more than a crush."

I pause, halting our progress across the gym floor. "Why do you think that?"

He stares at me and the familiar pull to him draws me closer to his side. "Because I recognize the look they're giving you and the feelings it evokes. It's the same way I look and feel every time I see you. Maybe it's a little more than their crush. Maybe it's a lot more."

My eyes search his, finding that he's speaking the absolute truth. A new wave of emotions falls over me, ones that I'm still not quite ready to address just yet. But the pull he has on me is so strong and I know in my heart it's more than a crush between us.

My eyes fall to the floor in an attempt to hide the emotions I don't want to show. But he won't have it. He tilts my chin up with his knuckle, looking deep into my eyes before dropping his lips onto mine. It's a chaste kiss, but it definitely doesn't lack the usual fire that's always burning between us.

A clearing throat sounds behind us, drawing our attention to Charles tapping his watch to Andrew.

"Yes, of course," Andrew says. I can't tell if he's slightly embarrassed or ashamed of our public show, but that doesn't stop the heat from crawling up my neck as well. Once again, I've made a spectacle of myself, letting my guard down and allowing myself to throw caution aside. I can only imagine what they're thinking of us now. I try to pull my hand from Andrew's, wanting to put some space between us but obviously he's not having it as he tightens his grip. Charles looks between us and smirks.

"Well played Tessa. You definitely gave those boys a run for their money. But now it's late in the afternoon and we must be going."

Only then does it dawn on me that it's a weekday as we

walk toward the front doors of the building.

"Don't the children have school today?"

"The children have a holiday from school this week. It was the most opportune time to meet with you and allow us to show you what the children do while they're here," Priscilla says.

"Well, I'm glad for that. These are all wonderful kids and they are so fortunate to have a place like this to come to," Kara says. I nod my head in agreement, thankful I don't have to try and talk again.

Andrew and I fall into step with everyone else, but he puts some distance between us and the rest of the group as we cross the parking lot. His thumb continually runs across the back of my hand and I don't know if he's trying to soothe me or soften a blow.

"Andrew, don't forget we have a board meeting at four," Charles says as he stands in the open door of his car.

"I just need to drive Kara and Tessa back to their hotel first since we arrived together. I'll do my best not to be late."

We say our goodbyes to Charles and Priscilla, agreeing to meet up for another tour tomorrow. Always the gentleman, Andrew opens the door for Kara as she slides into the back seat of his car. He quickly rounds the vehicle to open my door as I reach out for the handle. Once I'm safely folded inside, he climbs into the car and we head toward our hotel.

He seems distant as he navigates the streets though I'm not sure why. Perhaps it has something to do with our little public display of affection in front of his superiors. That really was quite stupid on my part, allowing myself to carry on like that especially in front of the kids. But every time I'm with him, all reason just leaves me. For the first time in my life, I'm acting on instinct instead of hiding away in the shadows, hoping to blend into my surroundings so I won't be noticed.

Then the ugly face of doubt confronts me. What if Charles spoke to him when I was playing basketball with the boys, advising him it would not be in the Foundation's best interests to be involved with me? Or he's probably wondering how to soften the blow when he cancels our dinner date for tonight. I worry my bottom lip between my teeth as I stare blankly out my window.

I listen as Kara talks in a hushed whisper on her phone in the back seat. More than likely she's talking to Christopher, giving him an update on our day so far. Hopefully, she leaves out my embarrassing gymnasium display from the conversation.

Andrew pulls the car up to the front entrance of the hotel, jumping out quickly to open our doors for us. We walk into the lobby, my arms hanging loosely at my sides. We pause at the sitting area as Kara turns to the two of us with a grin.

"Okay lovebirds, I'm heading to my room. Mr. Jameson and I have a date. Don't keep her out too long tonight Andrew," she says. I listen to her heels click on the marble floor on the way to the elevators.

Andrew turns to face me and I watch as his face falls slightly.

"Tessa, what's the matter? You look sad."

"Are you allowed to carry on a relationship with me Andrew? Is there some conflict of interest here or some unwritten decree that you shouldn't get involved with someone you do business with? I feel like something is off since we left the Center." My voice is small as I brace myself for the inevitable.

"What would make you think that? My professionalism and work responsibilities have no impact on my feelings for you. If I want to pursue a relationship with you, then I will. And I'll be damned what anyone else thinks." He gently cups my cheek, bringing my face up to meet his eyes. I swallow nervously as he silently beseeches me to listen to his words.

On an exhale, I brace myself for what I'm about to say. "I like you, Andrew. I've never had an attraction to someone as I do with you. You make me forget my insecurities and I get to be myself for a while, something that I haven't done in a very long time. And it confuses me because we barely know each other and that's when I'm at my most vulnerable, reading into lines that aren't really there. Does this make sense? I'm not making sense. And now I'm just rambling. I should really just stop talking."

Andrew's hands frame my face, his soft touch bringing the warmth I now crave. He bends down and places a sweet, addictive kiss upon my lips. A kiss that I could never get enough of regardless of how hard I try to fight it. He pulls me out of my head, letting my worries drift away and to put my trust in him.

"Tessa, you are an amazing woman and believe it or not you are making complete sense. I don't understand it either, but I am drawn to you in ways that I never thought were possible. It's a force that I'm not fighting and I hope you won't either." He wraps his arms around my waist, pulling me toward him while simultaneously nuzzling my hair. My arms wrap around his back, feeling the muscles beneath his sweater and sigh.

So it's not just all in my head.

"I'll be back at seven o'clock to pick you up for our date. Wear some jeans and a sweater if you have one." He pulls back and looks down at my boots. "And you'll probably want to wear a more comfortable pair of shoes than those."

I laugh as he places a sweet kiss on my forehead. It's not lost on me that he hasn't stopped kissing me since we've been standing here. Once again, I'm caught in a situation where I'm the subject of a little too much PDA. But with Andrew it just can't be helped.

"Jeans and a sweater it is then. I can't wait to see where you're taking me."

My fingers trail down his cheek, feeling his stubble start to form. He leans into my touch before turning to kiss the palm of my hand. Our eyes lock as I pull away from him.

"I will see you at seven, my lady," he says with an over exaggerated bow.

I giggle and attempt to do my best curtsy in return. "I shall be waiting with bated breath kind, sir."

He takes hold of my hand, kissing the top of it before turning to head for the doors. I watch his retreating form and sigh to myself, wondering how I was lucky enough to find him. But now I have something to look forward to and I wonder just what exactly he has planned for us tonight. I have a feeling it's going to be something fun and heaven knows I could use some of that right now in my life.

Chapter 8

THERE'S A LITTLE BOUNCE TO my step as I walk through the door of my hotel room and I know the reason behind it. It's the same reason why my face hurts from smiling. I have a date with Andrew. An actual date. Not something that was thrown together at the last minute or coerced by my troublesome friend. A date. Him asking me, a nobody, out for dinner. Nothing could break this high that I'm currently on.

I flop onto my bed and close my eyes briefly with the same stupid grin that's plastered on my face. The faint sound of buzzing has me opening my eyes though and looking around. What's that noise? I sit up and begin searching for my purse, which I must have dropped by the corner of the bed. I fish out my phone and see a missed call. My heart expands in the hopes that maybe Andrew had called but then I remember that he had a meeting to attend right after he left me in the lobby so that couldn't be it.

My finger swipes across the screen and I instantly regret looking at my phone. My dad. Perfect. My finger hovers over his number in a silent debate as to whether or not to return the call. He didn't leave me a voicemail so it couldn't have been that important. Turning my head I look over at the clock and doing a little mental math I determine it must be almost ten in the morning back home. So he either is just heading into court or just got out.

Somehow during my silent debate, my finger twitches and accidentally dials his number. Shit. I can't hang up now. He'll see my missed call and then call me back. I lay back down on the bed, the phone feeling like lead in my hands. I listen to it ring on the other side. It only takes two rings before he picks up.

"Tessa," he says.

I sigh. As usual, no happy or warm greeting from him. Like a typical lawyer, he's straight to the point.

"Hi, Dad. I saw that I missed your call so I wanted to return it."

My eyes close and I reach up to rub the spot above my nose, feeling the sudden onset of a headache coming. My dad hardly ever calls me just because he wants to talk to me. No, there's always some hidden agenda. Either it's him telling me how my life choices are all wrong and that I should better myself by following in his footsteps. Or he's berating me about my job, telling me that he can pull his strings for me to be something other than a secretary. The thought leaves a bitter taste in my mouth.

"It's nothing important. Sharon said that you were out of town on a business trip. I was just calling to see when you would be returning home."

I hear the rustling of papers in the background. The telltale sign that he's sitting behind his big, important desk, organizing his life and the lives of others. Because life is just that simple right? Everything belongs in a neat, perfect stack.

"Actually I'll be gone until late Friday night. Was there something you needed me to do when I get back?" The lack of enthusiasm is evident in my voice. I stopped trying to hide it from him a few years ago when I realized he never paid attention to what I said anyway.

"As you know, it's Sharon's fortieth birthday next week and I've decided to throw her a large party to celebrate. I was calling to invite you and a guest to the event."

Of course, he's going to throw her a giant party for her birthday. His little trophy wife is the center of his world and she gets everything that she wants.

He continues on even though I haven't said anything in response. "It's at the Millennium so it's going to be considered a formal affair. If you need money to purchase something appropriate for the event, I can have Natasha call you and she will set something up at one of the boutiques that she uses for these kinds of circumstances."

It doesn't surprise me in the least that he wants to deal with me through his personal assistant. I talk to her more than I talk to my dad. I could almost consider her a friend.

Almost.

"Um, well I don't have anything that would be good enough for the event so if you could ask Natasha to set something up for me I would appreciate it." My voice is small, feeling once again inadequate as a daughter. A formal affair? Just another reminder of how much I don't fit into his world.

"Consider it done. I'll have her contact you with the exact

details and everything else that you would need."

The loud click of his briefcase indicates that he's getting ready to leave. "I have to be in court now so I must be on my way. Enjoy your business trip. I will see you when you return." He pauses for a moment, letting his voice soften slightly. "Perhaps you can stop over and have dinner with us over the weekend?"

I rather dislike the family dinners he invites me to. It confuses me as to why he feels the need to bring me over. Surely it's just to feed his power trip or exert his will over me. It's the same thing every time I go over there. He will greet me and tell me that I can do so much more with my life. Then Sharon will wax on and on about how perfect their marriage and existence are. After that, I'll go home feeling insignificant and depressed. Boy, I can't wait for the weekend now.

"Sure Dad. That would be fine." Even though I know what the night will consist of, there's still that little part of me that doesn't want to disappoint my father. I wish that part of me would just go away sometimes.

"Please give Sharon a call when you return and let her know which day would suit you best. I'll talk with you soon."

"Okay, Dad. Have a good day in court. Bye."

There's no goodbye from him. Just a click and then dead air, indicating that he's ended the call. I toss my phone next to me and press the heel of my hands into my eyes. My headache is pounding full force into my head. Maybe a quick nap will help. I've got a couple hours to spare before Andrew gets here. I drape my arms over my eyes, allowing the dark to swallow me up as the memories begin to appear.

They're fighting again. The yelling is too loud. They're always fighting. But if I stay here maybe they won't see me. They always give me the look when I'm around. The sadness in Mommy's eyes is too much for me. But she always pushes me away when I try to hug her and tell her everything will be okay. So I'll just sit here with Dolly and wait. The yelling will stop. It always does.

I stroke my doll's hair, cuddling her close to my chest, whispering to her that everything will be okay. As long as I'm here nothing will hurt her. I pretend to feed her a bottle, blocking out the noise from the kitchen.

A door slams, causing me to look up. He's got a bag in his hand. But it's not the briefcase that he brings with him to work. No, it's much larger than that. He sets it down by the front door. I watch him from the living room floor, my knees tucked under my chin, Dolly pressed firmly to my chest. Another bag joins the first and then another. Three bags total.

He looks over at me but doesn't say anything. Why does he have all those bags? My cheek rests on top of my knees as I watch him get his coat out of the front closet. He shrugs it over his shoulders then slowly starts walking over to me. He looks sad. Why is he sad?

"Tessa, I have to go for a while."

"Why?"

"I just have to. You need to be a big girl for me though. Don't cry or carry on. That's what little girls do. And you're a big girl, right?"

I nod my head. Tears threaten to fall from my eyes, but I try to push them away.

"Yes, Daddy, I'm a big girl."

His finger traces my nose and he sighs. "That's my girl."

He stands back up and walks over to his bags, placing one

over his shoulder and clutching the other two in his hands after he opens the front door.

"Bye, Tessa," he says before walking out into the bright afternoon sun.

Something's not right. I sprint to the door, my face pressed against the glass as I watch him load the bags into his car.

"Daddy!" I yell.

He looks up and his face twists in pain. My hands bang against the glass, hoping that he'll come back.

"Daddy!" I yell again. He raises his hand and waves to me before he climbs into the car and pulls out of the driveway. I fling the door open and run down the sidewalk. My tiny legs carry me as fast as they can. The pain of the rocks digging into the soles of my feet doesn't hurt nearly as much as the pain in my chest. I stop at the end of the driveway and scream, tears streaming down my face as his car disappears from sight.

"Daddy!" I wail again.

He's gone.

Why is he gone?

Where's Mommy?

My hands push at the tears coming down my cheeks. My chest hurts. My eyes hurt. I walk over the rocks again and look down when the burning pain is too much. The red is seeping through my toes and onto the gray cement.

"Mommy!" I yell. But she doesn't come. It hurts so much.

I crawl on my hands and knees, not wanting to get blood on the carpet. That will make Mommy mad. The hard tiles on the kitchen floor hurt my knees as I crawl over to the sink. I wet a paper towel and press it against the cuts on the bottom of my feet.

It hurts so much.

I pick out the tiny rocks still stuck in the cuts and press harder to stop the bleeding. I look around the room, searching for the one person I want to find. But she's not here.

There's a noise coming from down the hall, almost like someone is crying. I check my feet again, placing a few Band-Aids on the cuts before I seek out the noise. I stop and collect Dolly, not wanting to be alone. My nose is still running and the tears are still there.

"Mommy?" I quietly ask.

Another noise comes from the bathroom and I push the door open slightly.

Her eyes are red and puffy. There's black running down her cheeks. She looks pale. She doesn't look like my mommy. She's huddled in the corner, pressed against the bathtub, her head banging against the wall.

"Mommy?"

"He's gone."

I slowly walk over to her, clinging tightly to Dolly. I drop to my knees and sit in front of her, hoping that she'll look at me.

"Are you okay, Mommy?"

The coldness of her eyes pierces me, holding me in my place. I scoot back a little from her, not liking the way she's looking at me.

"It's your fault. You're the reason why he's gone."

"What?"

Her head lifts off the wall and turns toward me again. She raises her hand, pointing a slender finger in my face.

"He couldn't handle it anymore. You were too needy. You took away his youth. He had loved me before you came. And now he's gone. Why did you have to exist? It's your fault. It's your *fault," she angrily sobs.*

Tears fall from my eyes once again. He left because of me. Daddy doesn't love me. Mommy doesn't love me. No, that can't be true. They love me. They have to.

I reach out for her, tears streaming down my cheeks. She hits me with her icy gaze and shoves me away.

"Get away from me! You ruined everything!" she cries.

I move further away, my knees scraping against the tiles.

"I'm sorry," I whisper.

"You ruined everything! Go away!" she screams.

Gut-wrenching sobs take over as I pick myself off the floor, holding onto Dolly's arm as she drags on the floor behind me.

It's my fault.

It's my fault.

I pick up Dolly and hold her in front of my face. Grammy gave this to me because she said it looks just like me. Brown hair, hazel eyes, rosy cheeks. She said it reminded her of her little angel.

I throw it across the room, watching it hit the wall, finally falling to the floor. The hurt won't go away. It's too much. My daddy left because I exist. He doesn't love me.

I crawl underneath my bed. My safe spot. My refuge. Placing my head in the crook of my arm, I let go and silently cry myself to sleep.

I startle awake. Holy fuck.

I gasp for precious air. My lungs feel tight and my eyes burn. Why do I feel like this? I drag myself off the bed and close the bathroom door behind me. The light flickers to life and the cause for my pain stares back at me in the mirror.

My eyes are puffy and red. Blotchy patches cover my

cheeks as if I had been crying for hours, which explains the dry and scratchy feeling in my throat. I look and realize my hair is a rat's nest, sticking up everywhere. What in the heck was I doing? Did I somehow stand on top of my head while I was sleeping?

I swipe hastily at the black running down my cheeks as the flash of my mom spewing her venom at me comes into view when I look in the mirror again.

"It's my fault," I whisper.

No, not now. I can't do this now. Andrew will be here soon and I need to get ready. These repressed memories need to go back into the tiny box in my mind, never to be opened again. They need to stay there where they can't hurt me anymore. Because if I don't feel them, they can't hurt me. If I don't acknowledge their existence, they're not there.

The first bite of the scalding hot water hitting my naked flesh clears my mind as I let the water run in rivulets down my face. It washes away the pain of the resurrected dream that I thought I had long buried. I stand under the spray until I'm convinced that I'll appear normal again.

The buzzing of my phone has me searching the room. Where in the heck did it land after I talked to my dad? I scramble across the comforter, my towel barely hanging on to me as I shove my hands under the pillows.

Three missed text messages from Andrew.

Oh crap, what time is it? The bright red lights of the bedside clock beam the answer that I feared.

7:10 pm.

I'm late! Oh God, I'm late! My thumb swipes across the screen, opening the first message.

I'm just pulling up to the hotel now, love. I can't wait to see you. ~A~

That was at a quarter to. The next two are time stamped a few minutes ago.

I'm down in the lobby waiting for you. I'll be the good looking gentleman in the chair with the goofy grin on his face. ~A~

I hope you haven't forgotten me, love. Text me back and let me know where you are. ~A~

Shit, shit, shit, shit, shit! I need to text him back, let him know that I didn't forget about him. How could I ever forget about him? My fingers work in double time, quickly typing my response but the knock at my door has my head shooting up instead.

The towel wrapped around my naked body starts to slip slightly as I open the door, thinking maybe Kara wanted to check on me. Instead, I'm greeted by the hard body that turns my own muscles into a quivering pile of mush.

Andrew's hands are tucked casually into his pockets as he rocks back on his heels slightly. A quiet gasp escapes his parted lips as he takes in my state of undress. I can feel the heat of his stare again as it travels across my body, lingering slightly on my chest before falling onto my face.

"Andrew, oh my gosh, I'm so sorry. I was just typing you a response," I say quickly, almost to the point of panting.

"Please tell me that you do not make it a habit of opening doors wearing just that. For if you do, I may be arrested for assault should anyone other than me ever see you like this."

I swallow hard, his eyes following the movement. A low noise can be heard and I know it's from him. It's then I realize that he's feeling proprietary of me as if my body is for his eyes only.

My head shakes from side to side, a slow smile playing on my lips. "No, I can honestly say that you are the only man that I've ever answered the door to wearing just a towel. So you should feel pretty special. But since I am in a towel and I'd rather not bail you out of jail, why don't you come inside so I can finish getting ready."

Without hesitation, he brushes past me, walking through the room and glancing around briefly before settling into the chair in the corner. My towel loosens again so I wrap my arms around my chest, squeezing it tight. I don't need to embarrass myself again in front of this man. A wardrobe malfunction is all I need to completely throw me over the edge.

The blood in my veins heats my cooled skin as I watch him drag his index finger across his lips, seemingly studying me as I stand there frozen under the heat of his gaze. I shift from foot to foot, unsure of what to say to him.

"I'll only be a few minutes. It won't take long. Promise," I say, backing up toward the dresser to retrieve the clothes I had picked out to wear. Holding onto them for dear life, I slowly back toward the bathroom, thankful that my towel did not fall off my body in the process.

Ten minutes later I emerge, fully dressed this time, as I make my way over to him. He hasn't moved an inch, still sitting there, silently assessing me and giving me no indication of what he's thinking. I slowly creep up to him, my hands wringing in front of me. My eyes search his face once more, desperately trying to find the words to bring him out of his apparent trance.

"I think I'm ready to go now. I'm usually not this ab-sent-minded or late. Well, not *this* late at least but I guess I fell asleep when I got back and lost track of time. Then I couldn't find my phone and you were texting me and . . ."

I don't get the chance to finish that thought as he pulls me into his lap, pressing his mouth against mine. He consumes me easily, stealing my breath as we move as one against each other. His long fingers thread into my hair, holding me to him as he licks the inside of my mouth. The warmth of his tongue touch-ing mine sends shocks throughout my body. My hands frame his face as we sit there just holding and kissing each other.

After a beat, he pulls back but the fire still burns brightly in his eyes. "You're rambling and speaking nonsense again. I was afraid something had happened to you while I was gone. When you didn't answer my text messages, I decided to come up here and check on you."

"You were worried that something happened to me?"

Andrew just nods, keeping his eyes firmly on mine. His hands run up and down my arms soothingly and I feel my whole body relax for the first time since he stepped foot into my room.

"What I wasn't expecting was for you to take my breath away. I have never seen a more beautiful sight in all my life than you at that moment."

The gentle touch of his palm against my cheek stirs some-thing inside me. It's not desire, which is there, but it's some-thing more, something I can't quite put my finger on just yet. The intensity of his words loosens up another brick from my carefully guarded wall. I lean into his touch with a soft sigh.

"Really? I find that hard to believe because I was a mess. I mean, my hair wasn't done, my make-up was washed off and I'm not even going to address the lack of clothing issue."

His lips find mine once more, halting my argument. "Too much talking. You are beautiful. I don't care if you believe it right now or not, but I will tell you that every minute I'm with you until you do."

I shift on his lap, my backside making contact with the growing bulge at the seam of his jeans. Andrew grunts and places me on my feet, discretely adjusting himself in the process. My eyes are drawn to his movements but quickly look away because I don't want to get caught staring at what appears to be the start of a rather impressive erection.

He rises from the chair and runs his hands down my arms. "Now if we don't get going soon, I'm going to have to revise my plans and they're going to involve that bed over there."

Andrew nods in the direction of my bed and another stirring happens between my legs. Do I really turn him on like that? Between the initial proprietary statement at the door, the low growls and the bulge in his jeans, it's becoming clear to me that yes, in fact, I do.

This knowledge makes me feel stronger, more confident that Andrew actually does care about me. With a final kiss on my nose, we lace our hands together as we leave the room, heading toward the lobby and out into the brisk night air of London.

"So where are you taking me?" I ask. Our hands swing in time with our steps while the wind blows my hair around, making it catch in my lip gloss repeatedly. Andrew laughs, retrieving the strands from my lips and tucking them behind my ear. His smile warms me against the cold wind, but I secretly want it to keep blowing if it means he'll always be tucking my hair behind my ear. Such a simple gesture and yet there's more to it than what meets the eye. It's intimate without being awkward, personal and yet something you can do in public without causing people to stare. I've never experienced this sort of positive attention from a guy before and I'm beginning to like it.

"You'll see when we get there. Tell me, what are a few things you'd like to see while you're in London?"

My lips twist to the side as I think about everything I could possibly want to do.

"Well, there's Buckingham Palace, Big Ben, the Tower of London, Westminster Abbey," I say, snapping my fingers when I forget the names of places and landmarks. Andrew helps me out with a few more names, making a mental checklist as I go.

"Oh, and I really want to ride on the subway."

He throws a quizzical look my way. "Subway?"

"You know, the underground train?"

He laughs. "You mean the Tube."

"Yes, that."

He kisses the top of my head as we approach a large station sporting the words Canary Wharf Underground.

"Well let's check one off your list right now."

I giddily jump up and down as we board the train. It's basically like I thought it would be; packed with people. But I equate it to riding the subway in New York. An experience you need to do at least once, simply to say you've done it.

We emerge from the Waterloo Station a few minutes later and start walking toward the water. The grip his hand has on mine increases as I see where he's taking me.

"The London Eye! You're taking me to the London Eye!"

I screech. He laughs and catches me as I jump into his arms, squeezing him as if my life depended on it. He holds me close to him, allowing his scent to calm me down as usual.

"Yes, love, the London Eye. I figured the best way for you to get a good view of London is from the top. I've reserved our tickets so we can enjoy it together. This is the best way to see the city at night."

Andrew sets me back down on my feet, cupping my cheek and kissing the top of my head. The public displays of affection don't seem to bother me anymore as we walk hand in hand to the pod indicated on our tickets, which he must have picked up before he came to the hotel.

I let go of Andrew's hand once we're inside, going straight for the giant fishbowl window. It's dusk and the city lights are twinkling over the river. It's just breathtaking to see. Andrew walks up behind me, wrapping his arms around my waist, pulling me into his chest. His warm breath tickles my ear as he plants a kiss on it.

"Stunning, isn't it?"

I turn around in his arms, placing a gentle kiss upon his lips. "It's amazing."

"Just wait until we start making the rotations. The view from the top is extraordinary."

The rest of the crowd files in and the waiters come around with glasses of champagne. I barely even notice that we have started to move until I glance out the window.

Andrew hands me a flute, clinking it with his and smiles. "To our first date. May we have many more dates together in our future."

There's that sparkle again, brightening his eyes as they

hold onto mine. It's the same sparkle that causes a fluttering in my stomach and the blood to rush through my veins at rapid speed. Deep down in my gut I feel the pull to him, lifting my spirits, taking me higher into the clouds.

I can't help but stare at him over the rim of my glass. He's dressed so casually in his jeans and button up shirt, yet he still makes it look so refined. And he's taking me out on the town tonight, making me feel like the most important person in the world. The new sense of confidence I've found flounders slightly as the nagging question of why me bounces back into my head, followed closely by the realization that we only have two more days together. Two more days of enjoying him, enjoying our time together and shared moments that make my knees weak and my heart flutter.

Andrew tilts my chin up with a push of his knuckle. Slight frown lines appear on his beautiful face as his eyes search mine. "Tessa? What's wrong? You seem sad."

I shove the unwelcome thoughts back into the black abyss and force a smile. "It's nothing. I'm just silly. I was thinking about the wonderful time we're having and how much I don't want it to end."

I give my empty champagne flute to a passing waiter before entwining my hand with Andrew's. "I'm so happy when I'm with you like it's the most natural thing in the world. I feel like I'm at home. Does that make sense?"

His thumb traces a line down my cheek, brushing across my lower lip. Multiple emotions flash through his eyes, likely mirroring my own.

"I do know what you mean. I lose my breath every time I see you or get lost in the depths of your eyes, praying that I'm never found. The connection we have is so strong it makes everything else just disappear."

My hands run up his chest, feeling every muscle as they climb and inch their way upward, finally linking around his neck. I step closer and press my face into the warm skin at the collar of his shirt. The heat radiating from his body warms me even though I'm not cold. No, the slight chill running down my spine is due to the subject we keep avoiding, or at least I do. But we need to address the rather large elephant in the room because at some point avoiding it will be too late.

"But I'm leaving in a few days. I'm afraid what we have, or what we could have, will be gone when I leave and I don't want it to be over. Not yet."

He pulls back and his lips quirk up into a smile. "We will have more than a few days together, love. I promise."

The rest of the ride was spent in his arms, holding me close against him, letting his words echo through my head, giving me the faintest amount of hope for a future with him. The details on how exactly that will work out are still up in the air but the confidence with which he said them has me wanting to believe him.

"Are you hungry?" he asks me as we walk down the street.

"Actually, I am. I could go for something light to eat."

"There's a small café near here that has the best sandwiches you'll ever have."

His arm is draped across my shoulders, pulling me close to his side as we round a few corners until we're standing in front of the small building. The delicious aromas coming from the doorway have my mouth watering and, as if on cue, my stomach rumbling. I clutch it with my hands and start to laugh because truly this only happens when I'm around Andrew.

He laughs and drags me inside the door. "We better get you some food rather quickly. I don't want you wasting away before my very eyes."

"I'm pretty sure that I am in no danger of that happening," I reply on an eye roll.

Andrew finds us a booth in the corner. I slide into the seat and am surprised when he slides in next to me, rather than across the table. Our shoulders and knees press together in the confined space, causing blood to rush to those areas, warming them instantly. The smell of his cologne is stronger and I resist the urge to lean into him but apparently Andrew has other ideas. He leans down and nuzzles his face into my neck, whispering sweet words of endearment, making me laugh at times as his breath tickles my skin and his hand rests firmly on my knee. My hand covers his and I close my eyes, savoring the moment.

The waiter clears his throat next to us, causing me to jump in surprise while Andrew just laughs into my hair at my reaction. How does a quiet girl like me go from blending into the background to engaging in public displays? I look over at Andrew as he orders food for the both of us and I know the answer to my question. It's him. He does it to me. He brings out something dormant inside me that has been aching to be released.

We refrain from another embarrassing show of affection and decide to learn more about each other instead.

"What about your family? Do they live close to you?" Andrew asks.

Our fingers play with each other and I bite my lip, wondering how I'm going to explain my family without going into too much detail.

"Sort of. My father lives in one of the small suburbs of Minneapolis, not far from my apartment. He's an Assistant Attorney General for the state so his plate is always full of court cases and meetings."

"And your mum?"

"My mom still lives up north. I don't get up there to see her very often. What about yours? Are you parents close?"

He nods and takes a drink of his water. "They are, actually. Still living in the same house I grew up in just outside of London. They both just retired and are starting to relax a little while enjoying the peace and quiet."

"Good for them. That must be exciting."

Andrew nods. "My dad is thrilled to finally have time to relax. My mum is less than thrilled to have him around the house all day long. I have a suspicion that she invents little things for him to do so he stays out of her hair. But it's just as well. My dad would go crazy if he had to sit around all day long with nothing to do."

I laugh and watch his facial features soften when he speaks of his parents. You can tell that he loves them very much and must have a close relationship.

"Do you see them often?"

"I try to make it up there when I can, which is only about every few months. But my mum is religious about calling me every Sunday morning, regardless of where I am. Unfortunately, that also means that she doesn't care about the time changes and sometimes finds me answering the phone at two o'clock in the morning."

"But that's sweet that she does that. It means she cares about you."

"That she does," he says.

I chew on my bottom lip and decide to ask the one question that keeps nagging me. "I hope you don't find this rude, but I have to say this. You don't sound anything like I would have expected an average British person to sound like. I mean, you don't speak with all those funny phrases and slang words that I have zero idea what they mean."

Andrew laughs, threading his fingers through mine before bringing my hand up to his lips.

"I was wondering if you were going to comment on that. You're correct. I don't use much slang when I speak because I've learned that no one else in the world understands me if I speak that way. So I had to train myself to speak more eloquently, more business-like, and less like a tosser who is constantly pissed, and looking for a good rogering while his life is all sixes and sevens."

I laugh so hard I have to hold my stomach. "I have no idea what you just said, but it sounds so funny."

He laughs and smiles with me. "That is exactly why I had to train myself not to speak that way. Could you imagine me walking into a boardroom and start spouting words like codswallop or wanker or worse, blow me? Which does not mean what you think it means."

"Stop," I say breathlessly. "I'm dying. No more. Okay, I get it. So you decided that sounding more American was better?"

"For the most part. When I'm at the pub though, my old habits tend to come out. Otherwise, my mates will give me hell all night."

"And we wouldn't want that, would we?"

He laughs again. "No, most definitely not."

I slow my laughter and just admire his face. He looks so carefree and happy when he's laughing. And I love the fact that he's laughing with me and not at me. Not to mention that his laugh is contagious, making me want to laugh with him all the time. And who doesn't love a man who can make her laugh?

We decide to move to safer subjects after that. He tells me of his days at Oxford and all the trouble that he caused with his fraternity brothers. I laugh some more at the stories, especially since I really cannot see him getting into any sort of trouble whatsoever.

And he's incredibly attentive when he listens to me talk briefly about my life back in the States. He keeps his focus on my eyes, never darting around or looking bored as I go on about the neighbors that I think are slightly crazy. Or the dog down the street that likes to come visit me whenever he gets off his leash. Of course, my stories are nothing compared to his, but that doesn't seem to matter to him. He's genuinely interested in everything that I have to say, treating it like it's the most precious information that he'll ever receive.

But as our stories progress, sadness creeps in again. The faint sounds of a ticking clock can be heard through the quiet murmuring of patrons and it seems almost symbolic as if it's counting down our time together.

I shake off the feeling, needing to bring my focus back to the present and just enjoy our date. We eat and laugh some more as I listen to him talk. He switches into a few different languages with some of the stories about his travels and that does something entirely different to me. Andrew's voice is sexy in his native British accent, but add other languages into the mix and it's just . . . oh, my. Words can't even describe it. Just listening to the way he rolls his R's or the fluent French he slips into is damn near the sexiest thing I've ever heard in my life.

We walk hand in hand back to the hotel in a comfortable silence. I think he's about all talked out and I know that I'm not about to give anything else up for tonight. I stop briefly and reach up on my tiptoes to kiss his cheek. He turns his head to me and smiles.

"What was that for?"

"For tonight. Thank you for dinner. You were right, it was absolutely fantastic. The best food I've ever had."

He leans in close. "Just wait until I cook for you back at my flat."

"You cook?" I say with a surprised tone. He laughs and kisses the end of my nose.

"Why yes, I cook. Don't you?"

I laugh and shake my head. "Does Macaroni and Cheese count?"

He barks out a loud laugh, drawing the attention of a few passing girls. They giggle as we pass them, but he doesn't seem to notice. Instead, he drapes his arm around my shoulders again as we continue our walk.

"That barely counts as food Tessa. Before you leave, I will cook for you."

My heart skips a beat as I imagine sitting around his apartment, being in his space as he prepares a lavish meal for me. Okay, not quite lavish but something more than cereal. The possibility of invading his personal space has me giddy once again.

"I would love that Andrew."

We walk into the quiet lobby of my hotel, still hand in hand, still silent and yet still communicating with each other. I've never met someone where I can have a quiet exchange and still understand everything. Body cues, the way our eyes stay locked on each other, simple caresses and accidental touches, all of it is a form of communication between us. Each of them let the other know what we're thinking and feeling, our wants and desires without needing to give it a voice. And in that particular connection there's something else that lies beneath, something larger than the both of us and am afraid to confront it.

Andrew holds me close until we reach my door. The ever present heat in his eyes burns through another layer of my resolve as I snake my arms around his neck, pulling him into me. Our mouths descend upon each other, nipping and sucking, tasting and savoring at the same time. He presses me against the door and swallows my moans as I feel his hips roll into mine. The air around us heats up and I swear there are fireworks going off somewhere in the distance.

We break away from each other, both breathless and resting our foreheads together. He tilts his head, pressing his lips against my ear before whispering in the seductive, quiet voice that I love.

"Have breakfast with me again? I want to spend as much time with you as possible before we meet everyone else."

My panting breaths bounce back against my face from the collar of his shirt. I press my lips against his warm skin, letting him feel my smile rather than see it.

"Yes, breakfast would be fantastic. What time?"

He pulls my head back to look into my eyes. "Nine. I'll come get you."

Our lips brush together once more before he takes a step back.

"Afraid that I'll leave you standing alone in the lobby?" I smirk.

He shakes his head. "Or maybe I'm hoping to catch you in just your towel again."

I laugh and put the keycard in the slot. "Don't bet on it. That may have been a one-time deal."

I open the door and lean into the jamb. "I will see you at nine."

"Goodnight, sweet Tessa," he says, closing the gap and giving me a final kiss goodbye.

I can never get enough of his mouth and am thankful that he's more than eager to give it to me. I can't think of a time where I've ever kissed someone as much as him.

And I wouldn't change it for the world.

"Dream of me," he whispers before he retreats with a wink.

And just like that he disappears around the corner, leaving me with my wits scattered about all over the hallway of the hotel.

Dream of him? If only I could. But with the promises that he's made tonight and the hope for a future, maybe I can finally let go of my dream man and focus on Andrew instead.

Chapter 9

THE BRIGHT SUNLIGHT PEEKS THROUGH the curtains, causing me to squint awake. A pounding ache spreads across my face as I open my eyes to discover what I already know to be true. The base of the bedside table is becoming a constant fixture of my morning vision and frankly I'm getting quite sick of it.

Why couldn't I dream of Andrew like he wanted me to? Is it truly that hard to dream of a man who is perfect in every way? Obviously he must have had a head injury at some point in his life.

Dragging myself into the bathroom, I reach for my giant bottle of Advil, shaking several little orange pills into my hand. Is it wrong that I never leave home without my five hundred count bottle? At this point in the game, they're more like Tic Tacs than ibuprofen.

My eyes fall onto my reflection in the mirror and I cringe at what I see. Dark circles ring my dull hazel eyes once more from a fitful night of sleep. My neck aches as I twist it from side to side, trying to get a good angle to examine the now darkening bruise on my cheek. Somehow in my extremely good luck I managed to hit the exact same spot as yesterday.

With a shaking hand, I reach up and lightly brush my fingertip across it, causing me to wince in pain. There is absolutely no way I'm going to be able to hide this from Andrew. It's already turning a nasty shade of purple and red. I close my eyes and sink to the floor, curling up into a ball against the shower door. Just once, I'd like to wake up and not have to hide some hideous bruise on my body. People will begin to think that someone is beating me. At least they would if there were someone in my life.

In desperate need of a distraction and to not lock myself in my head, I decide to sing my mood away as I pull myself off the cold hard floor. Plugging in my phone to the iPod docking station, I crank up my playlist to a level where I shouldn't disturb anyone else but can still be heard in the shower and sing my heart out. Just so I can block out every negative thought regarding the dream man and nature's cruel joke of keeping me single.

I'm just finishing my morning routine when I hear Kara's telltale knock at my door. With a laugh, I open the door and she comes barreling inside with a dreamy expression on her face.

"Oh my God, that man is insatiable! So much phone sex last night. We're on two different continents and he can still bring me to multiple orgasms. I think I may have carpal tunnel syndrome."

I can't help but laugh as she flops her perfect body onto my bed. One of the things I love about Kara is her ability to say exactly what's on her mind. "Ew, gross. There's a visual that I do not need Kara. So how is Christopher?"

"Amazing, as always. He was still at the office when I surprise Skyped him wearing nothing but my panties. It would have been better if he were in a meeting, but then he wouldn't have answered if he were. Oh, how that man rocks my world."

"Always the drama queen. Isn't it slightly dangerous sleeping with the boss? I mean what happens if you two break up?"

"Are you kidding me? You know that I've been fucking around with Chris for years. I think we're finally getting ready to make it public rather than hide it. You know, try the whole dating in plain sight and whatnot."

She pulls herself up onto her elbows and smiles at me. She always looks so happy when she's talking about her relationship with Christopher. I think I would be a nervous wreck if I had to hide my relationship with someone, forced to keep it a secret. But it doesn't seem to bother her too much, or at least she doesn't let on that it does. All I want is for her to be happy.

"I'm so happy for you, Kara. You and Christopher always looked good together I thought. Not that it's that big of a secret around the office that you two are together. I mean, the way gossip is around there I'm surprised you're not having a shotgun wedding due to some unplanned pregnancy. You know how it is when you work in an office full of women."

"Jealous bitches. They've been trying to get their claws into Chris for as long as I can remember." She moves her eyes across my outfit and gives me a reassuring smile, knowing that I'm nervous about how I look. "You look nice today. I love the outfit."

I look down at the tan corduroy pants and blue tunic

sweater and compare it to her gray twill pants, white button up blouse and multicolored scarf. "I feel underdressed compared to you though."

Kara scoffs and waves her hand at me. "Whatever. It's just another tour. Besides, it complements you perfectly. Oh, and speaking of work, Chris has requested that we have a meeting afterward with him so no dates for you tonight. Duty calls," she says, lifting her body from my bed.

She moves closer to me and I try to back away before she gets a good look at my face. Unfortunately, I'm too late.

"What in the hell happened to you?"

My hand covers the spot as I look down while I walk away. "It's nothing. I fell out of bed again and I think I hit the same spot as yesterday."

"What the fuck? It looks like you went a few rounds with a boxer and lost." She follows me to the bathroom where I try to cover it up again.

"It's not a big deal. Just help me try to hide it. I don't want Andrew to see it."

"You know, you should seriously talk to a psychiatrist about those dreams of yours. They could help you get rid of them. You can't go on day after day hurting yourself like this. It's not good for you."

Kara places her hand on my shoulder and I fight back the tears that threaten to fall. See a psychiatrist? That's all I need is for a professional to tell me how sad and pathetic I am. Or worse, they'll say that I'm just like my mother.

My eyes go wide and Kara's arm instantly wrap around me from behind. "Oh, I'm sorry Tess. I didn't mean to insinuate anything. It's just . . . oh, fuck me and my lack of a filter."

I turn and wrap my own arms around her, pulling her close. "It's okay, Kara. I know you didn't mean anything by it. But I'm not going to therapy. I just can't."

She pulls back and I can tell that she's forcing her smile. "Well, then maybe I'll buy you those bed rails that toddler's use. That way you can't fall out and hurt yourself."

We both laugh and all the tension that was in the room has now vanished as if it was never there. Leave it to Kara to always find a way to lighten the mood.

"But in all seriousness, I think you should talk to someone about them. It can't be good for you to continually have the same dream to the point of throwing yourself over the edge of the bed."

"Kara, it's just a dream. A silly idea of me being with a guy, whom I never get to see and is supposedly *the one*. Trust me, if I could dream about anything else I would. I mean, I've been begging myself to dream about Andrew for the past few nights and I can't even do that."

The cogs in Kara's brain are working overtime as I watch her face twist from side to side, deep in thought. "Tell me again what your dream man looks like."

With a huge sigh, I plant myself on the edge of the tub and close my eyes, recalling what I can of his features. "He's tall. Muscular but not bulky, even though I don't get to see much of his body, but somehow my fingers know what it looks like. His face is still in the shadows most of the time, but more and more pieces are starting to show. He has the bluest eyes with beautifully sculpted cheekbones and stubble across his jaw. I think he has dark hair, but I can't tell because of the shadows. And he's been calling my name more and more in the dream. His voice is low and seductive, but I can't tell where he's from. He doesn't sound like he's from back home."

My eyes open and I watch as her face lights up. "Hmm, okay then."

I narrow my eyes at her, as much as I possibly can without major pain setting in. "What is going on in that brain of yours, Kara?"

"Hmm? Oh, nothing. Nothing at all."

"Bullshit. I know you well enough to know when you've got your mind set on something. Spill it," I say, giving her my feeble attempt at a menacing glare. It's pathetic at best because let's face it, not even a mouse would run away from me.

She shakes her head as she exits the bathroom. "Nope, not going to tell."

I let out a frustrated groan and she laughs in response. She makes her way over to my desk and looks over the files before shoving them back into my bag.

"Everything still look okay with them?" I ask.

She nods. "Yep, everything is perfect. After we meet with Chris tonight, hashing out the final details, we'll be completely set for tomorrow's meeting. And Chris and I both agree that you do not need to attend, so you get to have the day off. Think of it as your reward for your hardass boss making you work late tonight."

My eyes brighten and dance as I clap my hands together. "Really? A full day to myself in London? Are you sure you won't need me?"

"Don't worry about it. Chris is flying in tonight. He said he wanted to be there for the meeting tomorrow so I've got my backup."

"When you said meet with Chris I assumed that we were doing this over the phone or Skype."

She shakes her head. The smile on her face brightens even more. "Nope. He's coming here."

I have the sneaking suspicion that he's coming here for more than just the contract signing and Kara is probably thinking along those same lines.

"A full day without work in London. I wonder what I'll do with myself."

Kara sticks her finger right in my face and her mouth turns down in a teasing scowl. "So help me God if you stay in this room and read I will kick your ass from here to Timbuktu."

"Oh you know me so well," I joke.

We both burst into a fit of laughter as I hear someone knocking on my door. I wipe a tear away from the corner of my eye but then another one threatens to form for an entirely different reason as Andrew stands in my doorway, looking as handsome as ever.

"Well, that is one way to answer the door love. Although yesterday was definitely better for a visual," he says, bending down to lay a kiss at the corner of my mouth. "But I do love to see you smile."

My cheeks flush as I move to the side, allowing him to step in. He pauses in front of me and I take the opportunity to stand on my tiptoes and brush my lips properly against his.

"Good morning, handsome."

He lovingly sweeps his fingertips across my cheek before we walk further into the room. Kara is leaning against the desk, bracing herself on her arms and an amused expression still across her face. The scent of his cologne swirls around me, a scent that I'm starting to recognize and love. Somehow he always smells good first thing in the morning. Well, okay, not the first thing because obviously he's had time to prepare and I have zero idea as to what he looks like when he first wakes up. Then that pleasant thought has my mind focusing on something entirely different as I move my eyes slowly up and down his body, wondering what it would be like to wake up to him every morning.

Andrew notices my stare and smirks. "See something you like, love?"

I flush a million shades of red and sit on the edge of my bed, gnawing on my bottom lip. He laughs and sits next to me, slinging an arm over my shoulders to draw me into his side.

"I'm just teasing. I love it when your eyes are on me," he whispers so only I can hear.

Kara looks between the two of us. The same stupid smile is gracing her lips. "So how was the date last night?"

"It was perfect. Andrew took me to the London Eye and then we had a small dinner at this cute little café nearby," I say, resting my hand lightly on his knee. I hope he doesn't mind the intimate gesture but with his arm around my shoulder my mobility is limited. My options are his knee or further up the inside of his leg and I don't think that would be appropriate.

"Oh! And we rode the Tube to get there," I excitedly say.

Kara rolls her eyes. "Only you would get excited about something like that. But I'm glad you had a good time."

Andrew's thumb traces little circles on my shoulder, causing my body to relax and melt into him. My bones feel weak and I lean my head on his shoulder. The rumbling of his chest indicates he's either silently laughing or making that low sexy noise of possession that I've noticed coming from him more and more. There's just something about that deep rumbling noise that's insanely hot. I'm all for women being independent and holding one's own but when a guy feels protective of you, it makes you feel as if you're the only person in the world that matters.

"So, Andrew, do you think you can show my girl another good time tomorrow since I gave her the day off?"

My eyes widen at Kara. Damn her and her meddling ways. I should have known there would have been a hidden agenda behind giving me the day off.

Andrew's arm tightens around my shoulder, pulling me almost onto his lap. "I'm sure I can think of some way to keep her occupied. Charles informed me during our meeting yesterday that I will not be needed tomorrow. So it appears that I am at your disposal to do with as you please."

I swallow past the lump in my throat, unsure if it's from nerves or something else on a more primitive level. But the thought of spending an entire day with Andrew has my insides dancing. No interruptions, no work, nothing. Just the two of us, playing the happy couple as we spend time together. Well, as happy as a couple who only has one day to spend with each other can be. I shake off the negative thought, determined to be happy with the remaining time I have left here with Andrew. I'll worry about what happens next when we reach that point. His cheek rests upon the top of my head and I sigh. This is going to be hard and I'm not as convinced as he is that I'll come out of this unscathed.

Kara stands upright and claps her hands. "Okay, enough of this lovey-dovey shit. I'm hungry. Let's blow this pop stand and get something to eat."

The three of us make our way down to the restaurant. On the way down, Andrew's hand never once leaves the small of my back. The heat of his hand permeates my sweater, igniting my skin once again in the way that only he's able to do. I've never had a reaction to anyone as I have with him. It's scary but comforting at the same time. It's a feeling that I've become accustomed to in this short period of time and I know that I'll miss it when I leave.

We're seated near the bay of windows and Andrew takes the seat to my right. I suspect it's because he wants to be as close to me as possible. Another thing that I've noticed is that he never sits across from me, always next to me, touching me in some way, shape or form. Not that I would ever complain about that. I'm like a starving person at a buffet. I crave his touch more than I should, but I can't help myself.

We chat idly about nothing and everything all at once. Kara is, of course, being her usual self, reciting story after story that leaves us in stitches. I hardly notice the waiter when he brings us our food. Heck, I didn't even remember ordering. But judging by the amount of food on my plate it must have been Andrew that ordered for me. Apparently he doesn't want to listen to my stomach growl today.

It is the most enjoyable breakfast that I've had in a long time, even more enjoyable than yesterday when it was just Andrew and me. But Andrew's hand has taken a permanent residence on my knee while I eat. He must know that I'm incapable of doing anything with my left hand though I'm not sure how he would know that unless he's been watching me that closely.

I turn my head to Andrew, placing a hand over my stomach. "I'm so full. Why on Earth did you order so much food for me?"

He looks down at my plate, noticing that I've only finished about half of it. He pins me with his blue eyes and a smile that doesn't quite meet them. "Because you don't eat enough as it is. Your stomach is always growling, telling me that you're constantly hungry. So I decided to fix that problem the best way I know how. By ordering your food for you."

Kara laughs and wipes her mouth with her napkin. "Finally! I've been telling her that for years and she never listens to me. Maybe now she'll actually take the advice."

I look down at my lumpy body and cringe. How can they not see what I see? "You both are crazy. I'm fairly positive that I need to lose a few pounds and gorging myself on food is not the way to do that."

Andrew's hand lifts from my knee and traces the contours of my cheek. "You are beautiful just the way you are. I wouldn't change a thing about you."

"Aww, you are just too good to be true, Andrew," Kara says. Then I see it, the familiar gleam in her eye as she looks at me. "So tell me, Andrew, do you enjoy elevators?"

I spit my water across the table, leaving a fine mist among the plate and centerpiece in front of me. Once again, Kara has me embarrassing myself in front of him. He pats my back while handing me a napkin to wipe the water dripping down my chin.

"It just so happens that I love elevators but only if I'm in the company of this beautiful woman to my left," he says.

I give him an incredulous look, unable to believe that he'd like to be stuck in an elevator with me, especially since I almost drowned while on dry land in front of him. Twice.

"Well if you ever happen to be in our neck of the woods, you should definitely ride an elevator with Tessa then. She has a thing for them." She smirks and resumes taking a drink of her coffee.

With extreme mortification still present on my face, I turn to look into Andrew's amused one. "Okay, the whole story is I'm usually packed into the elevator and cannot reach the button to hit the right floor. And I can't ask anyone to press it for me because, well, I'm me. So to avoid any further embarrassment, I ride the elevator until I can reach the buttons and choose the next floor before riding back down. It's really not that big of a deal," I say, twirling a lock of hair around my finger.

Andrew taps his lips with his index finger. "So you're telling me that you're too shy to ask for help? My poor damsel in distress."

He thinks it's funny? Can the ground just please swallow me up right now? He leans over, pressing his lips against my temple. The softness of his lips calms me down, and I feel the tension in my shoulders ebb away slowly. My eyes fly over to Kara, who just shrugs her shoulders and finishes her coffee.

"Bitch," I mouth to her. She blows me a kiss in response.

Kara decides to even the score by telling an embarrassing story about herself. I suppose I can forgive her now for the earlier stunt. Andrew links his hand with mine, pulling it into his lap to rest on top of his thigh. My breathing picks up slightly and I try to focus on anything other than the appendage my hand is near.

After Kara pays for breakfast, not without major grumbling from Andrew, the three of us climb into his car and begin our journey into the late morning traffic. Kara's cell phone chirps behind me and I don't have to bother turning my head to ask who it could be.

"Christopher?"

"I swear that man never sleeps. He says he's on his way to the airport so he can catch his flight over here." I can hear the giddiness in her voice as she quickly types out a response to the text message.

I reach over and lace my hand into Andrew's, having the dire need to have skin on skin contact with him. Kara and Chris have such an enviable relationship. Yes, it's mostly in secret but the way they are when they're together, it is borderline magical. I've never seen two people more in love with each other.

Andrew gives my hand a gentle squeeze before bringing it to his lips, kissing each of my knuckles in response. He must know my thoughts. The twinkle in his eye tells me so.

It's a bit longer of a drive than yesterday to get to the building. It's a similar structure except there aren't as many children running around that I can see. He parks his car next to Charles' in the nearly empty parking lot before rounding the car, holding open the doors for Kara and me.

He rests his hand firmly on my lower back as we stroll through the front doors where we're greeted instantly by Charles and Priscilla.

"Good morning, ladies. How are you feeling today?" Charles asks with a smile.

Kara shakes each of their hands and smiles. "We're doing well, thank you. It's been a very eventful morning already, but we're both eager to see what you have in store for us."

She's fidgeting more than usual. I'm guessing it has to do with her anxiety over Chris coming here tonight, although I'm not sure why. Then again, I don't know what it's like to be in love with someone and then have to be separated from them for any amount of time. Love is just a confusing lie in my experience, but somehow it hasn't jaded me. What happened with my parents and my relationship with them hasn't deterred me from believing that love is possible for people like me, the nobodies of the world, the unloved and unwanted.

Andrew's hand slides easily around to my hip, pulling me in closer to his side. It's as if he has a direct link to my thoughts because he always knows exactly when I need to be held tighter. Or when I need him to gently caress me in the way that he does. Or when I need to be left alone with my thoughts even though he does it reluctantly. But each and every one of those things does not go unnoticed and it makes my heart ache with an unquenchable need for him.

And like Alice, I feel as if I'm falling further and further down the rabbit hole, unsure if I will find my way back to reality or even if I want to.

"Excellent to hear. I'm sure you and Tessa will be most impressed with this facility. This one is more of a schoolhouse than a center like the one we saw yesterday. Because we're more on the outskirts of London, we decided to have a school for the children who are orphans. This is a quieter area and not quite as developed, which is why we need a facility like this one."

We walk through the hallway and the faint sound of voices can be heard in the distance. Artwork adorns the halls, beautiful bright pictures obviously done by the hands of the children who live here.

"This school is for all ages. Our teachers are paid through grants we are given by numerous corporations, private donors, and even some government agencies. The children get full medical and dental care through the government programs available, as well as all their meals," Priscilla says.

"That's amazing. So all of these children are orphans? Do they stay on premise or do they arrive from elsewhere?" Kara asks.

Priscilla turns and smiles. "The dormitory is actually the building behind this one. We have workers who stay with the children once they leave here and take care of them. All of the dormitories are equipped with everything the children need, such as cafeterias, gymnasiums, a playground and recreational area, so on and so forth. We take excellent care of the children while they're here waiting to be adopted by loving families. Our goal is to make it as smooth of a transition as possible."

I'm unable to speak as I continually gaze at all the pictures along the walls, vaguely paying attention to anything that Charles and Priscilla are saying. This is getting a little too close to home for me. I may not have been an orphan, but it sure felt like I was most of the time. The past comes creeping back to me, unbidden and unwelcome, as I remember that fateful day when my whole world crashed down upon me.

Chapter 10

"TESSA?"

I look up at Mrs. Walsh with a perplexed stare. I'm not making any noise or disturbing the class in any way. She's clutching a note in her hand as she looks at me with sad eyes. She motions for me to join her at her desk. I start to stand, but something about the way that she's looking at me tells me that I should bring all of my stuff with me.

I gather my books and pencils into my arms, clutching them tightly against my chest as I make my way to the front of the class. Her head is down as she hands me the note.

"They'd like you to report to the office as soon as possible," she whispers, placing a gentle hand upon my shoulder but it feels like lead.

I don't try to talk because I know it won't do any good. I'd probably break down and cry right in the middle of class and I don't need to throw more fuel on the fire. School life is already hard enough as it is. The constant jabs and stares of my daily harassment at the hands of my peers. It's a ritual that I will never be rid of but one that I've grown accustomed to, as sad as it is.

With a shaking hand, I take the note from her and give the slightest of nods before I walk through the door and down to my prison sentence. I know what this is about. I've feared this day would come for the past few years. But all of my efforts to conceal and hide have obviously slipped through a crack somewhere, exposing what I didn't want anyone to see.

Sitting in Mr. Richards' office are two people dressed in neatly pressed suits; one male and one female. Their expressions could be construed as kind only I see them as cruel. I know it's not meant to be that way, but I'm trapped with no escape in sight. My feet halt my progress, leaving me standing like a statue in the doorway.

"Tessa, please have a seat," Mr. Richards says, motioning me to the empty chair next to the two social workers.

"I can't," I whisper.

Tears threaten to fall. My ears and face burn with humiliation that this has to happen in front of my principal.

"Please Tessa, we just want to talk with you," the lady says. Her voice is soft and soothing, but it feels like barbed wire to my ears.

She stands and carefully leads me to the chair by the elbow. My books are still tightly clutched to my chest as I sink into the hard fabric, knowing my fate is already sealed for me.

"Tessa, my name is Nancy and this is Mark. We're with the Child Protection Services. We'd like to speak with you for a moment if that's all right?"

My eyes dart to Mr. Richards as he sits behind his desk. I shake my head. I don't want him here to see this. He catches my hesitation and stands abruptly from his chair.

"I'll wait outside. Please let me know if you need anything," he says. He places his hand on my shoulder and I shrink further into myself at the touch. He retracts his hand as if he burned me. I hear the click of the door as it closes, sounding like a jail cell in my mind.

"Tessa, we just want you to know that you're safe. You understand that, right?" Mark says.

I stay stoic and quiet. Tears threaten to fall once more, but I fight them off. My eyes stay focused on their neatly polished shoes. Why does this have to happen now, right here, in the middle of my school day?

They nod their heads and continue. "We received a report that you do not have power at your house. Is that correct?"

I don't answer.

"We also received a report that you don't have any running water."

Again, no answer.

"You've been seen at the food shelf on almost a daily basis and occasionally at the shelter. Tell me, is this true?" he asks.

Silence. I won't acknowledge their statements because even though they're true, I know what that will mean. And really it doesn't matter if I confirm or deny them because either scenario will lead to the same result. And I've been trying to avoid that for almost eight years.

"Tessa, we really just want to help you. It's okay. You don't have to be scared anymore."

I shake my head. I was never afraid. I had everything under control. All I needed was a few more months and then I would have been in the clear. We would have been okay.

"We've been to your house and you should know that your

mom, well, she's not there anymore," Mark says.

My head snaps up. Where is she if she's not there? An unexpected pain lances through my chest.

"She's been committed to the hospital because she's a danger to herself and to you."

"No," I whisper. My head shakes violently back and forth and I can no longer hold back the tears. They're streaming freely down my face in fierce torrents, splashing across my notebook as it falls away from my chest.

"Tessa, I know you don't want to believe it, but she is. It's not good for you to be in that kind of environment. She's incapable of taking care of you or herself."

"I do it. I take care of us."

Nancy frowns. "It's not your responsibility. You're not the adult here. She is. Even though the house is surprisingly tidy, you cannot live there. There's no heat, no power, no running water. It's not safe. I don't even know how you managed to survive the winter like that."

"We're fine." I was going to settle up the utility bill next week. We're only a couple months behind. But the city turned it off anyway. "Just, please, bring her back home. She doesn't want to be alone."

She doesn't want me either, but I leave that part out. I can't believe this is happening to me, to us, to my world as I know it.

"We can't do that Tessa. She was ranting about wanting to die because your father left and that you were in the way," says Mark.

Blackness swirls around me. She told them. She actually told them that she didn't want me. My fate is sealed. I have no one. A loud sob escapes my lips as I cry into my hands. The sound of *my books crashing to the floor doesn't even register as I fall to my knees, hiding behind my hands as the tears leak through the cracks of my fingers.*

They don't move from their chairs. They just let me have my moment to break down as my world comes to an end. The only way of life that I know is now changing and I can't say that it'll be for the better. Am I glad my mom is going to get the help she needs? Possibly. Am I mad that we were ratted out to social services? Undoubtedly.

I stay sitting on the floor, allowing the sadness to take over until I'm comfortably numb. A feeling that I'm well acquainted with. Numbness means nothing can hurt me. Numbness means nothing is there. Numbness means I'm alone.

I hear the muffled scraping of their chairs against the carpeted floor. I watch as their shoes approach me. Polished, black, perfect shoes. My gaze lands on my dirty, nasty sneakers, the ones I found in the dumpster behind an apartment building near our house. They're a size too small but I took them anyway. Someone obviously didn't want them and I desperately needed them.

Mark comes into my line of vision, sadness etched across his face. "It's time to go, Tessa. We've found a place for you within the city so you can stay here and graduate."

Perfect. Staying in town, allowing myself to be the continual target of everyone's frustration and hatred. They don't seem to understand what I go through here or what this will do to me. The torment will only get worse once everyone knows that I've been placed into the hands of the State, forced into the system that I never asked to be a part of.

"I want my dad," I cry.

Nancy frowns. "We have been unable to locate him just yet.

We've left several messages but have been unsuccessful in reaching him. Until we're able to get in contact with him, you have to come with us."

He doesn't want me either. He's avoiding me, not taking any calls regarding my safety or welfare. My mom was right. It is my fault. Another wave of pain crashes into my chest. I'm alone, unwanted and unloved.

"Tessa, honey, it's time to go," Nancy says as if I'm a wounded animal. But I am. I'm deeply wounded. But there's no fighting what's going to happen. It's already done. I just need to face it head on and hope that the next few months go by swiftly so I can leave this town and never look back.

They flank my sides as I stand and gather my books. I keep my head down as we exit the office, heading toward their town car that's parked out front of the school. A few kids in the hall stop and stare as I walk out the doors, their whispered words echoing in the halls as if they were speaking into a microphone. Nancy places me in the backseat and I look out the opposite window, away from the small crowd that has formed outside, away from the judging eyes of my peers.

"Are you ready Tessa?" she asks.

I don't respond because it's inconsequential if I'm ready or not. This is going to happen one way or another. Maybe if I don't fight, they might take it easy on me. We drive out of the lot, toward my new hell located just outside of town, on a little hobby farm.

Trees line the dirt driveway. The smell of animals invades my nostrils, causing my lips to turn down in disgust. I want to go home.

We stop in front of an old farmhouse. The white paint is

peeling away from the siding. The front porch looks sunken into the point where it could fall right off from the main structure. Unkempt bushes line the front of the house. In the distance is an older dilapidated barn with a hole in the middle of the roof.

I look back and forth between Nancy and Mark and begin to cry again. They cannot seriously leave me here. I'm safer back at my house with no power or water.

"I know it looks rough on the outside but believe us, looks can be deceiving. The inside is much nicer," Nancy says, ushering me towards the front door.

I place one foot in front of the other, forcing my legs to carry me up the stairs. A middle-aged woman opens the screen door before I get there. Her hair is swept neatly into a bun. She has a blue floral dress on with a red apron covered in flour draped over the top. She's wiping her hands off on a towel and a sweet smile plays across her face.

"Oh, you must be Tessa. Well aren't you a sweet thing," she says, enveloping me in a hug. I stand stiffly, not returning the sentiment. She pulls back and assesses me from head to toe.

"You look like you haven't had a thing to eat in ages. Come child, inside you go. You're staying with us now." She politely helps me walk into the front door, closing the screen behind us. "Don't worry, we'll take good care of her," she says to Nancy and Mark.

"We don't doubt that Mrs. Jenkins. If you have any questions or concerns, don't hesitate to call," Mark says. And with a nod between the three of them, the car pulls away and out of sight.

I stand in the front entryway, unmoving, as I assess my surroundings. Dead animals and fish adorn the walls, all staring directly at me, following my movements. The carpet is threadbare, showing a worn path of dirt tracks leading directly to what

I assume is the kitchen. It must have been a shade of teal at some point as that's the only color I can see besides brown. The furniture is straight from an old lady's house, all floral patterns in cream and pink beneath a thin layer of dust and dirt as well. An old-fashioned TV sits in the corner with the rabbit ear antenna sitting on top.

Mrs. Jenkins pushes me further into the house, toward the kitchen area. A large wooden table with multiple scratch marks occupies the far corner of the room. The metal cupboards are a dingy white, matching the linoleum on the floor.

I don't want to be here.

She turns to face me; the smile that was present previously has now faded to a slight scowl.

"So your job, while you're here, is to clean this house from top to bottom. That is payment for us letting you stay here. Every day. I want to see this place spotless and clean. You can start with the kitchen."

She picks up the mixing bowl she was working with and dumps it in the sink. The clattering of metal utensils echoes around us.

"There's no dishwasher so you have to do everything by hand. Well, come on. Get to it."

She turns to leave but stops, glancing over her shoulder. "And no dinner until it's done." And with that I'm left alone to my chore. I turn in a small circle and see everything else that I must have missed on my first glance. Numerous cast iron pots and pans lay dirty and crusted over with food on the stove. There are several stacks of plates crawling with bugs on them in the corner. The foul stench of a week's worth of garbage has my stomach revolting, threatening to spew the bile that's rising in my throat.

How is this better than my situation? This is so much worse.

Hours pass and I haven't even made a dent in the mess as she keeps bringing me more and more dirty things to wash. Then she informs me that I am to scrub the floors and the walls before I could even think about eating. That doesn't stop her from getting a plate of food for herself though.

A man's laugh startles me as I'm bent down on my hands and knees, scrubbing the corner by the table. I fall back onto my butt and I'm met with a disturbing set of brown eyes. He's very tall and overweight, allowing his gut to hang over the top of his filthy jeans. He's in a white shirt, covered in dirt and oil stains. The patches of hair on top of his head indicate he's probably blond, but it's hard to tell. He smiles, showing me his missing tooth on top and I shudder.

"So, you're the little thing they brought us. Well, that's good. Very good. Glad to see you're already working hard to pay your dues."

He snorts and spits into the sink, directly onto the clean dishes I just finished washing. My spirits sink lower, although I'm not sure how that's possible. I want to cry. I want to scream or run away, but I know it's useless.

Two more months.

That's all I need is two more months. Then I'll be eighteen and of legal age to take care of myself.

My eyes follow him as he wets his hands under the faucet and wipes them across the cupboards, leaving brown streaks of mud in their wake.

"No clean towels so that will do. Now move your ass and get to cleaning or you won't like what I've got planned for you," he says, grabbing his belt buckle. His tongue snakes out to run

across his lower lip before turning to leave. Another shudder runs through me and I whimper quietly to myself as I turn my focus back to the task at hand.

The tears mix with the bucket of disinfectant as I silently cry. I mourn the life I had. I mourn the person I used to be. I mourn the loss of my childhood. I mourn the loss of me.

Two months.

And not one day over.

Chapter 11

I SHUDDER AS I CLUTCH my arms tightly around my middle. My eyes close as the visions run rampant through my head. I can still remember every detail of that day, even though I tried as hard as I could to block it from my memory. But there are some things that you see that stay with you forever, some experiences you're forced to live through time after time as if they were etched into your very existence.

I feel Andrew come up next to me, leaning down so his mouth is pressed against my ear. "Are you cold, love?" he asks. His hands run up and down my tense arms, thinking that I'm freezing when in all actuality I'm fading into numbness. I fight the black that threatens to creep in, willing Andrew's light to shine down and clear away the memories.

His cologne surrounds me again, clearing my thoughts. His body heat permeates my soul, warming me though I'm not cold. He's fighting my demons and he doesn't even know it. My knight in shining armor.

I turn my head to look up at him, our noses inches from

each other. "Just thinking, that's all."

His lips press into my temple as we rejoin the others, still talking about everything that goes on in the school. I fade in and out of the conversation, too wrapped up in the artwork adorning the walls and the bitter taste of my memory still fresh in my mind.

The bright colored pictures lighten my mood with each one I see. All are of happy things and places. Many of them consist of rainbows and flowers, a few have unicorns and teddy bears. There's one of a puppy playing with a bone and another of a bright, colorful dragon breathing fire while flying in big puffy clouds.

"What do you say, Tessa?"

I crane my neck toward Kara, not paying attention to anything that is being discussed.

"Huh? Sorry, I guess I didn't hear what you were talking about."

"Charles wants to know if we wish to tour the dormitory. I think it's a fantastic idea, wouldn't you agree?" she says.

My nerves get the best of me as four sets of eyes wait for my answer. My fidgeting hands can't stay still long enough as they twist into each other in front of me. Kara notices my discomfort and mouths her apology while no one is looking. I give a slight nod.

"A tour sounds good to me. I would love to see where the kids stay and how they interact with each other."

"Splendid," says Charles.

Like a flock of sheep, we follow Charles through the remainder of the building, exiting onto a small cobblestone path that leads to a similar sized building. In the distance, there's a playground occupied by many children, all swinging or sliding together. The slightly cool breeze carries their laughter through the air, somehow making it feel warmer.

Andrew drapes his arm around my shoulders once again, allowing his heat to warm me without asking. He's so in tune with my body that he knows exactly when I need him. He kisses the top of my head and I allow this happy moment to erase my earlier depressed mood. The corners of my lips turn up into some semblance of a smile as I snuggle closer to his body. The rumbling of his chest indicates his satisfaction in this as his lips find my crown once more.

The five of us enter a side door that opens into a brightly lit hallway. Painted handprints with children's names written in calligraphy on the palm make up the front of each bedroom door on both sides of the hall.

"This is the residence hall. All of the children here are set up in rooms by similar ages and separated by floors for boys and girls," Priscilla explains.

"What is the age range for the children that live in the dorms?" Kara asks.

"We have children as young as age three in the dormitory since we have a preschool program offered at the school. The rule is they have to be able to attend school to be in the residence. All of the infants and toddlers that are too young for school stay at a separate location just down the road from here."

Kara nods her head as she walks over to one of the doors. There are four tiny handprints that are all painted pink and swirled with purple. I walk up next to her and lightly drag my fingertip across the names.

"I assume that your school follows the same guidelines as the public schools in regards to holidays and time off then?" Kara asks.

"Yes, we follow the same schedule as the public sector since a portion of our funding comes from the government," Charles says, casually shoving his hands in his pockets.

"So what are the children doing today since it's a holiday for the public schools?"

Kara's mind is working a mile a minute and now I know why she said we will be working late tonight. For us to try and get this to work back home it's going to take a lot of time. But the thought of helping children who have nowhere to go brings a small smile to my face. I'm just thankful that no one is asking me to voice my opinions because I'm not sure I'd be able to stop my voice from breaking or showing too much emotion.

My eyes fall on Andrew's before they drop to his lips as they curve upward into a smile. He's just listening to the conversations, but the pride shows on his face as Charles and Priscilla go into detail about what everyday life consists of for the children here. It has my insides melting instantly. He's passionate about his work, and it shows as I listen to him join in on the conversation. Just thinking about a man, a single man, who only wants to make the world better for children melts you to the core. And for someone like me, a hopeless romantic who falls quickly into her emotions, that is a very dangerous thing. But it's something I find myself not willing to fight for much longer. At least where Andrew is concerned.

I'm drawn to him, pulled by an invisible string by some unknown power. This man, this beautiful, caring, generous man, for some inexplicable reason, is interested in me. And the way he wants to change the world for the better has me tripping over myself, pushing aside my underlying fears, wanting to stand by his side and help him in this process.

I've never really put too much thought into fate but since he keeps bringing it up, it has me thinking more and more about it. Knowing my background, and knowing what his line of work is, this has to be more than coincidence. There has to be a reason why we're here together.

The feel of his hand wrapping around my hip causes my heart to flutter wildly in my chest and the muscles below my belly to clench with delight. The warm press of his lips against my temple has me sighing with happiness, my earlier gloom gone as I relax into his touch.

"Shall we see if we can find some of the children?" Priscilla asks.

"Oh, yes please. I'd love to have some interaction with them." I can't help the massive grin that's spread wide across my face. Andrew's fingers flex into my hip as we walk into a commons area located on the ground floor of the building.

Several couches and chairs are littered throughout the room. There's a TV in the corner surrounded by a small group of kids sitting on the floor. Several boys and girls are reading books and studying at a few tables in another corner while a few little girls are painting their nails and giggling nearby. There are multiple adults scattered throughout the groups, some of them assisting with the homework while others are playing board games or huddled watching the movie.

"This is the general commons room. This is where the children are able to come watch television, play games, hold study groups or just sit and quietly hang out together," Priscilla says, waving her hand in their general direction.

I have never seen a more well-behaved and quiet group of kids in my life. Even at the library in the high school, there was a constant hum of noise around you, distracting you to the point where you just gave up trying to get anything accomplished. But not here. Even with the TV on, it's quiet and calm. No one is running around trying to start fights or tattle on the other. Everyone is just sitting quietly or whispering secrets to another, perfectly content with their world as it is.

We leave the room and head a short distance down the hall, walking through a set of double doors that swing open to reveal a large library. I gasp quietly as I look around in awe. This was not what I was expecting to find when we first arrived for the tour. Large wooden bookshelves surround the massive space, each filled with different kinds of books. Tables and chairs occupy the middle of the room, along with a few smaller bookcases.

Along the back wall, there is a loft area where I watch several small kids climb the stairs. With my interests now piqued, I start walking toward the staircase, needing to see what will greet me at the top. I stop at the base of the stairs and look back toward Charles.

"Could I go up there and read a story to the kids?"

"Of course. I'm sure they would love that," he says.

Several emotions shift through me as I climb the stairs, gripping the railing tight. When the loft comes into view, I gasp at what I see before me. One wall has been painted with the image of a giant tree house, a beautiful mural with big leafy branches and birds flying around puffy white clouds. Another wall boasts a pond scene with ducks and swans swimming in the water and children throwing bread crumbs toward them. The wooden railing overlooking the library has silk ivy laced between the spindles. Multiple silk flowers in colorful clay pots are placed in front of the rail, giving it almost a fairytale appearance.

There are multiple bean bag chairs and plush rugs set up in the middle of the floor, occupied by several children silently reading to themselves. The oldest child I see doesn't appear to be more than eight-years-old with a few of them looking as young as four. All have their own books, flipping page after page in silence with bright toothy grins on their little faces.

My hand rubs the spot over my heart as I stand at the top of the stairs and watch them, completely overcome with emotions. With a tentative step, I walk further into their space, crouching down low to meet them at their level.

"Good afternoon. How are you all today?"

Ten tiny pairs of eyes all swing my way, each accompanied by big, beautiful smiles. They whisper their greetings to me, still keeping in mind that they're in the library and need to be quiet.

One little boy jumps up from his bean bag chair, darts over to me and smiles.

"My name is Dominic." He holds his tiny hand out to me and I wrap my much larger one around it, shaking gently.

"Hello, Dominic. It's nice to meet you. My name is Tessa. How old are you?"

He has curly red hair and a face full of freckles. His green eyes sparkle as he holds up his hand, his fingers splayed wide.

"Five? Wow, that's a whole hand full."

He nods his head, showing me all his teeth as he smiles. I

straighten myself upright as he takes my hand, leading me over to the rest of the children. They're all just too adorable as they watch me sit in the middle of the bright green rug in the center of the loft. I cross my legs and place my hands on my lap.

"Would anyone like me to read them a story?" I ask.

They all yell their approval as I bring my index finger to my mouth to remind them to be quiet in the library. Ten little fingers all mirror me in a shushing sound and I can't help but smile.

"Do you have a favorite book that you would want me to read?"

Several of them jump up and run to the bookshelves located along the far wall. The children that remain behind ask me questions, curious about my accent and where I'm from. I laugh as they compliment me on my outfit and how pretty I look. I'll take those kinds of compliments any day of the week.

A little girl returns, holding a familiar book out in front of her.

"We like this one a lot. Could you read it to us?" she asks. Her voice is quiet and small, a trait I find very familiar. I smile sweetly at her before she places the book into my hands.

"Of course. I would love to read this one. What's your name?"

"Amelia," she replies. My eyes travel over her and I fight the sadness in my heart. Her curly blond hair is pulled back into pigtails and she's wearing a frilly purple shirt with her worn jeans. She holds her hands behind her back as she swings back and forth, a nervous habit I would guess. Without thinking about it, I tap the end of her nose and smile.

"It's very nice to meet you, Amelia."

She giggles and joins everyone else around me. Several have pulled up some bean bag chairs while others are lying on their stomachs close to me. Amelia sits next to me, cuddling into my side. I turn my head slightly when I feel another pair of eyes watching me. I'm greeted by Andrew's smile as he leans against the wall, his arms crossed casually over his chest. That smile alone warms me up inside as I return my attention to the ten little people all gathered patiently around me.

I look down at the book and smile. The Country Mouse and the City Mouse. I remember this book. This used to be my favorite when I was little. My grandma said that I used to recite it by heart to her when I would visit. She'd try to throw me off by changing the story as she read it and I would always correct her, causing her to laugh and kiss the top of my head. The memory hangs heavy in my heart, but I shake the emotion off, needing to create a new memory now.

I hold the book out in front of me, showing the pages as I read the story. They all watch me intently; smiles plastered wide across their faces as they listen to me read them the book. A few of the kids are holding stuffed animals while others are just resting their chins in their palms.

A round of applause follows after I finish. Toothy grins greet me again as they beg me to read another story. My eyes fall upon Andrew as I silently ask if there's enough time. He shrugs his shoulders. I turn to glance over the railing of the loft to find the other three in our group, but they're not around.

"Where did everyone go?" I ask Andrew.

He pushes himself off the wall and walks toward me in that sexy, easy swagger he has. His hands are stuffed casually into his pockets as he approaches us.

"They continued on with the tour and then I believe they were going to head to the office. We didn't want to disturb your story time with the children."

He folds his body onto the floor next to me, tucking a lock of hair behind my ear. His index finger lingers on my cheek, causing the blush to appear on my face again. His mere touch always affects me so and I wonder if it will always be that way. Will I always feel this giddy when he's around? Will his touch always ignite my skin, my heart, my soul?

I can't help the giggle that escapes me though as I watch him try to get comfortable next to me. His long legs don't seem to want to cooperate in the small space the kids have given him. He looks at me with a laugh of his own.

"What's so funny?" he asks.

"Nothing. You look so cute sitting here surrounded by all these kids while sitting on the floor in your dress clothes."

It's his turn to flush this time as his eyes dart from mine to the kids surrounding us. I'm sure there's a part of him that wants to kiss me right now, but with ten little eyes watching us, it probably wouldn't be the best idea. Instead, he flashes me that dazzling smile of his and begins talking to one of the little girls who has suddenly taken a fancy to him. It's not surprising the girls are flocking to him. Heck, I'm flocking to him for reasons unknown other than it just feels right.

Another book is held out in front of me and I smile. Taking the book from the little boy, I glance down at the title and once again my heart drops into my stomach. I'll Love You Forever by Robert Munsch. Oh no, I can't read this book. It makes me cry every time I read it, regardless of how old I am.

"This one? You want me to read this one to you?" I ask,

praying that they change their mind.

Maybe they'll change their mind and find a Dr. Seuss book instead. Unfortunately, there's no luck in that happening.

"Yes, please. We love this book so much. Could you please read it to us?" says a little brown haired girl with glasses.

I sigh, resigned to my fate and pray I can get through reading this book with minimal tears shed. I quickly glance at Andrew and he gifts me with a tender smile that lights up his face. His hand covertly sneaks over to my leg as he brushes his thumb gently along the outer seam of my pants, silently reassuring me that I can read it.

Straightening my back, I prepare myself for the emotional ride that I know I'll be taking when I start reading. It's the lullaby part that kills me. But I always sing it in my head. It's a soothing melody yet that's part of the reason why I get emotional because it's so endearing and sweet. And that's exactly how I read it to them. I sing it.

All the kids listen as I read to them, the words sometimes getting stuck in my throat. I push them out anyway, just to see the smiles on their faces. Another round of applause is heard as I close the book. Andrew places his hand on my knee and it takes everything within me not to break down and cry. At least I managed to finish the book with minimal emotions showing. Andrew's hand squeezes my knee, a reassuring gesture of a job well done. My chest is heavy once again and I take a shuddering breath. My eyes close as I exhale, letting all the tension go with it.

Andrew stands and holds his hand out to help me up from the floor. A collective groan is heard from the kids, letting me know their displeasure.

"Could you stay with us for a little bit longer? We like to listen to your voice when you read," says one of the older looking girls as she pulls on my sweater.

Once again, my chest tightens as I remember the reason why the children are here. How I wish I could take each and every one of them home with me. I bend down and gently cup her cheek.

"I'm so sorry sweetheart, but I can't stay anymore today. I do want to thank you for letting me read to you all. I enjoyed it so much."

I stand up but not before they all gather around me, hugging me tightly, saying their goodbyes. A few of them land some sloppy kisses upon my cheeks, making me smile. Reluctantly I head to the staircase with a final wave goodbye. Andrew's right behind me, his strong hand placed on the small of my back.

The air around us feels warm and I don't know if it's from Andrew's close proximity or the emotional ride I just had from my little story time. I turn to Andrew in the hall, my lips twisted to the side.

"I could use some fresh air. How about you?"

My voice is full of unshed tears as I'm unable to hide them anymore. Between my past memories creeping back into my head, the book, and the children I'm just an emotional mess.

"Sure, love. Let's go this way."

He places his hand in mine, leading me down the hall to a side door. It opens up to the playground area where we're greeted with the laughter of the children playing on the equipment. I close my eyes and take a cleansing breath, blowing it out slowly.

"Thank you, Andrew," I say, squeezing his hand.

My eyes open and are instantly greeted with his, shining with the emotions that I'm trying to fight.

"No need to thank me for anything, Tessa. To see the smile on your face is all I want." He reaches up as his fingers tangle in my hair, dragging the strands slowly through them. "I never want to see anything but a smile on your face."

His words cause my heart to beat faster as they bounce around in my head. Why did he have to be so sweet?

Unable to keep myself away from the laughter, I walk over to the swings as several little girls ask me to push them. Andrew joins me, both of us laughing and playing with the kids as they rotate from the swings to the slide to the merry-go-round. Andrew doesn't dare follow them down the slide but of course he encourages me to do so. As if I could ever turn down a slide. It's surprisingly fast and I'm flung into the air when I reach the bottom. Andrew is there to catch me though as I stumble into his chest. His arms wrap protectively around me and his reverberating laugh shakes my own chest.

There's a small group of boys playing basketball nearby. Andrew raises his eyebrow to me and I shake my head. He laughs and pulls me toward the side door again.

"No basketball for me today. I'm still sore from yesterday," I say, reaching up to rub a sore spot on my shoulders.

He quickly moves behind me, rubbing the spot with his thumbs as I moan in pleasure. He hits a rather tender area then gently kneads the knot until it loosens. Another moan escapes me and he quickly drags me around the corner of the building, away from the prying eyes of the children.

Andrew presses me against the hard wall, his face nuzzling into the crook of my neck. My arms reach up and wrap around his shoulders, holding him close to me as he trails his lips gently up and down my skin. A mewling sound comes from the back of my throat and he rewards me with that possessive noise of his.

"Maybe later I can give you a full body massage to alleviate your sore muscles."

A shot of heat runs directly to my groin and I almost buckle underneath him. He keeps a firm grip around my waist, leaning into me further. His hip presses against mine and I feel a twitching underneath his pants.

"Mmm, that would be heavenly. But I have a meeting with Christopher and Kara tonight and I don't know when I'll be done."

"I understand, love. Don't worry. We have all day tomorrow to spend together. And I plan on spending every single minute of it with you."

My eyes find his as I attempt to find the words I want to say to him. But I must tread lightly because I don't want him to see the sorrow and pain I feel, knowing that tomorrow is our last day together and I don't want to let him go. Not yet. I'm tied to him, so completely and emotionally attached that I know I will shatter into a million pieces when I leave.

He runs his nose along mine, giving the tip of it a kiss. It's my most favorite gesture from him, so intimate and loving. My heart melts every time he does it.

A shiver causes my body to tremble and he wraps his arms around me tighter. "Come, let's get you inside. I'm sure Charles is pacing the halls by now, wondering where we are."

He tries to pull back, but I squeeze him tighter, unable to let him go just yet. He laughs and strokes the back of my head, kissing my forehead while doing so.

"Comfortable?" he asks.

My lips find the underside of his jaw before I pull my face away. His eyes are alight with fire as I nod my head and smile.

"Very." My eyes bounce back and forth across his face, burning it into my memory. I don't want to lose this. I want to live in this moment forever as he looks at me with his bright, beautiful eyes. The same eyes that I lose myself in every time that he's near me. Eyes that I want to look at me, exactly as they do now, for the rest of my life. I'm so gone. I can't fight it anymore. All I can do is admit the truth to myself and pray that I come out in one piece.

I'm falling for him. No, scratch that. I've already fallen head over heels for him. The thought alone scares and excites me though I try to hide it from him, unsure if he returns the sentiment. All I can do right now is reach up to caress his face. "I don't ever want to leave."

And with that, the last of my walls crumble down around me as his lips press against mine, bringing with them a warmth and promise of more to come. "Neither do I."

Chapter 12

CHARLES SMILES AS WE ENTER the office hand in hand, unable to pull ourselves away from each other for even the briefest of moments. My head is still up in the clouds after my realization of how deep my feelings for him indeed go. I shouldn't be so careless to let my emotions run away from me as they are. But the intense feeling of belonging is one that I cannot keep bottled up inside, pretending that it doesn't exist.

But as his thumb rhythmically strokes the back of my hand I know that my willpower has lost the battle. I haven't quite got the semantics of how this is going to work, him living here and me living there, but it can't just end after tomorrow. My heart won't be able to take it.

"How did the reading go? The children seemed very excited to have you up there," Priscilla asks.

"It went well. I had such a fun time reading to them. Thank you so much for allowing me to do that."

Charles waves his hand in front of his face. "Think nothing of it. Anything to bring them joy is what this is all about."

Kara turns to smile at me as she reads my face. I know I'm unable to keep it from showing every single emotion running through me, but I'm at the peak of my happiness after my low point from this morning. She gives me a knowing wink and I wish I weren't so easy to read. She knows what's going through my head.

"Well I believe we've seen enough for one day, don't you agree? Tessa and I need to get back to the hotel so we can hammer out these contracts for tomorrow's meeting."

With a nod, Charles leads the way out of the building toward the waiting cars outside. He smirks as we all shakes hands goodbye.

"I assume you arrived with Andrew?"

"Yes, Andrew was gracious enough to drive us again today. We're very thankful for his excellent chauffeur skills," Kara laughs.

Andrew shakes his head but gives a small laugh. "It's always a pleasure to escort two beautiful women around."

He releases my hand and pulls me to his side instead. My hand rests on his firm stomach and I refrain from flexing my fingers to feel the taut muscles underneath. My head turns as Charles laughs while helping Priscilla into their car.

"I couldn't agree with you more, Andrew. Until tomorrow ladies," he says before climbing into his car and driving away.

My perfect gentleman opens the doors for me and Kara before taking us back to our hotel. Kara is busy clicking away on her phone in the back while I stare out my window, Andrew's hand resting lightly on my knee.

"I think Chris will be landing later this evening since he

left at five this morning. But we'll already have our heads together and hopefully finished by the time he gets here, just to irritate him."

"I still find it funny when you call him Chris. He just doesn't seem like a Chris to me. But that could also be because he's my boss."

"I think it's weird that you call him Christopher. He's so not a Christopher. The only time I ever use his full name is when he's in trouble or I want to annoy the shit out of him."

We laugh and I notice Andrew's smile out of the corner of my eye. He's concentrating on the rush hour traffic and hasn't said much since we left. Then again, he hasn't said much today to begin with. I wonder if he's working out a plan in his head just like I am, wondering if there's a way we can make a transcontinental relationship work. I roll the word *transcontinental* around in my head over and over and each time I do, another weight gets added to my heart, allowing it to sink further into my stomach. I don't want to leave. My hand reaches out, seeking his, looking for the comfort that his touch brings.

Kara begins cackling in the back and I turn my head, throwing her a quizzical look. She thrusts her phone in my face and I have to tilt it back slightly so I can see what's on the screen.

"Get this! Okay, so you know how Collins was all pissy when I got this account? Apparently he went and pitched a fit to Chris about it. And you know how much Chris tolerates childishness. As punishment, he gave Collins the animal shelter contract and the new gastrointestinal surgery center account."

She retracts her phone and clutches her stomach, almost

doubled over in her seat. I join in and let out a loud, embarrassing snort in the process. My hands clamp over my mouth at the sound, causing me to snort again. Unable to resist, Andrew begins laughing as well, shaking his head. I look behind at Kara and this time she is fully on her side, lying across the back seat.

I wipe a few happy tears from my eyes as I calm down enough to talk. "That's too much. Hasn't Collins learned that he won't get his way by doing that?"

Kara sits back up and straightens herself out. "Apparently not. Oh, that was the best email I've had in a while. I'll have to thank Chris later for that."

My eyes roll to the ceiling and I can only imagine what she'll do to thank him. I'm sure it'll be completely dirty, knowing those two.

Soon enough, we're back to the hotel and Andrew escorts us to the lobby again. It still amazes me how perfect his manners are. I wonder if it's a European thing because the guys back home are never this polite and caring. Or maybe it's just me and the fact that I've never been with a man like that before.

"I'm going straight to my room to relax a little before we get cracking. Give me about a half hour before you come knocking Tess. Better yet, I'll text you to let you know when I'm ready for you." Kara turns her attention to Andrew and shakes his hand. "Andrew, thank you again for everything. I'm so glad we got to meet each other. Hopefully, I'll be seeing more of you in the future, outside of business that is."

"My pleasure Kara. I'm definitely sure we will see more of each other soon," he says.

There's a secret smile that passes between the two of them and my suspicions rise. What are they scheming? She winks at me before turning on her heel toward the elevators.

Andrew turns me to face him, wearing that goofy grin that I adore. He looks like the cat that ate the canary.

"So, tomorrow's our last day together," I start. He holds up his finger and places it gently over the tops of my lips, silencing me before I can get my full statement out.

"We will have more than tomorrow, love. My only regret right now is that we both must work tonight. I would give anything to ditch our responsibilities and just spend all my time with you."

An idea hits me and I chastise myself for not thinking of it yesterday. Of course, this would make life so much easier. The smile brightens my face as I drag him across the lobby floor to the front desk.

I cannot believe I'm even considering this or what he may think it means. But with everything that's swimming through my brain right now, it makes the most sense. It's impulsive. It's uncharacteristic. It's something that Kara would do, which only furthers my resolve to just do it.

The desk clerk looks up from her computer and smiles at us. "How may I help you, Miss?"

I clear my throat once before I lose my nerve. "I'd like an extra key for my room, please. It's room 816, should be under the name Martin."

She clicks a few keys on her computer before looking back up to us, her eyes smiling. "Just one more key for you, Miss Martin?"

She bats her eyelashes at Andrew and I resist the urge to roll my eyes. *Yes, he's gorgeous and yes he's getting my extra key. Back off chick.*

"Yes, just the one."

She swipes it through her machine and hands the key to me. "Is there anything else I can assist you with this evening?"

I shake my head and slowly smile at Andrew, giving him a glance that I hope he reads as seductive. "No, I have everything I need right here. Thank you."

"Of course. Have a good evening, Miss Martin," she says before going back to typing on her computer.

I press the key into the palm of Andrew's hand, dragging my lower lip through my teeth.

"This is for you. Use it, don't use it, it's completely up to you. But I wanted to give you the option to use it since I won't be able to see you until tomorrow. And that makes me sad."

My hand caresses his cheek, feeling the prickle of the stubble starting to form underneath. His arms wrap around my waist, pulling me to him.

"What I wouldn't give to steal you away and just lock ourselves in your room for the rest of the night. This key will be used, I can promise you that. But I'm not going to tell you when I will use it. You'll just have to be surprised when you see me in your room."

He hits the call button for the elevator as I struggle with the urge to pull him in with me, letting him take me to my room and do with me as he pleases.

"I had a great time today. I know it wasn't a date or anything like that but touring the school, playing with those kids, it really meant a lot to me. More than you will ever know."

A single tear slides down my cheek as I'm unable to fight back the emotions from earlier in the day. I know he's going to have to learn about my past sooner or later. My fear is that once he learns about how I grew up and the circumstances regarding my inability to surrender to my feelings or accept them from others, he won't want me anymore. But he cannot go into this blind and I cannot hide this any longer.

He cups my cheek and places a kiss on my nose. "Why are you crying, love? Today was definitely a good day. I loved watching you play with all of the children. When you read those books up in the loft, it took my breath away. Seeing you surrounded by them, speaking gently and effortlessly with them, it seemed like it was the most natural thing in the world for you. It makes me think things that I shouldn't since we've only just met." He leans in close, bringing our faces mere inches apart. "But know this Tessa. I am making plans for the future. And they involve you."

The elevator dings behind me and before I know it, he's shoved me inside, pressing the button for my floor. We're nothing but a whirlwind of hands and lips and arms and tongues, pulling at anything and everything we can on each other. His tongue dives into the warm heat of my mouth, licking and savoring as I do the same. Our hands wander the contours of each other's bodies, feeling the steady pulse of lust and desire beneath the surface. His erection presses into my stomach and I moan in response. He wants me. And I want him. The buzzing current surrounding us is almost unbearable, but the spell is soon broken as the elevator doors open up to my floor.

We pull away in a breathless pant, almost as if we'd just run a marathon. He straightens my sweater, pulled askew in the heat of our unbridled passion before escorting me to my door. I smooth my hair with the hand not currently occupied by his then let it flutter to my chest, my heart pounding a punishing beat against it.

"Let's see if your key works," I say, still affected by our elevator ride.

He places the key in the lock and as soon as the green light appears we both smile. It works. But just as quickly, he steps back, placing the key back in his pocket.

"If I go in there with you right now I won't want to leave. And you and I both have a busy work schedule ahead of us tonight so it's best if we don't tempt fate right now."

He drags his finger along the slope of my cheek. My body trembles at his words and at his touch. Oh, how I want this man.

"Okay then. I'll just wait until I see you next." I try to hide the disappointment in my voice, unsure if I've succeeded or not. He bends down and slowly kisses my swollen and bruised lips.

"Your lips are so soft right now," he says, pressing his forehead against mine. "I'm going to have a hard time concentrating on work while trying not to think about these." He trails his finger across them and smiles. "It's taking every ounce of restraint in me to not lead you into that room and lay you out on the bed."

"Well if I don't go in there we're going to make a scene right here in the hallway and I'm reasonably sure neither of us wants that."

The low groan of frustration coming from him has my lips quirking up with a hint of satisfaction in knowing he's suffering the same as me. He runs his lips across the back of my hand before letting it drag through his fingers.

"I will be counting the seconds until I see you again, my

sweet Tessa."

He backs away slowly and I can't help but bite my lip as I admire the sway of his ass while he walks down the hallway. I blow him a kiss before he rounds the corner and slip into my room, melting into a puddle of need and want as I slide down the wall and sit on the floor.

I need a cold shower.

My phone beeps in my purse, still lying next to the door where I left it when I finally emerge from the bathroom. I run the towel through my damp hair, shaking off as much water as I possibly can. Okay, the cold shower probably wasn't the greatest idea because now I'm freezing as I wander around in the fluffy bathrobe while adjusting the heat in my room. However, it did do what it was supposed to do and that was to chill down my heated blood after the way Andrew left. If I close my eyes I can still feel him pressed against me, his lips still on mine, his taste still on my tongue.

I'm going to need another shower if I keep that line of thinking up.

I pull my phone from the front pocket of my purse and smile. Two missed messages. The first is from Kara, letting me know that she's all relaxed and ready to go. I walk over to my bed and sit on the edge while typing my response, letting her know I just need to get dressed then I'll be over.

The second message shouldn't surprise me at all. Andrew's name shines brightly at me and my heart beats just a little faster as I open the message.

I'm sitting in this meeting and all I keep thinking about is you. ~A~

He has got to be the most romantic man on the face of the planet, hands down. It's like he's straight out of a chick flick or something. I want to type a response but he said he's in a meeting and I don't want to bother him. Then again, he was texting me while he's sitting there so maybe it's not overly important. My fingers fly across the screen, feeling the need to be a little naughty.

I'm just sitting on my bed while thinking of you. Hopefully, it won't be long until I see you again. ~T~

Nothing too dirty but still gives him enough room to draw his own conclusion as to what I'm doing. I drop the phone down on the bed before picking out my favorite lounge pants and shirt, pairing them with my sports bra and fuzzy slipper socks. So I'm going to look like a complete slob when Chris arrives but if I'm stuck sitting in a hotel room for who knows how long, I'm going to be comfortable doing it. The beep behind me has my smile appearing before I even read his response.

I'm picturing you on your bed right now and that is not helping me. It won't be long, I promise. ~A~

And my text did exactly what I intended it to do, let him do his own imagining. Score one for me! I leave the phone on my bed as I finish getting ready, blow drying my hair into a mess before placing it in a high ponytail. It's just work. There's no time for glamour, especially since Andrew will not be seeing me like this. At least I don't think he will.

I grab my laptop bag, phone, and key before heading next door. I knock once and she flings it open with a yawn. She doesn't even bother trying to cover it, which makes me chuckle.

"Tired?" I ask, walking into her room.

"Beat, actually. And it's only going to get worse because I know for a fact that I'm not going to get any sleep tonight."

I mock gag at her comment and she laughs with a wink.

"Again, gross. I really, really, *really* do not want to think about you two having sex right now."

I place my bag on her desk, taking out the laptop and files before plopping myself on her bed, my back resting against the headboard. She crawls up next to me, crossing her legs like mine and hands me a Diet Coke.

"Thanks," I say, pulling the tab back and hear the hissing sound of the carbonation letting loose. There's nothing better than that first sip of an ice cold Diet Coke. Okay, that's not true but to stay focused that's what I'm going to tell myself.

"I'm thinking we'll just order in some Chinese and start brainstorming," she says, flipping through her notepad.

"That sounds good to me. I'm game for just about anything right now because I need a distraction."

Kara's face lights up and I know that I've just said the wrong thing. "Looks like someone else has sex on the brain. A little bow-chica-wow-wow? Is he good? He must be good. I can't imagine a guy like him isn't good." I stare blankly at her, shocked into complete silence at her onslaught of questions. She quirks an eyebrow and tsks. "Tell me you've at least done some heavy petting."

My jaw drops and I can't stay quiet anymore.

"Seriously! No more talk of sex!"

I playfully slap her arm as she falls to her side, clutching her stomach and laughing. I shake my head and return my focus to my laptop.

"You are so frustrating sometimes Tessa. How could you not be all over that man? You must have the restraint of a virg . . ." She stops suddenly, realizing what she's about to say. Her face falls slightly as she sits up and looks at me with sad, regretful eyes.

"Sorry, I forgot," she says, bumping her shoulder into mine.

"It's fine. Let's just forget it and get to work. How about you call the Chinese place for food and I'll start organizing the notes and contracts."

She accepts my change of subject and heads to the phone, ordering what sounds like enough food to feed a small village. But even with the subject change, the words swim through my head. No, I'm not a virgin but that doesn't mean I like to talk about my lack of promiscuity. And honestly it's taken great restraint to keep my body in check around Andrew, even though I've wanted to succumb to it several times, most recently about an hour ago.

But sex makes me nervous and Kara knows why. She's heard the story of my introduction to the act and how unpleasant and degrading it was for me. A shudder runs through me and I brush off the subject, not wanting to dwell on it any more than I already have.

I arrange all the notes and spreadsheets in front of me, having done this many times with Kara previously. I know exactly what to look for, what she'll be asking about and how to quickly come up with the answer. We are a well-oiled machine when it comes to this and I can't help but exude a hint of pride in my work. Yes, it's not glamorous but it's not supposed to be. But I know I'm just as good at this as some of the others around

the office, even without the four-year degree that they have.
A half hour later there's a knock at the door. Kara leaps up
with her wallet in hand and gasps loudly when she opens the
door. Standing in her doorway, holding two large paper bags of
food, is Chris.

"So I ran into the delivery guy in the elevator and knew
this had to be you just by the sheer volume of food," he says,
walking into the room.

The instant the bags land on the table she leaps into his
waiting arms, raining kisses on his face and neck. She wraps
her legs around his waist and clings to him as a small child
would. He laughs as his arms wrap around her, supporting her
weight. Not that she weighs that much. She's easily one hundred pounds soaking wet.

I tilt my head to the side as I watch their reunion. They
truly are perfect together. A match made in heaven in my
book. I notice the door still propped open and realize it's that
way because Chris's luggage is lying on its side in the hallway. I
get up and remove the bag, dragging it into the room and prop
it up against the wall.

Kara's hands are still wound firmly in Chris's hair and she
hasn't allowed him to come up for air.

"God, baby, when did you get here?" she says between
kisses. He takes her lips into an all-consuming kiss, silencing
her completely. He tries to peel her off his body to no avail. It
appears she's glued to him and he may just have to deal with it.

"I just landed an hour ago. When I was talking to you this
morning, I was already in New York. I wanted to surprise you
by arriving early."

There's a sparkle in his eye as he looks at her. It's a sparkle that I've come to recognize more and more as of recent. I've seen the same gleam in Andrew's eyes when he looks at me and it gives me hope that there could actually be a future there for us.

Kara peels herself away from Chris but doesn't go too far. She's clinging to his arm, playing with his fingers with that same stupid smile on her face. It's the one that gives her away every time, the one that tells the world how hopelessly, madly in love she is with him. Not that I could blame her. Chris isn't a bad looking man. Quite the opposite in fact. He's tall and very young looking. You would never guess that he was in his early forties. Then again, he does take excellent care of himself. The only thing that would give him away is the smattering a gray hair at his temples even though the blond hides it almost perfectly.

I reclaim my spot on the bed and watch as he struggles to undo his tie with one hand. His jacket falls from his shoulders and hangs between him and Kara until she finally takes the hint and releases him long enough to hang up the clothes he's discarding. He stands to my side, holding out his hand in greeting to me.

"Don't worry about getting up Tessa. How have you been?" He playfully nudges my shoulder with his hand in the way that a big brother would pick on his little sister.

"I'm good, Christopher. Kara and I got a good start on the contracts and we've got a list going right now for what we need to do once we get back stateside."

"Excellent. That's what I like to hear from the Dynamic Duo. Right now, I need to run through the shower and take this airplane smell off of me."

He winks at Kara and she smiles. "I'm just going to go help him scrub his back." She giggles as she follows behind him and I hear the distinctive click of the lock behind her.

"Gross!" I yell at the door. I seriously doubt that they heard me though.

I roll my eyes and return my focus to my laptop, clamping down on the pencil in my mouth, probably leaving teeth marks in the wood. There's one email, in particular, that seems to have gone missing and it's beginning to piss me off. I puff out a breath, shooting the pencil across the bed, watching it land on a stack of papers and roll off the side.

My phone quietly beeps somewhere and I start the daunting task of lifting up multiple stacks of paper, trying my best not to disturb them if at all possible. Finally, I find it, buried underneath the largest stack and smile when Andrew's name appears on the screen.

I'm stuck at work and I'm so lonely. How about you? ~A~

My teeth draw my lower lip between them, thinking of a response. I opt for the same tactic as last time, sending a message that's open to interpretation.

I'm still working too. Actually, I'm spread out in bed right now, surrounded by reports. ~T~

Within seconds, his reply comes across.

I'm very jealous of the reports that are lucky enough to be in bed with you. I'm hoping soon that will be me instead. ~A~

My eyes close as I imagine what it would be like if Andrew were here right now. The press of his hard body against mine, the smell of his cologne wrapping me in that safe cocoon, his fingers traveling over the hills and valleys of my body as he learns it.

No need to hope. I'm fairly certain it's a sure thing. How soon can you be here? ~T~

I shouldn't tease him like that, even though I really do want him in my bed right now. It's all my mind has been thinking about since he left me in a puddle of hormones just a little bit ago.

Say the word and I will be there now if you'd like. ~A~

My eyes drift to the massive stacks of paper and I groan. Why oh why do we have so much yet to do?

You have no idea how much I wish I could right now. I have a feeling it's going to be a while before I'm released from my forced servitude. Plus Kara and Chris are "getting clean" right now so I'm on my own. ~T~

I hop off the bed to retrieve my pencil, shoving it behind my ear as my missing email finally appears. I hit print and listen as the wireless printer across the room spits out the document. By the time I return to my spot, my phone beeps once more.

Just so you know I'm imagining all kinds of things I'd like to do to you right now, my sweet Tessa. I will hurry with my work so it'll be closer to my time dedicated to you. ~A~

Damn, if my heart didn't just stop beating.

I will try to do the same. I miss you. ~T~

Not as much as I miss you. It won't be long now, love. ~A~

I place my phone on the nightstand, needing to keep it away from me so I don't get continually distracted by Andrew. Focus. I need to focus so I can get out of here.

Kara and Chris emerge from the bathroom almost an hour after they went in. She's flushed and grinning from ear to ear and yet Chris looks as cool as he did when he first entered the room. Both are in their lounge clothes like me, giving me a little relief that I'm not the only one ready for a lazy night. Chris runs his hand through his damp hair and smacks Kara on her ass as she passes in front of him. She gives a slight yelp but bounces over to my spot, picking up a few papers in the process.

"How's it coming there, Chickie?"

"Everything is set up and organized. I'm just going through the contracts now to make sure that everything is in the right places and spelled correctly," I say around a forkful of Kung Pao chicken. Kara leans over to grab one of the takeout boxes and starts munching away.

"Wow, this is good," she says, wiping some sauce that had dribbled off her noodle onto her chin.

"Yeah, it's even better when it's warm."

She turns and laughs at me. "Sorry, he was dirty. I had to help."

"Help, what? Make him dirtier before he gets clean?"

"Basically," she says, shoving more noodles into her mouth.

"Again, gross."

Chris takes the box from Kara and kisses her lips. "You do know I'm standing right here ladies?"

Kara leans over and grabs another carton. "Yeah, we know. We just don't care."

He sits next to Kara and pulls her into his lap. She settles into his chest and sighs with a look of sheer contentment.

"Almost have everything we need Christopher. Shouldn't take too much longer."

He rolls his eyes at me. "I really wish you'd call me Chris.

I always feel like I'm in trouble or brokering some huge deal when someone calls me by my full name. We've known each other for four years now, Tessa. Plus you're one of the few that know about Kara and me, although that won't be a secret much longer."

There's that gleam in his eye again. She reaches up to stroke the side of his face before turning to dust her lips across his jaw line. They're so cute and considerate of each other. It's almost sickening to watch sometimes. Then I wonder if people have been thinking that about me and Andrew during one of our many public displays that we keep having. But Andrew and I have yet to even come close to their explosive love story. Ninety percent of the time those two are all mushy for each other. But that other ten percent is when the sparks really fly. When they fight, it's epic. Have you ever wondered what would happen if you take a firework and replace the gunpowder with nitro instead? Just watch them during a fight. It makes World War II look like a kids fight on the playground.

Yet somehow they make it work. Two incredibly frustrating and stubborn people who belong together. Fate couldn't have done a better job with them if she tried.

"Not until we get this project underway. You better swear to me Chris or so help me I will make you pay for it."

She pokes her fork in his face, giving her stern look, challenging him to fight. He laughs instead, kissing the side of her head.

"Okay baby, I swear. Once this gets off the ground, we will let everyone know."

Kara puts her food carton on the table and claps her hands. "Okay, enough is enough. Let's get this done so Tessa can get back to her room and you can remind me of why I keep you around."

"Well, that sounds like the best incentive yet. Let's do it."

"Again, for the one millionth time, gross," I laugh.

We sit on the bed, passing papers to each other, jotting down stuff in the notepad and, of course, laugh together. My fingers move furiously across the keyboard as I copy down everything they've written, fixing minor typos and moving a few paragraphs around.

Three hours later I hit print for the last time. My stiff legs scream in discomfort as I make my way to the printer. I hand the paper to Chris, who puts it on the bottom of the stack.

"That's it. We're finally done," he says.

"Thank God." I bend at the waist, touching my toes and allowing the vertebras to stretch in my back. Kara hops off the bed and stretches out her leg, shaking it before moving to the other one. A heated glance passes between them and suddenly I feel the temperature rise in the room. This time it has nothing to do with me.

"And that's my cue. Are you sure you don't need me tomorrow?" I ask, packing up my laptop bag. Kara hands me my phone and key and shakes her head.

"No, for the last time, we do not need you. Chris and I will take it from here. You are under orders to take the day off tomorrow and spend it any which way you feel the need to with Andrew."

My face heats up as I shuffle from foot to foot. Chris gives me a puzzled look.

"Who's Andrew? Did our Tess finally meet someone?"

I roll my eyes and sigh. "I met Andrew on the plane over

here. I didn't know that he was the head of operations for the Foundation until that initial meeting."

"You mean Andrew Parker?"

He wraps his arms around Kara from behind and rests his chin on her shoulder.

"Yep, that's him. He's perfect for her. Just the epitome of what a perfect gentleman should be. It was love at first sight for both of them," Kara says.

"So what are you saying? I'm not a perfect gentleman?"

"I'm pretty sure that you'll be proving my point in a few minutes."

I need to get out of here. I open the door and turn to say my goodnight. They barely acknowledge my departure as I listen to Kara's surprised yelp as she's tossed onto the bed.

My room is still dark as I slide into it, remembering not to bolt the door just in case Andrew decides to come over tonight. I place my laptop bag on my desk and get ready for bed. I leave the bathroom light on and crack the door a touch so it's not pitch black in my room. I turn down the bed and snuggle into the softness of the sheets, closing my eyes lightly while paying attention to every single noise I hear.

Within a few minutes, I hear the clicking of the door and the bolt sliding into place. His feet move across the carpet quietly and he drops something at the end of the bed. Another round of rustling goes on before I feel the bed dip next to me. I smile as his arm snakes around my middle, pulling me into his chest and kissing the back of my head.

"Are you awake, love?"

"Mmhmm."

"I couldn't stay away any longer. I had to be next to you."

My arms cover his, pulling him tighter around me. "I'm glad you didn't stay away. I missed you."

"I missed you too, love. We don't have to do anything except sleep. I promise."

"Just hold me," I whisper.

"Always." He nuzzles his nose into my hair, inhaling deeply as I relax into him. He draws tiny circles across my stomach. "There's nowhere in the world I would rather be than right here holding you in my arms."

A million emotions fly through me, each one tied to the man who's wrapped himself around my body and my heart. He's so sweet and caring and mine. Well, not mine, but I feel like he's mine.

Our peaceful reunion is interrupted by a loud thumping noise against the wall, followed by Kara's unmistakable moans, filling our quiet room. Good gravy, does she not have any decency?

I laugh and turn in his arms to face him, letting my hand run down his cheek in the way that I love.

"I take it Christopher made it here just fine?"

I nod. "He's reminding her of why she keeps him around if I remember right."

His eyes light up with laughter. I just love his eyes. The cool blueness, even when ignited with fire toward me, draws me in every time. I would be content to do nothing but stare at them daily, allowing myself to get lost in their depths.

He leans forward, pressing his lips against mine. It's soft at first. Like a first kiss between lovers. He takes his time, slowly molding my lips to his. My hand reaches up, allowing my fingers to trail through his hair as our mouths reacquaint themselves with each other. He tastes of mint and Andrew, something that I can't describe only that it's a taste unique to him.

A flash of something familiar sets in but I quickly wave it off, not wanting to get distracted and lose the feeling I have right now, at this moment. My tongue gets bold, running across the seam of his lips in an attempt to deepen the kiss but Andrew pulls back and gives me sweet little pecks instead.

"Not tonight, love. You asked me to just hold you and that's what I'll do."

And I'm gone. Done. Stick a fork in me, cast me to the side, send me down the river, finished. He's not going to try anything with me because I asked him not to. He's unlike any other man I've been with and I know for a fact that after this, there will be no one else for me.

My hand falls onto his chest and it's just then I realize that he's still wearing a shirt and his boxers. He really didn't have plans for anything more unless I wanted it. My heart sighs as the unnamed emotions come to the surface, begging for release. They're on the tip of my tongue, but I choke them back down. I'm not quite ready for those to be vocalized just yet.

He rolls onto his back, pulling me closer to his side in the process. I tuck my head underneath his chin and place a kiss in the middle of his chest. We laugh at the wall thumping, which is still going on and I hate to admit but is quite impressive. He kisses my temple and whispers his goodnight as my ear rests over his heart, letting the rhythmic beating of it lull me into a peaceful night sleep.

Chapter 13

MY BODY FEELS SURPRISINGLY WARM and comfortable as sleep slowly fades away from me. The feel of the soft mattress is still beneath me, the sheets still covering my body instead of tangled around my feet.

I didn't fall out of bed last night.

A smile crawls across my face, delighted at this little revelation as I stir. But strong arms wrap around me tighter, holding me to the hard body in front of me. One eye braves the morning light as the most beautiful face in the world slowly comes into focus. His eyes are still closed. The thick black lashes are fanned across his cheeks. His morning stubble has my fingers itching to touch it. I open my other eye to get the full effect.

He's smiling.

Either he's still asleep and having a good dream or he's awake and enjoying my early morning voyeurism. Privately I hope it's the latter. I try to move my legs, only to discover that his are wrapped around them as yet another anchor.

"I think you're attempting to get away from me before I have the opportunity to see what you look like first thing in the morning," Andrew says. The amusement in his deep, raspy morning voice is so sweet that I can't help but giggle.

His eyes blink open. Bright blues find my curious hazel and I watch as his whole entire face lights up like the sun coming over the horizon.

"And just as I imagined, you are the most exquisite sight anyone could see. Exactly how I want to start my days, looking into your beautiful eyes with sleep still lingering behind them."

He closes the distance between our lips, sealing them together. A sigh falls quietly from me when he explores my neck with his mouth.

He's here.

In my bed.

And we're both still fully clothed, yet I've never felt more naked. His words linger in my still sleepy brain. He thinks I'm the most beautiful sight first thing in the morning. And we haven't even had sex yet.

But then the scene from my dream pops into my head, bringing me back down from my high. It was different this time. I was able to see more of his face, the distinctive slope of his nose, and his perfectly sculpted mouth. He's still approaching me from the shadows, causing me more frustration but for some reason a sense of belonging as well. The image still isn't as sharp as I'd like. I swear it's hanging on the edge of my mind, teasing me that there's something familiar about this shadowed being.

It could be the fact that I didn't fall out of bed last night as to why I feel different about the dream. Or it could be my subconscious trying to let him go with the realization that Andrew is here now to fill the void in my life. The need for my mystery man is no longer a necessity. Andrew is here, seemingly ready to take on the role of the main man in my life. He hasn't said quite as much, but he's alluded to it enough times where I have to think that's what he wants.

His nose circles mine, bringing me out of my thoughts and back to the present. I kiss him on the end of his nose in the same way he does to me, my most favorite of his gestures of affection. Well, at least the most decent in public. His arms wrap tighter around my middle, drawing me closer to his body.

"I like this, sleeping here next to you. For one, I didn't fall out of bed and hurt myself like I do every morning."

I try to laugh it off. Andrew's smile slowly fades from his face instead.

"I would never let anything happen to you while you're in my arms and in our bed. I wish I knew what your dreams are about that cause you so much distress at night."

He cups my cheek and stares into my eyes, searching for the answer to his question. I'm afraid to vocalize my dreams, afraid that he won't understand or worse, that it'll scare him away. But if we have any hope of a relationship he needs to know everything about me. With a shaking hand, I tuck a strand of hair behind my ear and attempt to swallow past the lump now formed in my throat.

"I know you do that when you're nervous, tucking your hair behind your ear. You have nothing to be afraid of with me. I want to be the one to protect you every day, be the light that chases away your nightmares in the dark. Your knight in shining armor, for lack of a better term."

I blow out a breath, letting go of my fear in the process. "They're not nightmares. At least I don't think they are. My subconscious is trying to tell me something but the message is vague and I can't see the whole picture at times. The last few nights though, the picture has been getting sharper, allowing me to see a few more pieces to the puzzle. I'm hoping that means something good is going to happen in the future. But there's a face that keeps coming from the shadows and my mind's eye won't let me fully see it. I think that's why my body is so restless at night. It's trying to see what's coming, but it can't."

My fingers pick at his shirt while I try to explain to him what I think the dream means without actually giving away too much. How does one explain to the man who is currently occupying a bed with them that they dream of someone else every night?

Andrew looks down on me, his thumb running down my cheek, gently easing my mind into the calmness that it craves. "Our minds have a funny way of interpreting dreams. This face that you regularly see could be a person blocking a path you're trying to take or it could be the person you're supposed to run to. The shadows are just your mind trying to keep it at bay, keep some sort of unknown at an arm's length in a way of self-preservation." His hand cups the back of my head, pulling me closer until we're nose to nose. "But as long as I'm here with you I will do everything I can to keep you safe and to make sure that your dreams come true, whatever they may be."

If there was any doubt lingering in my mind before it is gone like the wind. My heart has fallen completely and effortlessly into his hands. It is now his to take care of, to mind, to guard. And I give it freely to him, without question or restraint.

This mystery man, this person in my dreams cannot hold a candle to Andrew. He would never lie in the shadows, always at an arm's length. No, he would be bursting through the darkness, never stopping until he reached me. That I know without a doubt to be true.

My fingers reach up and run through his dark hair, lovingly caressing him, trying to reassure him that I believe everything that he's said to me. He is my knight in shining armor, my light against the shadows of the dark. He's the one person I could never live without, the other half of my soul. It's crazy, I know. Believe me, I know how desperate I sound, but I'm a hopeless romantic and he's saying all the right things at just the right time.

Andrew's fingers mirror mine, threading the long strands of my hair in his, combing through it slowly before finally falling down to the sides of my neck. His fingers follow the trail, drawing circles down my arm before placing his fingers in mine. Our joined hands are lifted to his mouth as he places a gentle kiss upon each of my knuckles then clutching our hands to his chest.

We lay there, completely entranced with each other, doing nothing but staring into the depths of each other's eyes, the portal to the soul. Nothing is spoken. No words are necessary for communication between us. His body speaks for him and my body answers. Two matching hearts beating as one in the early hours of the morning.

Seconds, minutes, hours pass by with nothing else but the sound of our breathing. Finally, my stomach rumbles loudly, breaking our trance. Andrew laughs, kissing the tip of my nose as the heat of embarrassment flushes my face.

"I believe that's my cue to feed you. Though I must say it pains me to have to leave this bed. However, we have a busy schedule ahead of us and lying here all day is not part of that. But I am willing to adapt if need be."

My brows furrow as he smiles that dazzling smile of his. "What plans?"

He taps the end of my nose. "I'm giving you the grand tour of London. Well, as much as we can fit in over the course of the afternoon. I will not break our evening plans because I have something special in mind for tonight."

My whole face brightens at the thought of a special night with Andrew, my mind working furiously on what that could be. He leans over, softly kissing my lips before sitting upright and stretching his arms above his head. I mirror his action but instead of sitting up I'm still lying on my back. The feeling of not lying on the ground is too good to pass up. It's not every day that I wake up lying next to the most handsome man on the planet. That's incentive enough to stay in bed all day long.

With great reluctance, I slide up and lean against the headboard of the bed. He wanders around my room, pulling things out of his overnight bag that was placed at the end of the bed.

"Would you like to shower first? It'd probably be faster if you go before me since it may take me a while to get ready. You know how it goes with women in the mornings."

My legs swing over to the side, throwing the covers away from my body. He stills as his eyes roam over my newly exposed flesh, which isn't much considering the nightshirt I wear comes down to my knees. His lips twist into a playful smirk as I stand next to him.

"Believe it or not, I've never cohabitated with a woman before so I'm not familiar with the rituals of the morning preparations."

This little bit of information surprises me. But it also raises a few questions of my own that need clarifying. He's either a virgin, which I highly doubt, never had a lasting committed relationship or he's a serial one-night stand type of guy. The ones that I try to avoid at all cost because they lead to nothing but heartbreak.

"Are you saying you've never seen a woman get ready in the mornings or you've just never lived with one?"

My voice wavers slightly, the fear evident in the words that I've chosen. He stops what he's doing, dropping the pile of clothes on the floor and takes the few steps over to stand in front of me. The feel of his hands as he runs them up and down my arms calms my nerves.

He looks down at me, his face serious. "No, I've never lived with a woman before. Yes, I have seen them get ready in the mornings but I don't want to talk about other women while I'm here with you. As far as I'm concerned there was no one before you."

My heart flutters again in my chest at his words. He's too good to be true, knowing exactly what to say to make me feel like the most important thing in the world to him. So he has a past. Who doesn't? He's dated a few women before me. That's not surprising either. It was more surprising that he wasn't currently dating anyone when I met him.

"What did I ever do to deserve you?" I ask.

He gathers up his clothes again and kisses my cheek. "I've asked myself the same thing every day since we met. I won't take long."

He disappears into my bathroom and I slump back onto my bed. Reaching for my phone, I text Kara, letting her know that I have a giant bottle of Advil in case she needs it after the pounding she was doing against my wall last night. Kara texts back with her usual smart ass remarks, making me laugh.

It's too quiet now that Andrew isn't in the same room as me. I turn on my playlist, needing to fill the void and start bouncing around to the beat as Gavin DeGraw sings about being in love with a girl. Warmth spreads through my body as I wonder if Andrew feels the same way as I do about him.

I listen as I hear him singing in the shower, and I turn down the music so I can eavesdrop better. It's comical that he's singing along with the song I'm playing. Apparently I must have the volume up loud enough to be heard over the rushing of water. But I don't want to draw unnecessary attention to my spying. So I resume the volume it was at and busy myself around the room, picking out clothes that I think could be appropriate for our excursions. I don't like being unprepared for situations. Being unprepared means things can happen and for me that's never something good. The black cloud that follows me around generally sees to that.

A puff of steam comes out of the now open door and my mouth turns into Niagara Falls again as Andrew emerges from the bathroom. I swear he's walking in slow motion as he pulls his shirt over the hard muscles of his abdomen, giving me just the barest glimpse of his rock hard abs.

He sits next to me on the bed and begins lacing his shoes. My eyes close as his sweet, sexy scent surrounds me in the safety of the cocoon that he brings. It should be a sin to smell that good.

Andrew nudges my shoulder, flashing me that heartbreaking smile of his. "Your turn, love."

My head turns to acknowledge the statement only my body feels frozen to the spot. The heat emanating from him warms my skin even though goose bumps are present. He laughs and stands me up, patting me on the behind as I gather my clothes and disappear into the bathroom.

I close my eyes and inhale deeply. It smells of him, his body wash, his cologne and just him. I want to bottle this up and bring it with me so I'm never without this smell. Stripping out of my nightshirt I turn the water on and occupy the space that he was just naked in, feeling slightly dirty at the thought.

"Where are they?" I mutter to myself, tossing the clothes to the side for the third time. Great, I've forgotten to take my underwear with me. How do I go about getting them? Quickly dress sans underwear and retrieve them like it's no big deal? But then I remember his reaction to the time I answered the door in nothing but my towel and that drives me to repeat the action, hoping he'll respond in the same way.

I stick my head out of the door, looking around the room for him. He's standing by the windows, talking to someone in a hushed voice on the phone. I spy my missing pair of panties lying on the bed, exactly where my pile of clothes had ended up before I was distracted by him. My feet move quietly across the carpet, hoping for a sneak attack.

But just like me, his body must be in tune with mine because Andrew turns to face me as I approach the bed. He mutters something into the phone and then promptly ends the call. Clinging to the front of my towel, I bend over to pick up the panties and watch as the slow smile crawls across his face. He makes a move to come closer to me but I back away slowly.

"Time schedule, remember? I'll be right back," I say, quickly walking back into the bathroom but not before I notice the slight bulge in his pants that he's adjusting.

I break my own personal record for getting ready, having my hair dried and curled in no time flat. For once I feel perfectly made up with nothing out of place. I feel beautiful and confident, all because of Andrew. He makes me feel that way, even if I don't believe it half the time. I walk back into the room and instantly his arms wrap around me, pulling me close to him. His lips press into my temple and I nuzzle into his chest.

"Beautiful as always, my sweet Tessa. Shall we?"

He extends his elbow to me and I eagerly link mine with his. He escorts us out of the room, down the elevator and into the bright morning sun.

"You're really not telling me where we're going?" I ask, pulling my sunglasses out of my purse.

He shakes his head. "It's a surprise. A good one, I promise." He looks down at my feet and smiles. "I'm glad you decided to wear comfortable shoes today. We'll be doing a lot of walking."

I look around for his car as we walk past the valet and head down the street.

"You didn't drive here last night?" I ask.

He shakes his head again. "My plan involves many stops throughout the day and I didn't want to waste time by chasing down parking spots."

He's sporting his mirrored aviator sunglasses and a huge smile. He's very playful this morning. I love playful Andrew. He grabs my hand and whisks me easily into his stride. I'm surprised I'm able to keep up with him seeing as his legs are longer than mine.

We turn a few corners and arrive at a little café. There are a few wrought iron tables set up in a fenced-off area in front. The delicious smell of pastries drifts through the air, making my mouth water.

"Our first stop of the day. Let me feed you before we actually begin our journey."

He pulls me inside and I place my sunglasses on top of my head. It's small but quaint with only a handful of tables inside, each covered in a red linen tablecloth and black wooden chairs. The scent of freshly ground coffee smells almost as good as Andrew. Almost.

I walk over to the display case to review my choices. Everything looks so tempting and horrifically high in calories. I chew on my bottom lip, warring with myself on whether or not I should eat the sugary confections in front of me or just stick with a cup of black coffee. My body has been used to running solely on caffeine that this whole week has been throwing it off balance. I wonder if I could get away with just the coffee? Andrew would never let me do that though. He'd probably force feed me something if I didn't do it willingly.

Andrew's hand stays firmly on my back as I hunch over, carefully assessing each item in front of me. Do I pick the muffin or the croissant or the donut? Chocolate or jelly filled? Buttery or topped with cream cheese? Either way it's going to be a big hello to my jiggly thighs.

"Good morning. What can I get for you two?" the guy behind the counter asks, pulling my nose away from the glass display case. He's a little too chipper for this early in the morning for my taste. But then again I haven't had my first cup of coffee yet.

"I'll have an orange cranberry muffin and an espresso. Love, what about you?" he asks. His arm wraps around my hip, pulling me into his side as I make my final decision.

"Could I get a croissant and a vanilla latte, low-fat milk if you have it please?"

The young man behind the counter flashes me a bright smile and nods his head.

"Excellent choice."

I watch as he slides the glass case open, pulling out a ridiculously huge muffin and the mammoth croissant. It's flaking apart as he places it on the plate and I can't help the rumble of my stomach as he puts the two coffees on the tray with our pastries.

"Are you always this hungry?" Andrew whispers into my ear. I turn my head and shake it slightly.

"No, I swear my stomach never growls like this. It only does this when I'm around you."

He tucks a strand of hair behind my ear. "I think it knows that I'm here to take care of all your needs."

My mouth opens to say something only nothing comes out. I'm blown away by his words once again. How can his words cause warmth to run rampant through my bloodstream, heating each extremity and pumping precious air into my lungs that he knocks back out each time I'm with him?

The guy behind the counter clears his throat as he presents our tray with our breakfast on it. Andrew thanks him before grabbing it and leading me outside to one of the available tables. He places the tray on top and moves to hold out my chair.

"You don't have to pull out my chair for me every time. I

am capable of doing it myself you know."

His lips find the top of my head while his hands lightly squeeze my shoulders.

"I know, but that's what a gentleman should be doing for a lady. And you are definitely my lady."

His lady? He thinks of me as his? I refrain from bouncing in my chair as my eyes follow him when he pulls out the chair to sit next to me. He still doesn't like to sit across from me, which I absolutely adore. My body craves him more than I realize and I don't want the distance between us any more than he does.

My stomach rumbles again and he shoves the plate with my croissant in front of me.

"Eat."

My eyes roll to the sky at his gentle command. I break off my first piece and slide it into my mouth. It's buttery and flaky and absolutely amazing. It practically melts in my mouth as I savor it. Hands down the best croissant I've ever had. The sun shines down, seemingly agreeing that the pastry could very well be heaven sent.

My eyes wander to Andrew, watching as he peels the wrapper off his muffin and takes the top off of it, setting it aside. That little act brings a smile to my face.

"Saving the best for last?"

I laugh before taking a sip of my latte. His close proximity, as he leans into me, causes my heart rate to spike.

"Always," he says before planting a small kiss upon my cheek.

He pulls away and pops a piece of muffin into his mouth, giving me a wink in the process. We sit and eat in a comfortable silence, each enjoying our little slice of heaven next to each other. I break off another piece and hold it out in front of him.

"Want some?"

He smiles and opens his mouth, taking the piece from my fingers, licking them clean. His eyes dilate as his tongue gently glides over my fingertips, causing a new rush of heat to run through me. I pull back my hand and run my tongue over my dry lips. My eyes fall to his hands as he breaks apart the top portion of his muffin.

"My turn," he says, offering it to me.

I open my mouth, taking the offered piece and once again hum my pleasure at the sweet and tart taste. He smiles and runs his finger over his lips, the same one that was just in my mouth. I swallow and nervously bite my lip, finding myself in a new territory. There's a sweetness to our gestures, feeding each other pieces of our breakfast, our eyes never leaving the other as we make idle conversation. He's the most considerate man I've ever met. No one has ever treated me with this much respect and kindness. I'm almost afraid to embrace it. I watch his throat work as he drinks his coffee, somehow finding it highly seductive. Then there's a twinkle in his eye as he regales me with another story of his past. Apparently he wasn't the polished, pretty boy he poses to be now. I have a hard time seeing him with a messy mop of hair and braces, sporting dirty clothes while using large sticks as fencing swords. Just another little piece of him that he gives me and I cherish it with the others.

"I just realized. We've been together for the past four days now and I don't even know your favorite color," I say with a laugh.

Andrew laughs with me while twirling his coffee cup. "You're right. How silly of us to continue on without this epic knowledge." I laugh as he smiles at me. "My favorite color is blue, any shade of it. There's just something about the color that has a calming reaction every time I see it."

I nod my head and smile. "I can see that. My color is green. Sage green, to be more specific."

"Ah, so you're one of those then. A color snob."

The face he makes has me giggling like a teenager. "Yes, I am a color snob. Although I wouldn't dismiss any shade of green if presented to me. I would just be more drawn to that particular one."

He taps his lips, pursing them against his finger. "Sudden death challenge?"

I raise an eyebrow to him. "I'm afraid to know what that is."

Andrew leans over and smiles. "I fire a question at you and you have to answer as quickly as possible. Then you ask me something and I do the same. We keep going until one of us can't think of anything else, or we fall over laughing. Are you interested?"

I nod. "By all means. Let's play."

"Favorite food?" he starts.

"Sesame chicken. Favorite band?"

"Rolling Stones."

"Really?" I reply.

He laughs. "I was raised on the classics and it never quite left me. No commentary, by the way. Just questions. Okay, bucket list vacation destination?"

"Florence. Yours?"

"Bali. Favorite pastime?"

"Reading. Favorite sport?"

"Rugby. Lace or satin?"

I'm taken aback by that question. "Um, lace?"

He leans closer to me. "Breathless or excitement?"

I lean closer to him. "Breathless."

Andrew leans even closer, just a breath between our lips. "Simple or fancy?"

"Simple," I reply.

His fingers brush along my jaw and he places a sweet, simple kiss against my lips. "I knew that answer already."

"How did you know?"

"Because there's no flash to you, nothing screaming that you need the best of everything to be happy. You're the person who is perfectly content with enjoying life as it comes. You don't need the fancy cars or the glitz of excitement. You are the type of person who will try to make the best of any given situation."

I blink several times while staring into his eyes. "How do you know that?"

"I know that because I've watched you these past four days and listened to you talk, listened to your stories and watched your body language as you approach different situations. All of them tell me the person that you are. And they all say that you are someone that I need to be around for as long as you'll let me."

And with those words, I know for sure that this is it for me, that I am ruined for all other men, even if we cannot seem to make things work out.

And that small bit of uncertainty has me seeking out his

feelings for me. "Andrew, what are we? Are we dating or just messing around as a vacation fling?"

I run my finger around the rim of my coffee cup, staring intently at the brown liquid inside. Andrew reaches out, grabbing my hand, halting my nervous tic, bringing my fingers to his lips, gently kissing each and every one. He shifts his body toward me, leaning over to rest his arm across the back of my chair. The blues of his eyes draw me deeper into him as he lets go of my hand to gently trace my cheek.

"I think we're past dating, love. And we are most definitely more than a vacation fling. You can put whatever label you want on us but just so I'm clear, I am yours and you are mine. We belong to each other."

Then, at that moment, images flash before my eyes. Andrew and I getting married, the two of us sitting on the front porch swing, watching our kids play in the front yard. I can see us dancing in our living room for no reason other than to hold each other. I see sunsets and sunrises, both spent in his arms. I see parties and laughter, tears and comfort. I see a life that I've always imagined and in each scene he takes center stage. He's who I want to spend the rest of my life with.

I am his and he is mine.

And with that, the overwhelming need to place a name to the emotion becomes too much for me. It's love. It has to be. I've never really felt it before and I have no other explanation for it. This need, this compulsion to be next to him always overrides everything else. His happiness is what I want to live for, to strive for. But I can't say it out loud. Not yet.

I place my hand on his cheek and gently pull him into a kiss. The faintest hint of coffee still lingers on them, but the undeniable taste of Andrew still overrides it all. He smiles and strokes my hair.

"Thank you," I whisper against his lips.

"For what?"

"Well, for one, missing your connecting flight to New York. Two, for accepting me for who I am, even though I still don't think we know each other well."

"We know more about each other than I think you realize. And it should be me thanking you for allowing me into your life. I know it's been fast and you've been nervous about how things will work out between us. But I know you feel the same things that I feel. There's a light in your eyes that mirror my own. Some things are just meant to be."

Tears burn behind my eyes, threatening to fall. I hold them back because I don't want to turn into an emotional mess. Not yet. I just nod my head, acknowledging his heartfelt statement, agreeing with everything that he's said.

"This is a little too deep for this early in the morning," I say, trying to lighten the mood.

He laughs and my heart flutters at the sound. "I agree. Today is about fun. Are you ready to start our adventure together?"

Such a loaded question and could very easily have a double meaning behind it. But I take it at face value and wrap my hand around his outstretched one. The bus boy quickly picks up our tray and plates as we step onto the sidewalk, falling into our perfect stride, ready to start our adventure together.

Chapter 14

A NDREW SURPRISES ME AGAIN BY taking me on the Tube, a simple thing that excites me and it's sweet that he remembers. I think it's just an excuse for him to sit as close to me as possible in the crowded train. As more and more people enter the train, he pulls me onto his lap to free a seat for someone. The small child that now occupies my vacated seat smiles up at me as he wiggles into it.

I feel Andrew smile against my neck as he presses his face in the space between my ear and my shoulder. I love the way that he always has to touch me, always needing to have skin on skin contact. Truth be told, I need it as well. I lean my body into his, relaxing into his touch as we ride to a destination unknown to me. He's promised me an adventure and I wonder what that could entail.

Soon he leads me back to the surface, exiting the Westminster Station and back into the bright midmorning sun. We walk through the crowded streets, his arm draped possessively around my waist, holding me close to his side. The murmuring of people on their phones or talking to one another become the background noise as I see one of the most famous landmarks come into view.

"Big Ben!" I cry, craning my neck up to look at the massive structure. "Holy crap it's huge!"

He laughs at my childlike excitement and presses his lips against my temple. "Yes, it's not just a clever name. Come, let's take the tour."

I tilt my head to the side, twisting my lips as I do. "We don't have to. I mean, you live here and have probably seen it a million times. I don't want to make you do all the touristy things. I'm content just looking at everything."

He flexes his arm around me and smiles. "I don't mind being a tourist in my own city. All I want to do is see that beautiful smile of yours all day long while I share the city that I love with you."

"Sometimes I swear you're too good to be true."

He kisses the end of my nose. "I can say the same about you, love."

We walk over to the line for the tour and follow along with the group, playing the role of tourist and taking pictures with my phone of anything and everything I see. I snap several photos of Andrew without him knowing it while he takes several of me with his phone, including a few selfies of the two of us together.

We complete the tour with a newfound knowledge of the structure and the history behind it. Well, it's new to me. Andrew was telling me the history behind it before the tour guide even said anything, making me laugh at inappropriate times and garnering several glares from other patrons.

He leads me down the way, stopping every once in a while to take my picture, even when I'm holding my hand up to cover my face. Just random pictures really, nothing of importance that I'm standing in front of. I think he's making up excuses, telling me that the light is hitting me just right and he needs to capture it. Or there's a beautiful flower that I need to look at and asks that I tell him what it smells like. I'm on to his game, but I play along anyway because it's making him smile and I will do anything for that smile.

As we walk hand in hand down the busy streets, I can't help but admire the history surrounding the area. There are buildings that look to be centuries old and I wonder what tales those walls could tell. What they've seen and what stories could be written. I'm just in love with this city, even though this is truly my first time experiencing it.

Andrew joins in my favorite hobby of people watching as we point out a few interesting characters on our journey. Everyone seems friendly though, even offering to take a picture of Andrew and me together when we stop in front of a picturesque floral display. He buys me a single flower, kissing my cheek as we continue down the street.

We walk through Westminster Abbey, again taking the tour. I'm in awe of the history in this building alone. So much has happened here. To be able to walk in the same area as kings and queens has my excitement jumping to a whole new level. Andrew takes it in stride though, keeping me close as we tour the different chapels inside. I run my hands across the many marble statues, completely in awe by my surroundings. The magnificent paintings adorning the walls catch my eye, as well as the stained glass work throughout the halls. Andrew takes me through the museum, telling me about the history of the artifacts and I'm amazed at how much he knows about his country. I'm sure if I took him to places back home I wouldn't have the slightest clue where things are from or why they're in the museum to begin with.

After several more pictures together, he leads us back out to the street, joining the crowd at the St. James's Park Station. He doesn't even give me the chance to take a seat next to him this time. He just pulls me into his lap right away. You won't find me complaining about this seating arrangement.

His strong arms keep hold of me as he nuzzles into the crook of my neck, whispering words against my skin. I don't even fight the public displays anymore, not caring who sees us because the time we have together is precious and I need to take advantage of it whenever I can.

We exit at the Victoria Station, joining the large crowd of people with cameras in hand.

"Where are we now?" I ask. He takes hold of my hand and as we turn the corner, I see why everyone has their cameras ready.

"Is that? Is that Buckingham Palace?"

He gives me a full megawatt smile, causing his eyes to crinkle in the corners. "Yes, my dearest. That is the palace. It's kind of a staple for any tourist to see."

I wrap my arms around his neck and press my lips against his. He laughs when I tug him across the street, clicking away pictures with one hand as I refuse to let him go. We see the famous guards standing at their post and we have our picture taken with them. He wraps his arm around my shoulder as we walk around the perimeter, looking at the gardens just beyond the large fence. But he humors me and takes me all the way around so I don't miss anything.

"Shall we go to our final destination?" he asks.

I look up at him, my eyes squinting behind my sunglasses. "There's more to see? My gosh Andrew, I don't think I could take much more. I must have a million pictures on my phone as it is."

He laughs. The sound reverberates through my chest, warming it up as it's my new favorite sound. Well, it's one of my new favorite sounds.

"This one is special. Come, let's get back to the station."

We walk down to the station, still hand in hand. I glance up at him as we wait for the train and let my eyes roam over his profile. Such a beautiful face, perfectly matched with the beautiful man who captivates me daily.

"You know, I can sit on a seat," I say jokingly.

He tightens his arms around my waist and shakes his head. "That is not in the rules for the day. This is my day to pamper you and that is what I shall do."

"I don't need pampering."

He laughs a lighthearted laugh. "You may not think so, but I do."

I roll my eyes and it only makes him laugh more. "You're going to spoil me if you're not careful."

"Maybe that's my master plan. To spoil you so much that you'll never want to be rid of me. But I think you just deserve someone who will look after you for a change."

His words make my heart sigh and I snuggle into him. Minutes pass and I don't even notice the crowds anymore. Nothing is apparent when I'm caught up in Andrew's spell.

When I'm in his arms, the world feels right like nothing could hurt us. I want this feeling to last forever.

When we finally emerge to the surface, we're greeted by the lush greens of Hyde Park. He pulls me closer to his side and stops next to one of the massive trees.

"This is what I want to do this afternoon. I want to have a lazy day in the park with you."

My heart expands as he runs his hands down my arms, pulling me close to his chest.

"That sounds perfect."

He leads us down a path lined with lush green trees overhead. He points out the many gardens that line the park until we come across the perfect spot.

"There," Andrew says, referring to a large shady tree just in front of us. "That looks like a good place."

We walk to the tree and he gently pulls me down between his legs as he props himself against the large trunk. My arms drape over my knees, pulling them to my chest. But then I'm pulled back as warm arms wrap around me, anchoring my body to his. He's holding me like he never wants to let me go.

"So this is what you wanted to do the most with me today?" I ask, craning my neck to the side to get a good look at him. He leans into me, kissing my forehead with a slight smile. I relax into his body, letting my head fall onto his shoulder. Our fingers play with each other, gently twisting around and exploring the expanse of skin on each other's forearms.

"Yes, this is what I wanted to do with you today. I just want to lie here in the park with you, holding you in my arms."

That has to be one of the most romantic things anyone has ever said to me. Okay, so no one has ever actually said anything romantic to me before Andrew but still. To him, it seems to be the most natural thing to do. It's like second nature the way he fusses over me or makes sure that I never have to open my own door. That's just a part of Andrew, it's who he is and it's a part of him I absolutely have come to love and adore.

"I love it. Sounds like the perfect way to spend the day."

I lean over, placing a small row of kisses against his jaw before relaxing back into him. The slight chill of the autumn breeze hardly affects me, not with the heat of Andrew completely surrounding me, keeping me safe and warm. He's like my own personal blanket, sheltering me from the outside elements.

The sway of the branches mesmerizes me, watching them blow softly with the wind. The excited giggles of nearby children float with the breeze, along with the exotic fragrance of wildflowers. It's like sensory overload. I remove my sunglasses, casting them to the side, enjoying the sun's rays at they hit my face through the leaves.

"You travel a lot for work, right?" I ask.

He nods his head. "Not terribly often but enough. It all depends on if there's something that needs to be done at one of the centers or if I need to scout out new places to build one."

"Do you find it difficult being away often?"

"Sometimes. There are days where I would much rather be relaxing at home or out with my mates instead of sitting in hotel rooms in other countries. But it comes with the job."

"Okay, so where is the most exciting place that you've traveled to so far?"

Andrew pauses to think about his answer. "For work or for holiday?"

"Either one."

"Turks and Caicos. A bunch of my mates and I decided to go on a holiday there after graduation. We stayed on the Grand Turk Island at one of the all-inclusive resorts there. It was pure heaven. Lots of sun, turquoise blue water and white sand beaches everywhere. We even did some snorkeling at the coral reefs. It was a grand holiday before joining the Foundation on a permanent basis."

I smile and close my eyes, picturing those white sand beaches as he describes them. "That sounds like heaven. I'd love to go somewhere like that."

"What about you? Where's the most exciting place that you've traveled before?"

I give a nervous laugh and fidget with my fingers. "You mean outside of London?"

"Yes, besides here," he laughs into my hair.

"Well, I haven't really been anywhere before. I didn't travel much as a child. We didn't exactly do family vacations or anything like that."

"Why not?"

I sit up slightly and take a deep breath, blowing it out slowly. Well, it's now or never.

"I, um, didn't have what you would call a normal childhood. My parents separated when I was young, around the age of nine. I was a mistake, or at least that's what I've been told. They only stayed together for as long as they did because I was little. My dad started working longer and longer hours at the office. It was almost as if he was making excuses to stay away from us. Or from me at least.

"One day, during one of my mom and dad's many fights,

he had his bags packed by the front door. I wasn't sure what was going on. He just said that he needed to go for a while. He told me to not cry because I was a big girl. And then he left. I chased him down the driveway, crying for him but he never once turned around. Then that was it, he was gone."

A lone tear slips down my cheek as I rest my head on his arm. Andrew untangles me from his arms, turning me around to face him. The sadness etched across his face hurts me, even though it's me telling my sad sob story. He cradles my face, his warm palms resting against my skin while his thumbs brush away the tears that have now started to fall unbidden from my eyes.

But I can't look at him right now. I adjust my body, moving to lie down next to him with my head on his lap. Andrew reaches over to run his fingers across my scalp and down through my hair, a motion that's meant to calm and relax me. I feel anything but calm and relaxed as the memories begin to flood my mind. I swallow past the lump in my throat, close my eyes and continue on.

"My mom didn't handle it well. She told me it was my fault, that if I weren't around he'd still be there with her. That's a lot to take in as a small child, knowing your very existence was the reason your parents hated you and each other.

"After that, she became withdrawn and could barely hold a steady job. My grandma helped for a while but when she died it seemed to throw my mom completely over the edge. She withdrew from me more and more, not hiding her contempt for my existence like she used to. She'd remind me of how I ruined everything that was good in her life and how much of a burden I was to take care of all the time. It was too much to take sometimes so I spent a lot of time by myself, trying not to upset her. The older I got, the less my mom wanted me, although I don't think she ever wanted me to begin with.

"And school wasn't a reprieve for me either. I didn't always have clothes that fit right or were always clean so I would come to school slightly dirty or wearing the same thing more than once in a week. Needless to say, I was not the most popular girl in school. Unless you call being tormented by my fellow peers popular. They would find new ways to humiliate me by hanging lewd signs on my locker or tape those little pine tree air fresheners to it. They'd make animal noises behind me or push me into the mud puddles on purpose. I basically became the butt of every joke in school.

"It wasn't until my senior year that my mom fully withdrew from me and everyone else around her. I think she realized I was going to leave soon and she shut down completely. She stopped working, which made it difficult to keep ourselves out of debt. Somehow I managed to get a job my senior year. It didn't pay much, but it was enough so that I was able to at least get us groceries every week. But the bills kept piling up and soon the utilities were shut off because I couldn't always make the payments on time. I would beg at the churches for help and during the winter months they assisted in getting the power back on. But come springtime, they figured we could manage it ourselves so we struggled again and they were shut off. It was the lack of running water that was the worst part. I had constructed a makeshift outhouse behind the garage so we could use the bathroom during the time we didn't have running water. Luckily, none of the neighbors could see us because we were far enough away that no one really cared. And the only way I could shower was at school, making sure I arrived early enough so I could use the locker room showers before people came.

"On the days where my paycheck was a little bigger and after I put money toward our back bills, I would buy some clothes from Goodwill that moderately fit me. Or I'd go to rummage sales and find things there that were really cheap. But I didn't always have cash on me so sometimes I relied on dumpster diving."

His fingers still in my hair but I can't open my eyes. I don't want to see the sympathy or pity on his face.

"My sweet girl," he whispers, causing another errant tear to fall down my face.

"There's more. A few months before I turned eighteen, I was called to the office at school. Somehow social services found out about my situation and committed my mom to a mental institution. She made the comments that she didn't want to live anymore and she didn't want me, so they placed me in foster care. I asked to be put with my dad instead, but they weren't able to find him. Later I learned he had just gotten married to his second wife and had taken their honeymoon in Europe so they were completely off the grid and out of the picture. They probably wouldn't have taken me anyway. Sharon doesn't like kids.

"Social Services took me to live with the Jenkins' and it wasn't much different than living at home. They told me I needed to earn my keep, forcing me to clean their house and wait on them hand and foot. Their only concern was getting their paycheck from the state for giving me food and shelter. But otherwise they left me alone. I threw myself into my studies, which allowed me to graduate with honors. The day I turned eighteen I left and never looked back.

"But that also meant that I didn't have anywhere to go. I bounced around a few homeless shelters while working several jobs at once. But that allowed me to save up enough money to get my own apartment and enroll at the Community College. Things were finally starting to look up for me. I had a decent job, a place to live and was getting an education. I even made a few friends in some of my classes." I swallow hard and brace myself for the next revelation. "Then I met *him*."

A shiver runs through my body as I begin to recall that horrific event. Andrew's fingers continue to thread through my hair, trying to get my body to relax.

"Who was he?" he asks gently.

"Shane Rivers. He was my first and last boyfriend. I met him halfway through my first year of college. He started out nice, saying all the right things to get me to trust him. And for a few months things were okay. We didn't do anything physical and at first it was fine. Then he became pushy and impatient. I was still a virgin so I didn't want to sleep with him because I knew that I didn't love him. He laughed at that thought and told me it was my job as his girlfriend to keep him happy and satisfied. One night he came over drunk and said he was going to take what was rightfully his."

My voice catches at the last few words and Andrew holds onto me, letting me know I don't have to continue on. But I do because I need to say it out loud and he needs to hear it.

"We stayed together for just a few months after that. I didn't fight him again after that first night. There was no point. He made it clear it was expected of me to just do it, so I did it. I just turned off my feelings and went through the motions. The day he broke up with me, he did it in front of the entire student body, saying that I was the worst lay he's ever had. After that, I stopped talking to people and just kept to myself until I graduated and moved away."

More tears fall and Andrew brushes away each one. I still can't look at him. I don't want to. I know what I'll find and I can't bear to see the look on his face.

"So finally my dad stepped up, gave me a place to stay until I could find my own apartment and here I am. Moderately put together and somewhat functioning. Now you know why I am the way I am. It's also why I love what the Foundation does and stands for. I know I'm damaged goods. I get that. And now that you know all of this you'll probably want to run far away from me but . . ."

I don't get the chance to finish my sentence as he pulls me up and engulfs me into an all-consuming embrace. His lips repeatedly press against my head and I break down in his arms, unable to keep my sobs at bay. He allows me to rest my head on his shoulder, holding me until I can calm my body enough to look at him. I pull back, trying to look into his face for some sort of reassurance that he still wants me.

Andrew brushes the hair away from my face repeatedly before finally cupping his hands around my neck. "If I could take away your past I would. I'm so sorry you had to endure that growing up. You should have been loved your entire life. It's what you deserve." He presses his forehead against mine and sighs. "I may not be able to erase your past, but I will make sure your future will be nothing like it. You will know every day how much you are loved and cared for."

I wrap my arms around his neck and quietly inhale his scent. It immediately calms my body. A newfound peace settles in as I listen to his words.

"All I ask is that you don't treat me any differently than you have. I've moved on from my past and I don't like to dwell on it. I don't want pity or sympathy. I just want you to look at me the same way that you have these last few days, with that sparkle in your eye that tells me how special I am to you."

The look that crosses his face has my mind wondering what he could be thinking. But just as fast as it appeared, it was gone. He brings my lips to his, gently sealing them together. I try to deepen the kiss, but he holds back, making it soft and delicate, something that a lover would do.

"And I will, every day for the rest of my life. I promise this won't change how I feel about you. If anything it makes my feelings stronger. I told you, I am yours and you are mine. Nothing will ever change that, love. Nothing."

I feel a weight lifted off my shoulders for the first time in a long while. Kara was the only one who knew of my past, besides my dad. And now that Andrew knows and accepts it, I feel as if we can move forward together. We could actually have a shot at making this work.

I move to straddle his lap and pull him into the kiss that I so desperately need from him. That all-encompassing, soul-quenching kiss that I long for. A kiss that shows how much he wants me, and vice versa. He wraps his arms around my waist, pulling me closer, knowing exactly what I need and how to give it to me. The world fades around us, leaving us in that private bubble where nothing else exists.

We pull back, breathless and panting, but calm and satisfied. My head falls onto his shoulder as he runs his fingers lazily up and down my spine. We sit in silence, absorbing everything that we have to give.

I can tell the cogs in his head are working furiously because he's grinding his teeth, more than likely getting the courage to ask me something.

"So your father, he knows everything now?"

I nod my head. "Yes, he knows everything. When I arrived on his doorstep, we didn't talk much at first. Mainly because I hadn't heard from him since I was nine years old. But soon he found out about Child Protective Services and wanted to know what had happened that made them get involved. So I brought him up to speed, not leaving anything out because what was the point? It was over and done with.

"He told me once that he had no idea that was going on, that we were as poor as we were, struggling like we did. But how could he not? I mean did he hate me that much to never call and check on me or check on the woman that he once loved to make sure we were taken care of? But he still swears to this day he had no idea.

"Guilt must have been eating away at him because he paid for my student loans and offered to pay for my apartment. I declined, saying that I wanted to make my own way in the world. He also offered to pay for my therapy, but I again declined. Our relationship is strained at best. I didn't want him feeling obligated to take care of me, especially when I know that he doesn't want to."

Andrew raises my hand, placing a kiss in the center of my palm. "Guilt and obligation are never a good reason to help someone." He looks down and makes a face I've come to recognize when his eyes find mine. It's the look that mirrors my own face every time I see him when he steals my breath away. He doesn't have to say it. I know he feels it too. "Tessa, you will never have to know that life again. I will always be there for you. You will never have to be alone."

"Thank you, Andrew. You have no idea what that means to me."

I press my lips against his one last time before moving off him, laying my head back in his lap as we both sit in silence and watch the world moves around us. His hand draws small circles on my stomach while the other resumes stroking my hair. We do nothing but stare into each other's eyes, causing me to fall deeper in love with him.

Chapter 15

WE LIE THERE FOR WHAT feels like hours but in all reality it's just minutes. His fingers are still tracing lazy circles across my body, sometimes touching skin, sometimes floating above my clothes but never once leaving me. A part of me cannot believe that he's still here or even that he still wants me. Most people cast aside the damaged goods, waiting to find that perfect specimen that doesn't need any work done to it. Andrew, he's a fixer, a mender, unafraid of taking that broken piece and putting it back together until it's whole.

My heart feels full for the first time in a very long time. The slow, steady beat seems to be tattooing his name throughout my body, marking me forever as his. His words still swirl around in my head as he basically declared his love for me. Well, not in so many words but he's promised to be there for me in the future. Why would he be in my future if he didn't love me?

His hand leaves in my hair and I raise my eyes to look into his peaceful blue ones. A new light shines in them, giving me hope, giving me strength and courage that we can make this work.

"Shall we walk a little?" he asks. His finger traces an invisible line down my nose before his lips touch the end of it.

My favorite kiss.

"I'd love to."

Andrew helps me off the ground and we brush off a few pieces of dirt and grass from our clothing. His arm wraps around my waist as he leads me back to the path. I rest my head on his shoulder, feeling his lips press against my head with a contented sigh. We pass more gardens and a large fountain, making up several stories about some of the people we see along the way. But we don't talk more than that. I think we've officially hit the limit for talking right now.

He glances down at his watch as we turn another corner. "We should get some dinner since we somehow managed to skip lunch."

"I could go for some food. Where shall we go?"

"My place. I told you that I would cook for you before you left."

My throat becomes dry and I blink a few times, trying to remove the astonishment from my eyes. I thought he was joking before when he suggested that he'd cook for me.

"Okay," I whisper. I don't know what else to say. I would love to see where he lives, invade his space and find out more about the man who has stolen my breath away more times than I can count.

"What time is your flight in the morning?"

I look up, trying to remember what the itinerary said.

"Noon I believe, which means that Kara and I have to be at

Heathrow around ten or so."

The wheels are working overtime as I watch his eyes dart back and forth across my face. What is he up to?

He dips his head to my ear. His warm breath tickles the area just below and my eyes close involuntarily at the contact.

"If you wouldn't mind, I would love to be the one to bring you to the airport tomorrow."

He pulls my lobe into his mouth and a burst of liquid fire runs throughout my body, scorching every inch of it. It's impossible to focus on anything else when my body is pressed up against his like this, whispering words against my skin. Making me regret having to leave in the morning.

"I would love that Andrew. It's going to kill me to leave tomorrow and not see you every day. I don't want this to end."

He tilts my chin up, locking his eyes with mine. "Tomorrow will not be goodbye Tessa. I told you, this is not the end of us. This is just the beginning. We need to get over this minor bump in the road first before we can coast smoothly down the path to forever."

I think my heart just stopped beating. No, scratch that, my brain stopped working too, as well as my lungs because I can't breathe. Once again, he's stolen my breath, making me fall for him even more. I blink back the tears that threaten to leak out as he cradles my face in his hands, looking deep into my eyes as he places his mouth on mine, sealing his promise with a kiss.

"This is home," he says, opening the door to his flat.

He ushers me inside and I slip my shoes off before walking

further into the foyer. It's much larger than I expected it to be. I always thought London flats were tiny, cramped spaces. Not this though. It's at least two, if not three, times the size of my apartment back home.

It's an open concept design with dark leather furniture that occupies the living room area. The entertainment center is opposite the couch, surrounded by shelves holding his DVD collection and various other books and knick-knacks. The matching loveseat and chair creates a warm and cozy conversational area.

I notice several picture frames sitting on the tables. One looks to be of his mom and dad, taken on their wedding day. Another shows him standing with them in his Oxford gown, apparently taken at his graduation.

Several paintings and photographs hang on the white walls, adding some additional warmth to the room. Upon further inspection, I can see that the photos are of city scenes, taken at night or at sunrise. It makes me wonder if he took them while he traveled the world, finding the beauty in everything like he always seems to do.

He takes my purse from me, laying it in one of the chairs before coming up and wrapping his arms around me from behind.

"And you live here alone?"

It's a stupid question I know, but I can't believe that a single person would need this much space. He follows me into the combined kitchen and dining room area. It's a modern space filled with stainless steel appliances, sleek black cupboards, and a taupe granite countertop. It's the polar opposite of my kitchen, which still looks like it is stuck in the Seventies.

He places his chin on my shoulders and nods. "All alone."

The giant floor to ceiling windows draws my attention. He catches my gaze and walks us through the doors, pushing them open. A small patio set, complete with a table and four chairs, sits off to the side and is surrounded by multicolored plants in a fenced-in area. It's a great area, one that makes me think of summer nights filled with parties or lazy Sunday afternoons of sitting and reading a book.

He pulls me back inside and turns me in his arms. "There's one more space that I want to show you."

Grabbing my hand, he leads me down a hallway off from the dining room, pointing out a spare bedroom to the left and a smaller bathroom. He opens a door at the end of the hall, pulling me behind him as we walk into the middle of his bedroom. Again, it's much larger than my room back home. A huge king sized mahogany sleigh bed occupies the center of the far wall, tastefully decorated with a plush dark blue comforter and contrasting cream colored throw pillows. A six-drawer dresser sits between two doors on the right wall while a pair of nightstands flanks each side of the bed. There's a bench at the foot with the same cream color as the throw pillows, completing the entire set. I've never owned a bedroom set but could definitely see this as something I would choose. It's simple yet elegant, tastefully put together to make the whole room come alive.

"This is my closet," he says, opening the door to the left of the dresser. It's a walk-in, filled completely with everything one would need to be the COO of a company, and then some.

"Wow," is all I say as I drag a tie that's hanging on a large rack through my fingers. It's not surprising that even Andrew's closet is neat and tidy.

We exit the closet and walk through the door on the other side of the dresser. It's his en suite bathroom and I'm completely jealous of what he has. A large sunken bathtub sits against the back wall with a glass enclosed shower directly next to it. Bamboo flooring and modern fixtures make up the rest of the space. I suddenly feel like I've stepped into one of those DIY shows on HGTV. I've never seen a bathroom like this before.

He pulls me back to his room, sitting us down on the bed. Suddenly I'm nervous about being here with him. I start to fidget with my hair. He takes notice and grabs my hands, pulling them to his lips.

"So what do you think?" He looks nervous, possibly even more nervous than me.

"It's amazing Andrew. It's so much nicer than my tiny apartment back home."

He lets out a breath and pulls me close. I wrap my arms around him, feeling his heart beat against mine. This feels like home; as if I could belong here. It's a strange feeling to have, but it's there nonetheless.

He pulls me off the bed, keeping me close and nuzzles his nose into my hair. "If we're going to eat dinner we need to leave this room right now because I don't know how much longer I'm going to be able to keep my hands off you."

My cheeks redden as lascivious thoughts run through my mind on what he could do with his hands on me.

On that bed.

In this room.

Skin on skin.

Touching.

Loving.

Holy crap it's hot in here all of a sudden.

We walk back to the kitchen and he holds out a chair for me to sit in while he begins preparing our dinner. I watch him move fluidly around the room, pulling things out of the cupboards and the refrigerator. My cheek is propped up on my hand as I just stare and admire him. Forget people watching. I think I found my new favorite hobby. Andrew watching.

"Would you like a glass of wine?" he asks, wiping his hands off on a towel.

"Yes, please. A glass sounds fantastic."

He pulls down two glasses from an overhead rack and fills them from a chilled bottle of white wine he pulls out of the countertop refrigerator.

"I hope you like it. It's a Sauvignon Blanc. It'll go perfectly with dinner tonight."

I clink my glass with his and smile above the rim. "I don't know anything about wine so I'll take your word for it."

He makes himself busy around the kitchen and I take my first sip from my glass. The refreshing, crisp flavor floats over my tongue and I silently hum my pleasure. I feel bad just sitting here and drinking while he's busy placing items into pans, sprinkling olive oil over the top of whatever he just put in there.

"Can I help you with anything?" I start to stand from my chair, but he motions for me to sit back down.

"No, you are my guest. Just make yourself comfortable and relax. I've got this all under control."

He takes two chicken breasts out of their package, placing them on top of some plastic wrap that he's already set out on the counter. He puts another piece on top and uses his mallet to pound them down until they reach the right thickness. He washes his hands and then puts some spinach, cheese, and prosciutto in the middle and rolls them up, securing them with a toothpick. They get placed in a shallow baking pan and set in the oven.

He washes his hands again before turning to face me with a grin. Grabbing his wine glass he walks over and pulls out the chair directly next to me. I watch his throat work the wine down and momentarily lose myself.

"You're so much better at that than I am," I say, referring to the culinary magic he was just performing.

"It's one of my passions. My mother was always cooking in the kitchen and I took the time to learn from her. Of course, my food is nothing like hers but I'd like to think it is right up there."

He bumps my shoulder and we laugh. I twirl the stem of my wine glass with my fingers as we just look at each other, not needing any words to pass between us. My gaze once again falls to the large windows in front of us and I let a sigh escape my lips.

"It's such a beautiful space, your patio area. I don't have anything like that back at my apartment. All I have is a first-floor view of the street. I'd kill to have some grass or a sitting area outside that I could call my own."

I can feel his eyes on me as I continue to admire his outdoor haven. When my eyes finally fall back onto his, I catch him with a funny smirk on his face.

"What? Do I have something on my face?" I start nervously wiping my fingers across my face, praying that nothing embarrassing is on there.

"No love, nothing like that. I was just thinking to myself."

"About what?"

"About you."

"What about me?"

He leans closer, putting his head next to mine so we share the same vision field. "I look at my garden and I see wasted space. I hardly spend any time out there so I don't need it. But as I was watching you look out there, I could see that glimmer of light and I know you imagined so many things to do out there. You see things for more than they are. It's one of the things I love about you."

I cling to those words, repeating them over and over. *It's one of the things he loves about me.* That means there's more about me he loves, doesn't it? He reaches over and covers my hand with his.

"It makes me want to give you the world so I can always see that light in your eyes," he says.

I just stare at our hands resting in front of us. There's so much I want to say to that statement. I just don't know how to put it into words. My lips press together and I give a small shrug.

"When you grow up with practically nothing your whole life it makes you appreciate the little things and everything else that you do have. My apartment is small, but it's functional, clean and it is mine. It's my space where I can relax and be myself. That's all I really want. A place to belong."

I tug at my bottom lip with my teeth again and he reaches up to set it free. The sad look is back in his eyes. I need to change that quickly. I lean over and place a small kiss upon his cheek.

"Thank you for dinner," I say.

He looks at me with a raised eyebrow. "But you haven't eaten it yet. How do you know it's going to be good?"

I reach my fingers up and trail them gently down his cheek. "Because you're making it for me, doing one of those little things you do that make me go crazy for you."

He takes hold of my hand, placing a kiss in the center before looking up at me with a face-splitting grin. "Crazy, eh?"

I laugh and lean closer. "Yep. Stark. Raving. Mad."

He tries to close the distance between us, but the timer sounds in the kitchen, pulling our faces apart.

"Saved by the bell," he says before standing and walking into the kitchen to remove a pan from the oven.

I blow out a breath and take another sip of my wine. Saved by the bell? Did he not want to kiss me? Or did he mean that it was going to go further than a kiss and the bell saved him? I'm hoping for the latter because there's no way that I'm misreading his cues. Am I?

Andrew throws some broccoli and cauliflower into a steamer while he checks the temperature on the chicken.

"Where do you keep your plates and silverware?" I ask, tired of sitting around and not helping.

He jerks his head to the back, letting me know they're in the cabinets behind him. I find everything I need for two place settings and decorate the table, leaving the plates just to his side so he can put the food on them, as he requested.

"Can you pull out another bottle of wine? Ladies choice," he says, slicing the stuffed chicken breasts and putting one on each plate.

I open the door and find the same bottle that we had emptied, placing it on the table for us. Andrew's putting vegetables and potatoes on both of the plates, making sure that my plate has more than enough food. He walks them over to where I'm sitting, setting his down right next to mine. I refill his glass and raise mine to his.

"Cheers," I say.

"Cheers."

We clink glasses and again I find myself staring at him over the rim of my glass. I study his face as he takes a sip of his wine, watching him savor the flavor in obvious appreciation.

My senses go on overload again as I smell the delicious food he's made for me. Garlic and basil are the most prominent notes and as if on cue my stomach rumbles loudly. Why does it always do that in front of him? My hands cover my reddening face, trying to hide my embarrassment yet again.

He pulls my hands down from my face, letting his fingers linger just a touch longer. "No hiding from me, ever. You're hungry. It's nothing to be embarrassed about. Part of my job is to take care of you and that's what I'm doing. Now let me do it."

I nod because I don't know what else to do. His smile calms the fear away again and I begin to dig into my food, surprised by how hungry I actually am. And he was right. He's a wiz in the kitchen. I've never had a home cooked meal that tasted this good. Or at least one that was made for me by my date. Before I even blink my plate is picked clean. He laughs as I watch him wipe his mouth off with a napkin.

"Good?" he asks.

"Good? Andrew, it was incredible. I've never had a better meal than that. At least one of us knows how to cook. Otherwise, we would be living off of cereal and Macaroni and Cheese."

He laughs, filling my ears with that sound I love. Then I realize what I just said. Did I just imply that we'll be living together? Again, a filter would be nice.

The laughter dies down, filling the area with comfortable silence and the hum of expectation. His hand reaches up, freeing a few strands of hair that got caught in my lip, tucking them safely behind my ear. The soft pad of his finger trails down my cheek, down the column of my neck before resting on the space right above my heart.

I nervously swallow, my eyes darting to his. He's silently pleading with me and I know what he's going to say before he even says it.

"Stay with me tonight." His voice is just a whisper as he pulls me closer to him, pulling me onto his lap. His hands run over my body, tracing every line and curve as my own hands rest on his shoulders, keeping me balanced because I fear that I may fall over.

"But I still need to pack." Why is that the first thing that pops into my brain? An utterly sexy, handsome man who is way out of my league has just asked me to spend the night with him and all I can think about is leaving? There has to be something wrong with me.

"I promise to get you back to your hotel in plenty of time. Besides, I'll be driving you to Heathrow, remember?"

I nod, a smile forming on my lips. "I remember."

Andrew's forehead falls forward, pressing against mine. His lips are inches away from my own. One little shift in our bodies and we'd be kissing.

"Just say that you'll stay here with me tonight."

"Yes," I breathe.

I feel his smile rather than see it because his lips are instantly on mine, kissing me slowly and passionately, giving and not taking. A chill runs across my skin, making it pebble immediately as realization hits. I'm staying here. Tonight. With him. In his bed.

This is it. It's really going to happen. I'm going to freely give myself to Andrew tonight, something that I've never done before. It excites yet scares me, but I know Andrew. He would never do anything to hurt me.

"I've imagined you in my bed for the past few days. I'm so glad my dreams will be a reality tonight," he says in his sexy, low voice.

I squirm on his lap because the low, dull ache that is always present when I'm around him has turned into a full on pulsing throb between my legs. He groans slightly as he places me back on the chair, fishing out his cell phone in the process. It vibrates in his hand and his eyes nervously flick to mine.

"Sorry, I need to take this. It will only be a minute," he says, accepting the call and then walking away.

Not that I mind him walking away. I could watch him do that all day. Well, not the walking away part. I just want to see his ass flex as he walks because let's face it, he has a magnificent ass.

I decide to not be a lump this time and start clearing the table, washing the dishes by hand and putting them away. My head lifts and I see him still pacing in the living room, talking in a hushed voice into the phone. My eyes flick to the clock on the stove and wonder who could be calling him at this hour of the night? It's well after business hours. I shake it off, reminding myself that it's none of my business.

Andrew walks back into the kitchen as I'm rinsing out the bubbles from the sink. "You didn't have to do that. I would have done it," he says, pressing his lips against my neck.

I turn in his arms, wrapping my own around his neck. "I wanted to do it. I wanted to help."

His lips brush mine before he releases me, a smirk playing across his face. I watch him walk over to his stereo, scrolling through some sort of playlist before tapping the screen and walking back to me. The flat is filled with the sultry sounds of a guitar strumming, followed by the raspy voice of Bryan Adams. Andrew stands in front of me and bows slightly.

"My dearest Tessa, would you do me the honor of this dance?" he asks, holding his hand out to me. My lip disappears between my teeth, suppressing the grin I want to show. My hand falls into his and he pulls me close, our chests touching and faces just inches apart. We sway in small circles around the kitchen to the melody that's floating in the air.

Once again, I'm thrown by his romantic gestures. Andrew leans forward, pressing our cheeks together. I sigh and wrap my arms around him tighter. His breath is warm against my ear as he sings the lyrics back to me. I always knew his voice was sexy but when he sings, it puts it on a whole other level. If it were possible to lose myself even more in him, I would do it right now, at this moment.

We dance to several more slow songs, each of them having a man declaring his love for a woman. And I'm trying really hard not to read into it but I can't help it. He said he wants a future with me, that there will be many more tomorrows ahead of us, that I am his. How can I not read it as anything but a declaration of love? He doesn't have to say it because I know it's there.

A few more songs pass and he pulls me to the couch. He turns off the stereo and is now crouching in front of his DVD collection.

"Fancy a movie?" he asks, looking at me over his shoulder.

"Sure, I'm game for a movie. What did you have in mind?" I ask, tilting my head slightly.

His fingers run over the movies before pulling two out. He holds them behind his back as he stands in front of me.

"Comedy or action?"

As if that's a real question for me. "Comedy. Always a comedy."

He laughs and walks over to the player, placing the disc inside without letting me see which title he's chosen.

"Do you have any popcorn? We can't watch a movie without popcorn."

He turns to me and his eyes are dancing with delight and something else. Something mischievous.

"You are correct. We cannot have a movie without popcorn. Would you like anything to drink, love? More wine?"

He walks over to the kitchen and starts making a bag of microwave popcorn. The buttery aroma fills the air as I think about my drink options.

"Actually do you have a Diet Coke?"

He nods his head and pulls out a diet and regular Coke from the refrigerator. Grabbing the bag out of the microwave, he dumps the contents into a bowl and walks back over to the couch, handing me my soda before placing the bowl on the table in front of us.

"Thank you," I say, popping the top and taking that coveted first sip. He drapes his arm over my shoulder, pulling me into his side as he turns on the TV, but not before he hit play. Apparently I need to be surprised at his choice.

"So what are we watching?"

He winks at me. "Just some good old fashioned British comedy."

Part of me wants to groan because I'm afraid of what that could be however the other part of me lights up immediately as the opening credits roll across the screen.

"Oh my God I love this movie! It's one of my all time favorites," I say, practically bouncing on top of him. His lips find my temple and he smiles.

"You seemed like a Monty girl so I figured this would be a good choice."

There's no way that he could have known how much I adore this movie. I snuggle in close to his side, linking my hand with the one that's draped over my shoulder. And, of course, we're instantly in stitches just from the opening credits. It kills me every time I read the part about the llamas. Just sheer comedy gold.

We recite almost every line in the movie, throwing popcorn at each other's mouths, missing the vast majority of the time. It's fun and easy, just sitting here and watching a movie while eating popcorn. I've never done this with someone before, outside of Kara and our chick flick marathons that we have. But this is different. And it's because of Andrew.

When the movie ends, we're both clutching our stomachs, still laughing at each other and at the movie.

"The rabbit part at the end kills me every time," I say, wiping another tear from my eye.

"Do you want to watch another movie or do you wish to do something else?"

His fingers brush away the hair from my face and his touch stirs something deep inside me again. He's still cupping my jaw while his thumb brushes a lazy pattern against my cheek. My breath quickens and my palms feel clammy. And then everything south of my navel contracts as something flares in his eyes.

I crawl onto his lap, placing my knees on either side of his hips. He steadies me over him and I reach up to thread my fingers through his hair. My face dips down and I kiss him, softly, just like he does to me. His hands travel up my back before linking around my neck, anchoring me to him. I open my mouth, allowing his tongue to find mine, taking long deep licks inside my mouth.

I arch my back toward him, pressing my breasts into the hard muscles of his chest. Another groan escapes him, allowing me to swallow it with my own. Heat flashes through my veins as I gently rock against him, seeking him out and gasping when I make my connection.

He wants me.

He pulls back, panting slightly as he looks deep into my eyes, searching for an answer to a question he doesn't need to ask. It's already been decided.

"I want you, Tessa. Are you sure about this?"

My eyes dart back and forth, burning his face into my memory because I want to remember every little detail of this moment for the rest of my life. The way he looks with his hair all mussed up after my fingers have been pulling at it. The way his eyes are dilated with need and desire for me. The way his mouth is slightly gapped open as he drags precious air back into his lungs. The way his chest rises and falls as he pulls in that precious air, causing my breasts to move with him. His hands have a firm grip on my hips before they slowly run over and cup my behind, pulling me toward him again to elicit another moan from the both of us.

"Take me to bed, Andrew," I whisper.

He slants his lips over mine once more before standing up with me still wrapped around him. He walks us down the hall to his room, carrying me with ease. My heart beats wildly inside my chest only I'm not scared anymore. No, scared is definitely not in my vocabulary right now. Desire, lust, want, need. Those are all I'm feeling right now. And as he kicks the door closed behind him I know, beyond a shadow of a doubt, that I'm exactly where I need to be.

Chapter 16

Andrew lays me down on his massive bed, gently crawling over me, resting his weight on his forearms as he hovers above me. He brushes away a few stray tendrils of hair from my face before his lips brush mine again.

"I have dreamt of this moment ever since I first saw your beautiful face. But I need to know, are you sure about this? You know we don't have to."

I reach up, gently laying my index finger across his lips to silence him. "Now who's talking too much. I know you're concerned about my past and how it may affect me now. Please don't let that get between us. I want you. I've never wanted anybody or anything as much as I do right now."

My hands frame his beautiful face. I need to reassure him that this is what I want, what I need. Andrew is my future. He's who I choose. He is who I want to give myself to in every way. Tonight, tomorrow, and every day after.

The smile he gives me has me melting into a puddle again as his lips seek out mine, taking his time to savor me as my body molds into his. His hand travels down my side and his touch sends another round of tingles throughout my body. A soft moan escapes my lips as he moves to my neck, biting and sucking a trail down the column of my throat, stopping to twirl his tongue at the dip in the base. My hands don't know where to go so I just roam over every inch of him I can. I grab his hair, claw at his shoulders, then trail my fingers down to his biceps and hold on to them tightly.

Andrew drags his finger between my breasts, trailing them around each one, causing my nipples to tighten into hard little buds. "So beautiful," he whispers, kissing my neck. "The most beautiful woman I've ever laid my eyes on."

"Andrew."

He drags my shirt over my head, tossing it to the side. His eyes roam over the newly exposed flesh, followed by his fingers at a leisurely pace. They trace over the slope of my breast where it meets my bra before dipping inside, brushing up against my hardened nipple. I close my eyes tight and unabashedly moan at the contact. My body is wound up so tight I feel like it could snap at any moment. I don't think I've ever been this turned on in my life and yet I know it's because of Andrew and what he does to me. It's how he makes me feel and how I feel about him in return.

With shaky fingers, I reach up and start unbuttoning his shirt, concentrating hard on threading each one through the hole. He stills my hand, covering it with his.

"Love, are you alright? You're shaking."

He sits up, dragging me with him. My eyes stay cast downward, embarrassed that I can't pull myself together to get even this one thing right. I'm not nervous, but I can't stop shaking. I wish I could control my body a little more because I want this so much.

Andrew cups my cheek, gently raising my face to look at him. His bright blue eyes are almost completely hidden by his now dilated pupils. The fire I usually see within them is burning so bright that it calms my shaking hand. He traces my face with his eyes as if he's attempting to memorize it. But I crave his eyes upon me. It's like an aphrodisiac that I cannot resist. He looks at me with such admiration that I'm almost addicted to it like a junkie needing their next hit.

I blow out a soft breath and will my body to settle down. "I know. It's just, I want this so bad and I'm afraid that I'm not going to be any good at it. I don't want to disappoint you. I mean, I have zero experience in this department. Plus I'm damaged and broken. I just . . ." is all I can make out before his mouth comes crashing down upon mine. My hands rest against his hard chest as he pulls me closer to him.

"You're talking too much again," he whispers against my lips. "You are perfect to me and there is nothing that you could do that would disappoint me." He grabs a lock of my hair, running it through his fingers before tucking it behind my ear. My eyes close and I hum with pleasure as his skin makes contact with the shell of my ear. "We'll go slowly, at your pace. We have all night, love. This is about you and letting me take care of you, whatever your needs may be."

His words give me a renewed confidence in myself that I'm in control of what happens to us, something that was taken from me in my previous encounters. He wants to please me and I want nothing more than to please him.

I lean forward, closing the small gap between us and press

my lips softly against his. My fingers move back to the buttons on his shirt, easily threading them through the holes this time. Once the last button is undone, I gently push it off his shoulders, giving me my first real glimpse of his body. I break away from his mouth so I can admire it fully as I trace over each line of toned muscle. A groan erupts out of his throat as my fingers play along his torso.

His eyes meet mine as he cups my face, pulling my attention back to him. "Tessa," he growls out. I love the way he says my name, how it rolls off his tongue, dripping with desire, causing my own wetness to increase between my legs.

Andrew lays me back down on the bed, his body half on mine, half on the mattress. His hand brushes my stomach and my muscles clench with need. I want more of his touch. I want more of everything he has to give me. My hands do their own wandering on his stomach, tracing that delicious six pack of his, skirting around the waistband of his jeans. With a roll of his hips, his erection presses into my side, showing me just how much he wants me.

He pops open the button of my jeans, slowly pushing them over my hips. His lips leave mine, dragging them slowly down the center of my body. He pulls my jeans off my legs, throwing them next to my discarded shirt. My fingers move to his belt, unbuckling it with ease and dexterity that I didn't know I possessed. I free him from his jeans, sliding them down his legs, using my feet to pull them completely off his body. He gives a slight chuckle and smiles against the skin at my stomach.

"You're better at this than you think, love."

I flush at his compliment, letting my own giggle fill the room. He silences it quickly as his lips move to the waistband of my panties, running his tongue along the edge. My fingers twist in his hair as my legs fall to the side, opening myself up for him.

His warm breath hits the small cotton panel separating me from him, causing my hips to move involuntarily. He runs his nose down the center and my breath hitches in my chest.

"You smell so good Tessa. I could spend days just inhaling your sweet scent."

Oh. My. God.

He loops his thumbs into the waistband, dragging the scrap of material down my legs, setting me completely free. His eyes light up the room with a passion so hot that it burns into my very soul as he looks up from between my legs. He climbs back up my body, reaching around behind me to unclasp my bra, setting my breasts free.

My hands rest on his shoulders as his mouth finds mine again. Our tongues tangle with each other as our hands roam our bodies. He massages my breast, taking a nipple between his thumb and index finger, gently pinching it. Pleasure spikes go straight to my core as I cry out into his mouth.

Boldly I reach into his boxer briefs, dragging them down his hips and he helps me take them off the rest of the way. I look down slowly, taking in his fully naked form. Michelangelo's David pales in comparison to the godlike specimen that is Andrew.

Looking at his perfect body I become self-conscious of my own. I move my hands to try and cover myself. Andrew shakes his head as he drags them away.

"Please, don't. I want to see you, all of you," he says, running his lips against my jaw.

His hand roams over my skin again, causing another round of goose bumps to appear. The reverent touch he gives me sends shocks down to my core, igniting the fire within me that begs to have all of him.

"Andrew, I . . ."

The room begins to spin as his tongue makes first contact with the sensitive and wet folds between my legs. I've barely even registered that he had moved that far down my body but with every lick, every nip he delivers to me, my mind blanks and empties. Making Andrew my sole focus and the pleasure he's giving me.

My hands fly into his hair, tugging and anchoring at the same time. He laughs lightly as I feel the rush of air against my swollen and throbbing flesh. Stars appear before my eyes when the first clench of my muscles happens. It's intense, it's almost too much to bear.

He adds a finger, expertly massaging me from the inside and I come undone. I loudly call out his name and fall from the heavens, spiraling down to Earth from a sensation I've never known.

Andrew kisses a trail back up my body, allowing my senses to come back to me. He pays close attention to each breast on his way back to my mouth. The taste of my arousal is still lingering on his lips as he slants his mouth over mine.

"You are so beautiful when you come. I must see it again."

I'm panting as my body tries to relax again. A new round of need builds though as he hovers over me, the swollen head of his cock pressing lightly against my opening. My hips roll instinctively toward him and he stills.

"I want to feel you, all of you Tessa, without anything between us."

"I'm on birth control," I say, looking directly into his eyes. "I trust you. Please, Andrew."

I'm begging and I don't care at this particular moment. I know it's a little reckless and risky however I know in my heart that he would never intentionally do anything to hurt me. The thought of anything other than skin on skin doesn't cross my mind. I want to feel him, all of him.

He pulls up on his knees, positioning himself at my needy center as my legs wrap around him, inviting him inside me. With one fluid move, he sinks inside me as my eyes roll to the back of my head.

"Oh God Tessa, you feel amazing," he says, slowly inching his way inside my slick entrance.

It's the most incredible feeling I've ever had in my life. The fullness, the feel of his hard length stretching me has my legs shaking all over again. My muscles grip him firmly as he buries himself to the hilt. He pauses, waiting for my body to adjust to him.

His head drops to my ear, his breathing erratic and hot against my skin. "You feel so good," he says, sliding in and out of me. He picks his head up and takes my mouth, our tongues twirling in time with his thrusts. My hips instinctively meet his as the muscles in my stomach tighten again.

"Oh God, Andrew," I say breathlessly against his mouth.

I'm there, standing on the edge of the cliff, ready to fall over into the intense pleasure I'm getting from Andrew. He presses his forehead against mine, eyes locked together. Our skin is slick with sweat as he moves faster inside me.

My eyes flutter closed briefly as I teeter precariously on the edge of sanity. "Eyes open Tessa. I want to see you when you come again."

My eyes flick open and fall upon his, heightening my own pleasure until it becomes too much. It's too intimate, too passionate, too intense. Within minutes, I shatter into a million pieces, falling over the edge while never breaking eye contact. I cry out Andrew's name over and over, feeling nothing and everything all at once. Andrew's eyes never leave mine as he thrusts several more times inside me, following in his own release.

"Tessa," Andrew growls against my neck, his movements slowing as he milks out the last of his orgasm.

My limbs feel heavy, but I tighten my legs around his narrow waist, holding him close to me. Our combined heartbeats begin to slow, our breathing returning to normal. I trail my fingers lightly up and down the muscles of Andrew's back, feeling them flex and ripple as he adjusts himself on top of me.

When he pulls out, I instantly feel the loss. My hands move around, pulling his mouth to mine, tasting of Andrew and yet still of myself. Andrew brushes the hair away from my face again and smiles before placing several small languorous kisses upon my lips.

"Perfect. You are an angel sent from above, destined for me alone. How do you feel?"

Words cannot even begin to describe the feelings I have swirling inside me. "Good, amazing, tired, sweaty." I can't help the giggle that escapes my lips and he joins in my laughter.

"Are you sore?"

My shoulders shrug in response. "A little, but it's not bad."

He rolls off me, pulling me to his side. My finger traces

patterns along his chest. His lips kiss the top of my head, causing a new wave of dizziness to hit me. I'm still riding the high of what we just did, relishing in the fact that it was the single greatest moment of my life.

I listen to his heartbeat beneath my ear as I slowly begin to drift off to sleep.

"I love you, Andrew," I whisper into the air.

He says nothing, only pressing his lips against my forehead as I drift off to another world, hoping that my future is as bright and happy as I dream it to be.

Chapter 17

I WAKE UP WITH A warm feeling wrapped around my heart, as well as a pair of strong arms around my body. Andrew is kissing my forehead, slowly dragging me from the incredibly peaceful sleep that I was enjoying for the second night in a row. *Another night without falling out of bed.* I'm beginning to think that perhaps maybe Andrew is a good luck charm in warding off that dream of mine.

My mind recalls the events of last night, bringing a smile to my face. My skin tingles as Andrew runs his fingers up and down my side. I remember the feel of his lips on my body, the gentle way he made love to me as he made me come twice, the way I said I love you before I drifted off to sleep . . .

Holy shit, what did I do? Did I really? No, I couldn't have. I wouldn't have. Panic grips my heart as I recall the fuzzy moments before sleep came over me. Shit. I did, in fact, utter those three little words, dropping them like a bomb. And he never responded. He never once said anything back to me or even acknowledged that I said them. Maybe he didn't hear me. Maybe

I'm off the hook and it'll be like I never said them.

Then the nagging voice that I had pushed away for the last day came back and screamed loudly in my head. *Or maybe he doesn't feel that way about you.*

My eyes are open wide with shock as I fully come awake. I look over and a bright pair of blue eyes is looking back at me. He leans down and softly kisses my lips.

"Good morning, love. How did you sleep?"

The gravelly tone of his voice slowly begins to ignite something inside me. I tamp it down because I'm still trying to sort out the warring emotions inside my head.

"Good. How about you?" I bite my lip as I watch the smile brighten his whole entire face.

"It was the best sleep I've ever had because I woke up next to a hazel-eyed angel still naked in my bed."

I flush at his comment as his arms wrap around me tighter. He has to return my feelings. I mean everything he said yesterday and what we did last night . . . that has to count for something, right? Okay, so he didn't exactly say he loved me nor did he ever sound like he was going to, but still. The signs are all there, right?

Oh God, I've made this whole thing up in my head, haven't I? Humiliation begins to form in the back of my mind and I tense in his arms. He must notice the change in me because he pulls back slightly, a frown drawn across his face.

"What's wrong, love?"

I shake my head. "Nothing. What time is it?"

He looks over at the clock. "It's around six. We still have a few hours before we have to get back to the hotel."

His lips trail down my throat and I suppress the whimper

that threatens to come out. I try to pull away from his arms, but he holds on tighter.

"Are you trying to get away from me?"

He laughs against my skin as his lips continue their journey. I wiggle some more and it causes his head to pull up.

"No, nothing like that. I just, um, have to use your bathroom."

I play with the edge of the sheet and watch the smile crawl across his face. Doubts still clog my brain, trying to desperately remember if he ever said anything last night.

"Yes, of course. Take your time. Feel free to help yourself to anything you find in the bathroom."

His fingers comb through my hair and I begin to let my guard down a little. Maybe I'm over-thinking this again. Which I know I have a tendency to do when I feel stressed or unsure. He kisses the end of my nose as I sit up and throw my legs over the side of the bed.

His phone beeps on the nightstand next to him. I watch his brows furrow together as he reads the message. Who would be texting him this early in the morning?

It's none of my business, I remind myself as I walk into the bathroom, shutting the door behind me. I stare at my reflection in the mirror and tilt my head to the side. There's a new glow to me that wasn't there yesterday. My skin has a beautiful pink hue to it like it's in a permanent state of blush. But then my brain reminds me of my verbal mistake from last night and how he never responded.

Maybe I am just a one night stand for him, a conquest to get into his bed before I leave. A stray tear falls from the corner of my eye as the harsh reality of my situation comes to light. I opened myself up to him last night and he didn't return it.

I root around in the drawers of his vanity, looking for a spare toothbrush. Surely he must keep a few around. And I found it, along with about five others. A stockpile of tooth-brushes still sitting in their packages lines the bottom of the drawer. Why would one person need that many toothbrushes? One or two spares I could see but five? Unless . . . unless he has many overnight guests that would need them in the morning.

Bile rises in my throat, threatening to come out at any moment. I need to shut off my brain because if I don't I will drive myself insane.

"You're reading too much into this Tessa," I whisper to my reflection. She scowls at me and sticks her tongue out. Man, my reflection is a grumpy bitch this morning.

The high I was on slowly dissipates as I freshen up and start the water running in the shower. Maybe getting clean will help remove the doubts out of my brain. At the very least it'll relax me a little.

A soft knock on the door startles me a little and I watch as Andrew's head peeks around the corner. He looks at me with that same feral need from last night and my thighs instinctively press together.

He chuckles at my reaction as he opens the door more, walking into the now steamy bathroom and standing before me in all his naked glory.

Holy. Fuck.

He's perfect. No, he's more than perfect but I'm not sure there's a word that can accurately describe him at this moment. I mean, I saw him last night, but the light was muted. But here in the brightness of the bathroom I get my first real glimpse of

Andrew's naked form.

And. It. Is. Amazing.

My eyes travel across the vast expanse of muscle and tanned skin. The shadow of stubble on his jaw adds to his sex appeal as I trace every inch of him with my gaze. I feel like I'm drooling as I slowly travel down his chest, his stomach, his . . . holy shit how did that thing fit inside me last night?

He laughs and moves slowly toward me. My eyes follow the sway of his body as it gets closer and closer to me. My lip disappears between my teeth and I swear the temperature in the room has increased about twenty degrees. The steam of the shower surrounds us, creating a fog that mimics my clouded mind. I just can't think when he's standing there naked in front of me, causing a rush of heat and wetness to build between my legs.

"So I thought maybe I'd join you in the shower and promote water conservation." He leans in close and my breath hitches as his lips graze my ear. "The best part about getting clean is the fun you have getting dirty again. And right now as I look at you leaning against the counter of my vanity wearing nothing but that dazzling smile of yours, I want nothing more than to get you dirty."

Andrew guides us behind the glass wall and adjusts the temperature of the water so we don't scald ourselves. His hands travel along the planes of my body before coming to grip the soft flesh of my hips. I look up into his eyes and decide to just lose myself and worry about the consequences later. My hands frame his face as I pull his mouth down to my own. The kiss is soft yet there's an underlying hunger in it, one that feeds my need for him as my tongue traces his upper lip.

"God, Tessa," he says against my mouth. Suddenly his hands move to cup my behind, lifting me off my feet and pinning me against the slick tiled wall. I wrap my legs around his narrow waist, feeling his erection press against my needy core. His lips travel along my neck and collarbone, nipping and sucking as I cling to his shoulders while pushing my head back against the wall.

His mouth encircles one of my nipples and I cry out from the sheer bolt of pleasure. My back arches away from the wall, letting him draw it further into his mouth. I grip his hair, holding him to me as he switches to the other breast, giving it the same attention and causing the same unbridled reaction in my body.

The tightening in my belly has me rocking against him, seeking out some kind of relief. He nuzzles between my breasts and I can feel his smile against my skin.

"Andrew, please," I beg. I don't know how much more I can take of the sweet torture he's exuding on my body. The need for him to be inside me is so great that I can't even feel the water beating against our skin anymore. I feel nothing except Andrew.

He adjusts his position, putting the head of his cock directly at my slick entrance. "You ready, love?" he asks, looking deep into my eyes to make sure that I'm ready.

I nod my head as the words get caught in my throat. Within seconds, the world feels like it's falling away from me as I feel every inch of him filling me. My tight inner walls grip him greedily as he slowly pushes deeper and deeper inside me.

My elongated moan echoes against the walls of the shower when he's finally buried to the hilt. He buries his face in my neck, slightly biting down on my shoulder as he stills, allowing my body to adjust to him. My breaths are short and panting so I cling to him more, pulling him closer, needing to feel every part of him.

He finally begins moving in his slow, lazy rhythm; bringing me slowly to the edge I want to freely jump off of just to feel the sheer high it brings. His fingers dig into the soft flesh of my behind as he picks up his tempo, thrusting me further up the slick wall. I squeeze my eyes shut as I try to hold off on my impending orgasm, waiting to tip off the edge until he's ready to fly with me.

His breaths are sharp against my neck and I can feel him swell even more inside me. He's right there, ready for me. That thought alone has my legs clenching around his waist even more as I let go and erupt around him, crying out his name as I fall into oblivion. Andrew follows right behind me, pouring himself into me as he grunts into my shoulder while simultaneously nipping and sucking against my skin.

Stars appear as well as the lightheaded feeling that I wish for, allowing my mind to blank and do nothing but feel this moment. But the moment is lost as he pulls out of me, placing me on my feet again while still pressing my body against the wall.

I tilt my head up to look at him and he breaks my heart with his smile. A smile that I'm going to miss as the cruel reality catches up to me again.

"I do love making you dirty Tessa. I wish we could stay here all day and do nothing but get lost in each other's bodies."

I force the smile upon my face as I lick a stray drop of water sliding down his neck. "Me too. I can't believe today is the day."

He places his finger over my lips, silencing me immediately. "Let's not discuss that right now. It's time to get you clean so we can spend the morning together."

He grabs his body wash and lathers his hands, sliding them across my body, making sure nothing is left unclean. Andrew pays close attention to my more sensitive areas, knowing that I must be slightly sore after our ministrations this morning and last night. I follow his direction and lather up my own hands, running them up and down the defined muscles of his body. It proves difficult, trying not to start another round of passion as my fingers wrap around his still semi-erect cock. Although I wouldn't object to a round three at this point. I'll take whatever he can give me.

Soon enough, he shuts the water off and grabs a towel for the both of us, gently running it over my body for me. He wraps the towel around my naked body and pulls me closer to him. I reach up and run my lips over his as an expression of gratitude.

"You're too good to me," I tell him. He gives me that lopsided grin of his and I giggle.

"Never. I can never be too good to you."

"Well if you keep this up I'm going to expect this sort of treatment every day and we both know that's not going to happen."

My heart twists in pain as I'm reminded yet again of my departure and his silence and avoidance of the subject or my verbal blunder of last night. Both make me sad but for two very different reasons.

He strokes my cheek, forcing me to tilt my head up slightly to his. "You know you make me so happy Tessa. There's not a moment of this past week that I would change."

His blue eyes sparkle and I fight the urge to break down and cry, mourning the loss of something that hasn't even happened yet. For now I'm here and so is he. For now I'm in his arms. That should be enough. But it's not. I'm addicted. I'm pulled to him on the cosmic level that I can't even fathom my days or nights alone anymore. He makes me want to reach out and take life as it comes to me rather than hide in my hole, watching it pass me by.

He makes me want to be more than my past.

The annoying sound of his phone ringing on the counter has both our heads turning in unison to it. Hmm, I didn't even notice him putting it there when he came in. Then again, I was distracted by his naked body. A three ring circus could have performed in here and I wouldn't have noticed.

I glance over and see a female's name before he quickly sends it to voicemail.

"Shouldn't you get that?" I ask.

He shakes his head and twists his lips to the side. "It can wait until later."

Until later. He means when I'm not here. It can't be more than an hour after we woke up. No one calls this early in the morning without a reason. And with his quick brush off of the subject it has my suspicions running rampant.

"Andrew?"

He types out a quick message and places his phone back on the counter. "Yes, love?"

Should I voice my concern or just let it drop? Seeing as I'm leaving soon, there's no point in causing a fight before I'm gone.

"Nothing."

He presses a quick kiss to my forehead before grabbing his chirping phone again and walking back to his room.

He's obviously busy this morning with whoever is messaging him. I watch him walk into his closet, pulling things out to wear for the day. My mind blanks out as I blatantly stare at him, watching as he slides his jeans over his perfect ass. I need to sit before I fall over.

Andrew looks over his shoulder and smirks at me. "Give me another few minutes and I'll start on our breakfast."

I nod and he walks back into the bathroom. I gather my clothes off the floor, thankful that they were not overly wrinkled in their haste to leave my body last night. The beep of his phone piques my curiosity again as I slide the shirt over my head.

I shouldn't look. It's none of my business. Besides I wouldn't like someone looking at my messages. But my feet have a mind all of their own as I walk over to his dresser and look at the screen as it illuminates in front of me.

Andrew, it's imperative that you call me. I'll be over in an hour. It can't wait any longer. I need to see you. Evie.

Evie? Who is Evie? I run through the list of members at the Foundation and none of them has that name. Did he lie when Kara asked him if he had a girlfriend? Or is this an ex who still lingers about? And what does she need to talk to him about?

My stomach twists as the past comes back to haunt me. He used me to get his way. That's the reason he didn't say anything back to me last night. He's already got someone waiting for him for when I leave.

I wrap my arms around my middle, forcing the tears away. I won't cry about this. I'm sure there's a perfectly good explanation for all the text messages and phone calls he's had since we woke up. Right? I mean, women always text early in the day, especially to guys they don't have any interest in. That's a blatant lie and I know it. There's only one reason a woman texts first thing in the morning and it isn't to say hey let's be friends.

I hear him fumbling around in the bathroom and I decide to alleviate his obligation to me. With a new sadness in my heart, I exit the room to gather up my things. I should just go. It would be easier on everyone involved if I just disappeared. He can meet with Evie without having to worry about getting rid of me and I can go back to Minnesota to live out my existence alone, as it should be.

I give his apartment one last look as I sling my purse over my shoulder and quietly close the front door behind me. I'm guessing it'll take him a few minutes to figure out that I've left so I decide to start walking until I can find a taxi to drive me back to my hotel. Luckily I didn't have to walk too far as one passes me and I flag it down, asking them to drive me there as quick as possible. The cab driver nods his head and I'm thankful that he's also not in a talkative mood. I don't think I would be good company at this moment as my heart splinters inside my chest.

Slipping the driver a few pounds to cover the fare and a tip, I run to the front doors and climb the stairs, not wanting to wait for the elevator. Images of my rides with Andrew come crashing into my brain and I stumble slightly on the stairs, catching myself against the railing.

My phone rings again for the third time and I ignore it. I

need to hurry and pack my things and get to the airport before he comes to find me. Another wave of pain hits me as I open my door, finding my room in exactly the same condition that I left it in the morning before.

We kept the Do Not Disturb sign up so my bed is still unmade. His duffle bag sits right at the end where he left it before whisking me away to our adventure around London. I close my eyes and tears threaten to fall as I can still smell his cologne in the air. But I remind myself that he was never mine and that it truly was a vacation fling after all.

I quickly throw my things together, pulling out every drawer to make sure I don't leave anything behind. His duffle still sits there and I stare at it, wondering what I should do with it. He still has his hotel key so he could come and get it when he's done seeing Evie.

Even the sound of her name in my head makes my stomach turn. I picture her as some tall model-type woman with cascading blond hair and looks that would make any man leave his spouse on the spot. They probably have had a love affair for years and were the perfect photo ready couple. Perhaps an on again/off again relationship. Maybe she's trying to rekindle something. Why else would she have been corresponding with him all morning?

I write a quick note, thanking Andrew for my time here and that I won't forget him but also asking him not to contact me because it'll be too hard. I tuck the note safely between the handles of his duffle and swipe my hand across the top.

A lone tear falls from my eyes as I turn and leave the room, sparing myself a final glance to cause me more pain. My door slams louder than I intend as I walk down the hall, brushing away the tears that are now falling freely.

"Tessa?" I hear Kara call down the hall to me, her voice soft and confused. I turn my head but keep it cast down so she can't see my red-rimmed eyes. "What are you doing here? I thought you were with Andrew."

I sniff once. "I was. And then he was getting messages and phone calls all morning from an Evie. The last one I looked at without him knowing it and she said she was coming over within the hour. I wanted to spare him the embarrassment of having to explain me to her so I left."

Her face drops as I brush away another tear. "There must be some misunderstanding. He said he didn't have a girlfriend."

I shrug my shoulders. "Yeah, well, he could have said that so he could pursue me this week. It's not like he'd be the first guy in history to omit the full truth to get a girl into bed."

Her eyes fall onto my suitcase by my side. "Where are you going?"

"The airport. I'm just going to wait there so he can't find me and make it more awkward than it already is."

"Has he called you yet?" she asks.

Just then her phone starts ringing and I hear Chris calling out to her from their room, saying that it's Andrew. My eyes grow wide and I start shaking my head from side to side.

"Please, Kara. Please don't say anything. I just need to get out of here."

She grabs me by my shoulders and holds me at arm's length. "I don't want you traveling around London by yourself. Stay right here. Let me grab my purse and I'll come with you. Just please don't leave yet."

I nod my head but keep staring at my feet. I feel defeated

and almost numb like the world is moving around me in slow motion. Kara runs back into her room and I can vaguely hear her talking to Chris. I wrap my arms around my middle as she asks him to bring their stuff to the airport behind us. Within minutes, she's in the hallway again, carry-on and purse in tow.

"Kara, you don't have to cut your morning short due to me. Really, I'll be okay. Spend your time with Chris. I don't need a babysitter. I am capable of taking care of myself. I've been doing it for years."

The familiar sad look in her eyes has me turning my head away. I don't want pity or sadness and I know she can't help it right now. She feels sorry for what I'm going through, even though there's a good possibility that I'm probably making this all up in my head. But then that text message appears before me and I close my eyes, hoping to keep myself in check so I don't break down in the middle of the hallway.

Kara places her hand on my shoulder and helps me to the elevator. "I know you'll be okay, but I won't be if I know you're out there wandering around by yourself. And let's face it; you're not exactly in the best frame of mind right now."

I can't argue with her statement as she guides me through the hotel and into a waiting town car. How she got one ready for us, I don't know but I'm sure it was when she and Chris were talking in her room. We pull away from the curb and I press my head against the cool glass of the window. Out of the corner of my eye, I see a familiar vehicle pull up. I know who that is without having to verify that the tall, dark haired man exiting the vehicle is indeed the man that I'm running away from. Just knowing that he's there is enough to make the floodgates open and the tears begin streaming down my face.

Kara pulls me into her side, rocking me gently as she rests her cheek against the top of my head. I cry silently, not wanting to draw more attention to myself, even though it's just us and the driver. The city that I've come to love over the past few days passes by me in a blur, a fitting end to my week here. I've experienced so much over this week and actually grown a little too. I've become slightly less scared, except my fleeing right now. I've learned that it's okay to put myself out there because even though I don't know the outcome I will never try new things if I don't. And if I fall, I can pick myself back up.

We pass through the airport, following the crowd like sheep in a flock. I respond to simple commands, giving people my ID when asked, responding to questions appropriately, doing my best to keep myself together when they ask me if I enjoyed my trip. And I did enjoy it, every second of it. I wouldn't regret a single minute of my time here, even though I'm leaving in heartache.

Once we get past security and into a zone where only ticket holders can be, I finally relax with the thought that I'll be home soon. Kara, bless her heart, keeps trying to engage me in a conversation as we sit in the first class lounge. Only I'm just not up to talking yet. It's still too fresh in my mind.

My phone beeps in my purse and I ignore it, just like I've ignored the numerous phone calls since we left the hotel. I'm sure he's going out of his mind, but I don't understand why. He's got Evie. Why would he keep wasting his time with me when there's someone here that he can see every day?

"Aren't you going to at least acknowledge that text message? You can't avoid him forever Tess," Kara says, placing her hand on my knee.

I sigh. "I know. But for now I don't want to. Maybe later. He'll stop eventually. I asked him to stop with the letter I left him in my room."

She tilts her head to the side and gives me her disappointed look. "You left him a letter? That's it? No advanced warning that you were just going to run away from his apartment, no 'hey I'll call you every day until we see each other again' message. You took the chicken way out and left him a Dear John letter saying to leave you alone?"

I chew on my lower lip as I think about what she just said. "Okay, so it's kind of a dick move on my part."

"Kind of?" she asks incredulously.

"Okay fine, a massive dick move. But let's face it. He's here, I'm there. And this Evie, she's here and can give him what he needs. I was just getting in the way. Besides, why else would a woman be messaging a guy early in the morning if it isn't about a bootie call or she's not hung up on him?"

"Common courtesy would be to let him give his side of the story."

"I know."

She shakes her head. "And you, my friend, are drawing assumptions, and you know what they say when you make assumptions."

I half-heartedly laugh. "Yeah, I know. But I'm not prepared for this right now. Let me get back to the States and clear my head. We both knew this was coming, that I was leaving today. So I'm making it easier on everyone without the awkward goodbye."

Kara throws her head back on a loud groan, pushing the palms of her hands into her eyes. "You're right. Giving the poor man a heart attack instead because you vanished without a word is way better."

"Stop making sense, please. And I thought you were on my side."

She wraps her arm around my shoulder and hugs me. "I am on your side. That's why I'm fighting you on this because it's my job to point out when you're acting stupid."

My phone beeps again and I'm almost tempted to look at it. Instead, I power it off so it stops making noise.

"He's not going to go away just because you're pushing him too. You know that right?"

"No, I don't know that. But there's an ocean between us so that will help. He'll get over it, I'll get over it and life will move on back to normal."

She rolls her eyes and her lips move to a flat line. "You're not my favorite person right now."

"Yeah, well, get in line. I'm not my favorite person right now either."

We sit in silence, not needing to say anything more. We both agree that I'm completely stupid and handling this wrong. And even if there weren't an Evie in the picture this wouldn't have been an easy departure. It would have hurt ten times worse.

Chris rounds the corner and places a kiss upon Kara's head. He slides into the seat next to her and they strike up an easy conversation. I'm glad that she's distracted so she can focus on something other than me. And I need to focus on something other than Andrew.

I look to the empty seat next to me and our first meeting plays before my eyes as if it was a dream. The way he looked and carried himself and how considerate he was when we sat next to each other on the plane. I'll miss that. I'll miss him.

They call our flight number and we board the plane, quickly finding our seats in the front. Kara offers to sit next to me, but I brush her off, telling her it's okay and that she needs to sit with Chris. I stare out the tiny window as I watch the other planes take off and arrive on the tarmac. When the announcement comes that we're getting ready to depart, I can't help but glance over at the empty seat next to me. A reminder of what I'm leaving behind.

Once we get the all clear to turn on our electronic devices, I pull out my phone and switch on my playlist. I lean back in my chair and close my eyes as the first song fills my ears. The quiet voice of Daniel Bedingfield has tears pricking my eyes. *Are you fucking kidding me?* Of all the songs on my playlist, this is the one that comes on. My hands fly to my chest as the pain of what I've done washes over me. We fit together so well in everything that we did. And he kept saying that fate brought us together, that we were made for each other, yet I ran away.

I press repeat on this song, torturing myself as a reminder of how much of a coward I really am. I found love and I ran at the first sign of difficulty; without talking to him, without allowing him to explain, or if there was even anything to explain.

I caused this pain.

Me.

All by myself.

Oh God, what have I done?

Epilogue

I FEEL ON TOP OF the world right now, the master at his game. Nothing can take me down from the high that I'm feeling. My dearest sweet Tessa loves me. She loves me. I wasn't anticipating her saying that at all but the emotions that were swirling through my head when those three most precious words fell from her perfect lips had my mind momentarily stop to process it all. I've warred with myself on this matter for the past few days. She's my perfect angel, sent from above at just the right moment when I needed her. And I've loved her from the moment I saw her.

Tessa. My dear, sweet Tessa, who lights up my life in ways that I never knew were possible. And yet at the same time she hurts in ways that no woman should ever hurt. It's understandable that she has trust issues. Who wouldn't have them, given her past circumstances? But now that I've found her I'm making it my life's mission to show her that yes, she can be loved and that she deserves love.

I grip the edge of the vanity, allowing myself a few more

moments of silence before I go out there and beg her to stay the weekend with me. I would ask her to stay here indefinitely with me if I had the choice. I know that's not a realistic possibility yet. We just need more time together. She is my it, my end all, my forever. The thought of her leaving on that plane in just a few short hours has my heart constricting in ways I never thought were possible. But that funny little organ has a way of wreaking havoc on your body and mind. And this beautiful creature that's waiting for me in my room has it beating with a new purpose in life.

I brush my teeth one more time, just to make sure that they're clean enough because I plan on kissing her until the moment security tears me away at the gates. Just the thought of her lips on mine, her sweet taste floating across my tongue has my jeans tightening at my crotch. I close my eyes, calming myself down before I walk out there.

"Are you ready, love?" I call out to her from behind the closed door. She doesn't say anything back. Perhaps she's already waiting for me in the kitchen. We did have a rather vigorous morning and I'm sure that she's built up quite the appetite. My appetite is slightly different. It's more carnal and primitive, fueled by passion and need. A need to keep her by my side for a long as I can.

The door swings open and I can't help the grin spreading across my face. I glance over at the bed, messed up completely with the blankets all askew and pillows not where they're supposed to be. Visions of the last few hours play before my eyes; her naked form beneath me, her heated breath panting against my skin, her fingernails raking across my body as she called out my name. I will never be able to sleep in that bed without thinking of her and the magical night we spent together.

But an eerie sense of dread creeps into my chest. Something feels off. I stop and listen for any movements or noises coming from the kitchen area.

Silence.

Maybe she decided to sit out on the patio. It's a bit nippy out this morning. Although she may be used to that since she does live in Minnesota. My feet carry me down the hallway as I wait for any indication that she's still here. But there's nothing. The curtains are still drawn over the patio doors. The coffee maker is off. There are no dirty dishes indicating that she already had something to eat.

I move quickly throughout the flat, opening doors, calling out her name. Where could she be? I asked her to wait for me. She wouldn't have left, would she?

"Tessa?" I call out again, panic lacing my voice. Each door I whip open turns up the same result. Nothing. I run my hands through my hair, gripping it tightly at the root and holding myself back from ripping it completely out of my head altogether. I storm back toward the living room, desperate to find any trace of her. But there isn't any. She's vanished, disappeared without a note or a reason why. Why would she leave me like this?

I check the chair where she laid her purse last night and it's missing, along with her shoes. That's my confirmation, like a dagger to my heart, the loud cry before there's silence. She's gone.

I run to my bedroom, needing to grab my phone and keys. A message alert appears on my screen and I swipe my finger across it to see who it's from. Maybe she's letting me know where she is.

Andrew, it's imperative that you call me. I'll be over in an hour. It can't wait any longer. I need to see you. Evie.

Is it possible she had seen this before she left? I'll admit the message is suggestive, but she doesn't know the reason behind it. She doesn't know that there's a minor issue with my best friend's family. Something they would like me to look into. Apparently something has happened since I first spoke with Evie this morning. Would this one text message be enough to scare Tessa away from me?

My mind travels back to what she told me of her last relationship, the way her supposed boyfriend used her, treated her like rubbish and then dumped her like she was filth. I shove my phone into my pocket and run my hands over my face. This is bad. She's already a timid, insecure woman and if she happened to misconstrue the message it may have sent her running.

No. I won't let her leave. I need to clear this up, make sure she understands how I feel about her. Bloody hell why didn't I just tell her this morning how I felt. Then she wouldn't have felt the need to be jealous or suspicious.

Fate has another plan for me apparently because the bloody wench has shoved every slow driver in front of me, blocking my way to reach her in time. I know where she is and I know where she's going to end up. The question is which do I choose first? I keep dialing her number, begging her to answer but every time it's the same result; her voicemail.

The tires screech to a halt in front of her hotel, almost hitting the town car that is leaving the front entrance. I do not need to add an accident to my morning. A morning that started out fantastic, waking up to Tessa wrapped safely in my arms, feeling her warm body pressed against mine. It took everything that I had in me to wake her this morning. She looked so peaceful as she laid in my arms. Her lips would curl into a smile as I stroked the side of her cheek then snuggle into the warmth of my body even further.

Several people block my way to the elevator as I bump into them, mumbling an apology of sorts while doing so. My foot taps impatiently on the marble floor as I will the damn thing to hurry its descent. I need to find her, pull her back into my arms where she belongs and explain everything; if there's anything to explain.

"Fuck it," I exclaim as I take the stairs up to her room. Reaching into my back pocket, I pull out her room key, anxious to get inside and see her. But before I even get to her door, a tall man emerges from the room next to hers. A man that I should know because I have dealt with him several times through video conferences.

"Andrew?" he says as I rush past him.

"Not now Mattson. I need to speak with Tessa."

He shakes his head. "She's not there."

Now he has my attention, turning to fully face him. His face falls as he takes me in. I'm sure I appear to be a mess, but my appearance is inconsequential. I have one thing on my mind and that's my hazel-eyed beauty.

"What do you mean she's not there? Where is she?"

He sighs and drops the bags to the ground. It's then I notice that it's not just his bag that he is carrying. Several suitcases fall to the side and I know that they are Kara's. Unless Chris has a penchant for bright pink luggage, which I highly doubt.

"She's already at the airport with Kara. She came back upset this morning, crying hysterically about something. I didn't catch it all, but Kara told me that she was taking her to the airport and that I'm to meet them there."

Then that's it. I'm too late. My back falls hard against the wall as I slide down, holding my head in my hands while bouncing on my balls of my feet. Chris joins me against the wall but not at my level. His legs cross at the ankle as he looks down at me, shoving his hands into his pockets.

"Look, I don't want to get in the middle of this thing between you two. I don't know what happened. But I know that Tessa's hurting right now. I also know that she has a tendency of overreacting and creating issues that aren't there. If that's not the case, then I suggest you walk away because I can't allow you to hurt her. She's been hurt enough."

I shake my head and look up at him. "It has to be a misunderstanding. We were so good. I thought we were in a right place. Everything was perfect yesterday and right away this morning. She never let on about being unhappy, except for having to leave today. But then I received a text message that she must have seen and misinterpreted it somehow, causing her to run."

Chris chuckles quietly under his breath. "Yeah, that sounds like something she'd do."

"I swear to you that I don't want to hurt her. If she doesn't want anything more to do with me, then I will grant her that privacy. It will be the hardest thing I ever do, but I will do it for her."

I lift off the ground and match his stance against the wall. He turns his head and tilts it slightly in my direction. "You love her?"

"More than life itself," I answer without hesitation.

He pats my shoulder and turns to leave. "Give it a few days. Let her cool off and sort things through. It could very well be the stress of having to leave that pushed her to this. As I said, it doesn't surprise me."

I nod my head and watch him pick up the luggage. "Oh," he says, turning back toward me. I cock an eyebrow in response. "Don't give up. If I know Kara, and I do, she won't let this drop. She's seen you two together and knows that Tessa has never been this happy before. And I'll do what I can to help as well. Hang in there."

And with that he turns to disappear down the hallway, leaving me to think about what he said. From what I know of Kara, I know that she can be tenacious and stubborn, never settling until she gets her way. Perhaps she could be an asset to my cause.

I slide my key into her door, listening to the latch click to indicate it's open. But I am unprepared for what I find. Everything is the same only it's not. Her stuff is gone, along with the air in the room. The bed is unkempt still from our one night together here. I've never been more content just sleeping next to someone in my entire life. I walk further into the silence, my spirit falling with each step. The only noise present is the sound of blood rushing through my ears with each frantic heartbeat. My duffle sits on the edge of the bed, exactly where I had placed it. I glance closer and find a note tucked at the top.

My unsteady hands unfold it as I read the heartbreaking note written in her beautiful script.

My dearest Andrew

I'm sorry to leave, but we both knew it was going to happen one way or another. A relationship between the two of us would never work out so I saved us the heartache and the trouble. This is difficult for me as I've enjoyed every moment of my time here and I want to thank you for giving me the best week of my life. Please don't try to contact me. It will only make it worse.

Take care of yourself.

Tessa

The note falls from my hands as I sit on the edge of the bed, feeling more like I'm sitting on the brink of a precipice, waiting to fall. I cannot accept this brush off or believe she doesn't care about me. I know better. I know she's scared and feels like she's alone. But she's not. Even if I'm not there physically, I will always be there. I just need to show her.

My head hangs in my hands, propped up on my knees as I think of a way to get her back before it's too late.

Acknowledgements

This book has been a process and an adventure, to say the least. I started writing it in October 2013 because I had this story stuck in my head and it wouldn't be happy until it got onto paper. The thought of ever publishing it didn't cross my mind at first. But after the many persistent voices of my friends who encouraged me to take the leap, here we are today. It has been an amazing journey from the beginning, one that I will definitely not forget. And I am so thankful to those that pushed me to this point because this truly is a dream come true.

There are so many people to thank that I really hope I don't forget anyone! If I do, please know that I love you more than life itself!

Of course, I'd like to thank my husband first. He's been a great source of support, telling me that whatever I need to just take it. Whether it comes in the form of him taking the kids for a while or emotional support when I'm feeling down, I know he's got my back. And from that support, I found the courage to believe that I could do it and that he will support me in my crazy adventure.

Billie, you've been with me from the beginning, reading this book chapter by chapter, even through the incredibly rough draft that I picked apart and put back together. Without your help and insight, I probably wouldn't be here. You've been one of my biggest cheerleaders and one of my best friends. Thank you for pushing me to do this, for believing in me and for picking me up when I was having my down days.

Patricia, Tara, and Stacy, you have been my lifesavers! The amount of support that you have given me is unbelievable at times and I have no idea how I was ever fortunate enough to find you all! All your help, all the notes and suggestions and offering to help me when I needed it means more than you will ever know. Your support and friendship have been a lifesaver and I love you hard for it!

Amanda, Andi, Gloria, Heather, Jenn, Melissa, Samantha, Stephanie, and Stephanie: your videos and messages of encouragement have helped me so much that words don't even exist to describe it. Your love and support show me the true power of friendship and faith. I have no idea how I was lucky enough to become friends with all of you but whether you like it or not, you're stuck with me for life!

And, of course, I need to throw a shout out to the Vixens because they truly are the nicest and most wonderful people that I know!! Thank you for showing your support and keeping everything positive! #VixenLoveForever

Murphy, you have no idea how happy I was that Tara suggested you to me. Your work on this cover is absolutely amazing! I came to you with zero ideas of what I wanted for the cover and you turned it into the most beautiful creation, capturing the feel of the book entirely! Thank you for all your help and for putting up with my non-stop emails.

And to you, my readers, THANK YOU from the bottom of my heart for taking the chance on this book! Without you, this wouldn't even be possible. This has been a dream come true and I'm so happy to finally share Tessa and Andrew's story with you!

About the Author

Jodie Larson is a wife and mother to four beautiful girls, making their home in northern Minnesota along the shore of Lake Superior. When she isn't running around to various activities or working her regular job, you can find her sitting in her favorite spot reading her new favorite book or camped out somewhere quiet trying to write her next manuscript. She's addicted to reading (just ask her kids or husband) and loves talking books even more with her friends. She's also a lover of all things romance and happily ever afters, whether in movies or in books, as shown in her extensive collection of both.

You can find Jodie at:

Facebook: www.facebook.com/jodielarsonauthor
Twitter: www.twitter.com/jlarsonauthor

79512282R00167

Made in the USA
Lexington, KY
23 January 2018